THE THINNEST AIR

OTHER TITLES BY MINKA KENT

The Memory Watcher
The Perfect Roommate

THE THINNEST AIR

MINKA KENT

THOMAS & MERCER

Published by Thomas & Mercer, Seattle

www.apub.com

Amazon, the Amazon logo, and Thomas & Mercer are trademarks of Amazon.com, Inc., or its affiliates.

ISBN-13: 9781503953406 (hardcover)
ISBN-10: 1503953408 (hardcover)
ISBN-13: 9781503951891 (paperback)
ISBN-10: 1503951898 (paperback)

Cover design by Shasti O'Leary Soudant

Printed in the United States of America

First edition

For Q, G, and C—my reasons for everything. And also for J, my reason for everything else.

CHAPTER 1

MEREDITH

Thirty-Six Months Ago

Anyone who claims chocolate cake is better than sex has never had the privilege of Andrew Price between their legs.

The snow-dusted Eiffel Tower stands tall outside our hotel window, and most of our bedding lies in a tangled mess on the floor.

This . . . this is a honeymoon.

Andrew climbs over me, his lissome runner's physique sheened and glowing, and when he kisses me, I taste myself on his tongue.

He likes that I'm adventurous, carefree.

Correction—*loves.*

He also loves that I'm almost half his age, wielding a libido that hasn't yet peaked and a body made for bringing the schoolboy fantasies of his divorced, middle-aged mind to life.

Running my hands along his muscled torso, I smile.

I love him. I love him a million times more than I ever thought I could possibly love another human being, and I don't expect anyone to understand, least of all my sister. Greer is convinced we've got some sugar daddy arrangement, that it's all for money and show, but she couldn't be more wrong.

I can understand Greer's concerns.

In the past six months, Andrew has paid off my student loans, bought me a car, and placed an entire privileged world at my fingertips. But she isn't there at night, witnessing the tenderness in his touch, the lingering kisses. She'll never know how it feels to lock eyes with Andrew Price from across the room and feel the ground shake beneath my unsteady gait.

He does something to me. Something no one else ever has.

With him I'm loved. I'm safe.

And that's how I know it's real.

The fancy cars, lavish dinners, and closet full of couture are nothing more than niceties. If he lost everything tomorrow, I'd still be by his side, dressed in rags and loving him nonetheless.

"More champagne?" He climbs off me, heading toward the minibar, and I miss his warmth, his subtle, musky scent. He's my addiction, one I fully embrace with eyes wide shut because when you love someone, you trust the process. You fall hard. And you don't look back. That's what makes it so intense, so magical.

Rolling to my side, I bend my knees and rest my head on my hand, admiring my perfect husband and quietly appreciating how every square inch of him officially belongs to me now.

No other woman can touch him the way I can.

No other woman can make him feel the way I do.

And he knows that.

"Yes, please," I say, my heart fluttering when his stare lingers on my body. He appreciates me, appreciates that I'm his. Before Andrew, I was always drawn to men my age, mistaking their arrogance for confidence.

Andrew isn't arrogant. He's successful, self-assured. But he isn't entitled. He simply knows what he wants and isn't afraid to go after it.

I'm so glad he wanted me.

He fills two glasses to the top and returns to bed, bubbling flutes in his hands.

"You're going to love me forever, right?" My lips curl into a teasing grin to disguise the seriousness of my question. I take a sip, letting the airy froth sit on my tongue for a moment. I want to remember this. I want to feel everything, imprinting this into my memory for always. "No matter what?"

Andrew takes a sip, his amaretto eyes locked on mine. "What kind of question is that?" He presses his lips into my forehead, exhaling before cupping my cheek in his hand. "You're my wife, Meredith. It's you and me. Forever. You're stuck with me."

Now is when I choose to ignore the fact that I'm his third.

He claims his first one doesn't count. They were young and fresh out of high school. Since they were divorced by the time he graduated from college, there were never any children involved. Andrew says he barely remembers that time in his life, and he always seems to struggle to remember her name, squinting as if he has to think on it. He was too busy studying and boozing it up at Notre Dame, opting to play rugby in his spare time rather than take his young sweetheart on cheap, college-town dates.

Erica came next, though I try not to think of her if I can help it, and I sure as hell won't let her ruin this beautiful moment.

She detests me.

But the feeling is mutual.

"Say that again." I roll to my back, keeping my flute upright and draping the sheets between my legs.

"Say what again?"

"Wife." I take a sip, hiding the grin I haven't been able to lose since he kissed me in front of three hundred and seventy-six of our closest friends and family.

Andrew takes the spot beside me, dragging his palm along his dimpled chin as he smirks.

"You're my wife," he says, taking his time.

Staring up at him, I study his chiseled jaw and boyish good looks. He has the eyes of a much younger man, but the salt and pepper at his temples is a sexy bonus. And he's crazy smart. He can talk about stocks and bonds and equities and securities in a way that intimidates even the top brokers in his field.

"You're the hottest thing I've ever seen," I say, reaching my hand to his face and dragging my fingertips along his perfect lips. "I can't believe we're married."

Seven months ago, I didn't know Andrew.

Six months ago, I was waiting tables at a café in Denver when he came in with a group of men, all in dark business suits and solid ties. I took his order first, and his hand grazed mine when he passed me the menu. He smiled. I smiled. Everything else faded away for a single, endless moment.

"It happened so fast, didn't it?" he asks, tucking one hand behind his head as he stares at the ceiling, basking in afterglow. "Guess I couldn't stand to let you get away."

I knew Andrew was going to be different from the rest when our first date didn't consist of burgers, beers, or baseball. He wore a suit and tie when he picked me up. When we arrived at the restaurant, he approached the hostess stand, confirming our reservations, and when we ordered our meals, he knew exactly which wines would pair with mine.

During the entirety of our date, not once did his eyes wander to a single passing beautiful woman. He held every door. Used "please" and "thank you" when appropriate. Didn't utter a single word about any of his exes. And not once did he check his phone in my presence.

In the hours leading up to our date, I was worried we wouldn't have anything in common. From what I gathered via a tiny bit of social media stalking, he was a single father with two children. He worked in finance. And he didn't spend much time online, his last Facebook post being four years ago.

Breath. Of. Fresh. Air.

After dinner, Andrew whisked me off to a symphony, fetching me wine at intermission and waiting for me outside the ladies' room without complaining once.

When my left high heel broke as we were walking to his car that night, I found myself with a twisted ankle. That's what I got for borrowing my roommate's cheap shoes. But rather than slip his arm around me and let me hobble back to the car and ending the date on an awkward note, he carried me in his arms like a groom would carry his bride. People gawked at the scene with their old-money stares and sour faces, but Andrew didn't pay them any attention.

His only concern was *me*.

When he took me home that night, he helped me to bed, got me ice and aspirin, brought my phone and plugged it in to the charger, and then he stayed until I fell asleep.

That's the kind of man Andrew Price is.

And I've yet to find a single twentysomething-year-old man with half the class as the man who captured my heart when I least expected it.

He's everything I never knew I wanted.

Everything I need.

Rolling closer, I rest my cheek on his chest, listening to the steady, constant thrum of his heartbeat and inhaling the indulgent scent of his bare skin as my body submits to a wave of exhaustion.

I'm spending the rest of my life with Andrew Price.

And that makes me the luckiest girl alive.

CHAPTER 2

GREER

Day Two

"Harris." I pound on his door until my knuckles grow numb, inspecting the bloom of red on my skin that nearly matches my chipped manicure. It's 7:00 a.m. on a January morning, the sun still hiding behind the horizon and a thicket of shiny Manhattan high-rises. The wind is relentless, the cold unforgiving. I'm sure he's still nestled warm in his bed, but my flight leaves in three hours and common courtesy is a luxury I don't have. "Answer the damn door. I know you're home."

This would be a hell of a lot easier if I still had a key, but last year I decided we needed to set boundaries so we could move on emotionally, which meant I had to move out. It isn't normal for two people who've been broken up for years to still live together, to still sleep in the same bed like some sexless married couple and attend their friends' weddings as each other's plus-ones.

But aside from everything that's happened over the past decade, Harris is still my best friend, my confidant, and one of the few people I actually like on this narcissistic, egocentric excuse for a planet.

And maybe a part of me still loves him more than I'm willing to admit out loud.

A muffled voice sounds on the other side of the door, and within seconds, it's flung open. Harris's tortoiseshell glasses are crooked on his face, and he smells like stale bedsheets and a hard sleep.

"What? What is it?" He squints at me, dragging his palm along his barely there five-o'clock shadow. Creases from his pillow mark his cheek and forehead.

"You didn't answer your phone." The tiniest part of me is irrationally insulted by his unavailability.

"I was sleeping. It was off."

"There's been an emergency. I'm leaving for Utah." My matter-of-fact delivery is a ruse that he'll probably see through, but it's all I can do to keep from falling apart on the outside.

Showing emotion isn't my forte. I'd rather suffer through a thousand pelvic exams than shed a single tear in front of another person. Besides, tears aren't going to find my sister.

His sleepy gaze comes into focus as he drags his hand through his messy onyx hair. "Utah? What, is it Meredith?"

"Yes." My arms fold. "Meredith is missing." Saying those words out loud for the first time almost knocks the wind from my lungs. To think them is one thing. To say them makes them real.

She's been here for everything, always.

The highs and the lows.

My biggest cheerleader.

And now she's not.

"What happened?" Harris lifts a brow, then squints, as if he's about to watch a train wreck unfold.

"She was supposed to pick up Andrew's kids from school," I say, gaze focused on his bare feet. "Never showed. Her car was found in the parking lot of a grocery store, the driver's door open and her purse and phone on the passenger seat. No sign of a struggle. She just . . . disappeared."

"Shit." He tucks his chin against his chest, rubbing the back of his neck.

"Anyway, I was just coming to tell you I don't know how long I'm going to be away, so you'll have to take over the shops for a while." I hate to put this on him when our business is in dire straits, but we don't have a choice.

A decade ago, Harris and I were fresh out of grad school, up to our noses in debt and finding it nearly impossible to land jobs in the face of the Great Recession, so we maxed out every credit card we had and opened a tiny coffee shop in Brooklyn. Two years later, we opened another in Chelsea. Then one in the East Village. Today we have five altogether. It was insane and exhilarating and stressful and still somehow blissfully wonderful because we were doing it all together. The two of us. Side by side.

But times are tough.

Competition is stiffer than ever, with new coffee shops popping up all over the place, run by social media–savvy millennials and started up with bottomless loans from their well-heeled parents.

This past Christmas, some new place called the Coffee Bar opened just around the corner. The owner invented a whole special menu of holiday movie–themed drinks inspired by films like *Home Alone* and *National Lampoon's Christmas Vacation*. BuzzFeed ran an article on them, and it went viral practically overnight, with people lining up for blocks just to try a "Keep the Change, Ya Filthy Animal" latte, which was nothing more than a glorified pumpkin spice latte with salted caramel. Or a "Cousin Eddie's Full Shitter," which was an iced mocha with an extra shot of Turkish espresso. None of the drinks were inventive by any stretch of the imagination, but we couldn't compete with a viral sensation.

Our December profits sank by 40 percent, and they continue to fall with each passing day. We were looking at shutting down at least three stores over the coming months until Meredith offered me a loan.

I didn't want to accept the help.

But I also didn't want to lose my livelihood.

Or Harris, whose current expression resembles that of an eyewitness to a fatal car accident.

"All right. Yeah. I can handle everything here. Just keep me posted, will you?" he asks.

I pause, lingering outside his door. He never cared much for Meredith, though he never explicitly said that. It was just in the little digs he'd make here and there, making fun of her for her social media addiction, her affinity for tabloid articles, and wearing too much makeup and too little clothing. He mostly hated that she was overtly sexual, but that was on principle. Raised by two Harvard-educated women's studies professors alongside three older sisters, Harris was a staunch feminist.

"Jesus. I hope nothing happened to her." His gaze falls, his words barely a whisper.

Funny how all those old misgivings no longer matter once shit gets real.

"I'll keep you updated on everything," I say, if only because I imagine I'm going to need his rational demeanor to keep me sane until I find her. He was always good at that, always good at putting things in perspective and talking my anxious ego down from the ledge. "Just . . . keep your phone on from now on, please. Even in the middle of the night. I'll only call when I need you."

The moment I turn to leave, the warmth of his palm clasps my wrist.

"Greer," he says, head cocked to the side. His touch is a comfort I can't allow myself to enjoy, not under these circumstances. "I'm sorry."

"Sorry?" I lift a brow, looking him up and down. "For what? She's not dead; she's missing."

He says nothing.

"And I'm going to find her." I've never said anything with so much conviction.

"I know you will. Look, I'm here if you need me." He pulls me into his arms, crossing a line he drew years ago.

Being in his arms again is a momentary catch in the midst of a never-ending fall. He still loves me; I know he does.

Just as I'll never stop loving him, he'll never stop loving me. His proposal to go our separate ways came after years of placing our relationship on the sidelines as we gave everything we had to our business. All our time. Our energy. Our passion. At the time, we were too far deep to see it, and by the time we noticed, we were too far gone. We'd lost our spark, settled for comfort over excitement, and we deserved more.

At least that's what Harris said.

The breakup took months, but it came as no surprise. I have my own issues, and Harris is a complicated man. It was always something I liked about him. He's deep. A thinker. They don't make them like him, at least not in mass production.

There's a melancholy sweetness and an air of sadness swirling together as I breathe him in the way I always used to. Part of me wishes he were coming with me to Utah, but someone has to stay back and keep the business going. The two of us leaving for an undetermined amount of time isn't an option.

"Call me when you land," he says.

"I'm going." I pull myself away from Harris and grip the purse strap over my shoulder, turning to leave after giving him a parting glance.

The unfamiliar gnawing of helplessness and uncertainty threatens to sink into my bones, but I draw in a deep breath, stride toward the elevator, and head toward my waiting cab.

I'm going to find my sister.

CHAPTER 3

MEREDITH

Thirty-Three Months Ago

"I can't believe you live here." Greer drops her bags on the marble-tiled foyer, her eyes floating to the top of the two-story entryway and landing on a Schonbek chandelier, complete with sixty-five lights glimmering through thousands of teardrop crystals. "Sure beats those shoe boxes we grew up in."

"Can we not?" I ask.

Greer's icy blues land on mine. "Can we not *what*?"

"Can we not make a big deal about the house?" I bite my lip, fingers interlaced on my hip, brows raised and head tilted.

As soon as Greer told me she was coming out for a visit, my stomach twisted into knots for days. It turns out the human body doesn't always know the difference between excitement and anxiety.

"So I'm supposed to pretend that you didn't pick me up in a Bentley, take me to a Michelin-starred restaurant for a five-course dinner on your husband's dime, and bring me back to your multimillion-dollar ski chalet?" Greer smirks, like she's razzing me, but I know her. There's a layer of something beneath her teasing tone, though what it is exactly I haven't a clue yet. Doubt? Skepticism? Disappointment? Jealousy?

It's not like I'm asking her to be proud of me. None of this is anything that I've earned or necessarily deserve. I married well. I got lucky. And I own that. I just want her to know that someone's taking care of me now.

And that I'm no longer her burden.

Wrapping my arms around her tense body, I squeeze her tight until her shoulders relax. "I love you, G. And I'm glad you're here. I just want us to have a good time."

My sister exhales. "We will. I'm sorry for gawking. It's just . . . this life you're living is insane. You're so young." She pulls away from me, her eyes locking on mine.

"It's not unheard of to be married at twenty-two," I say. "And you can't control fate."

"I just hope you don't forget who *you* are and what *you* want, you know? I didn't raise you to be a kept woman."

I reach for her bag, winking to keep things light and to keep this conversation from having a mother-daughter dynamic.

"I believe we already had this conversation," I remind her. "The night before my wedding?"

Her eyes roll. "I know, I know. You love him. He loves you. Everything's perfect, and I have nothing to worry about."

My lips pull up at the sides. "Glad you were listening. Want to see your room?"

The security system beeps twice as I wheel her bag through the foyer.

"What's that?" she asks.

"Andrew must be home." I glance toward the kitchen, waiting for the sound of his calfskin oxfords shuffling across the floor, his keys chinking on the counter, and the gentle whoosh of the wine fridge as he retrieves our nightly bottle of red.

"Mer?" he calls a moment later. "You home?"

"In here." I wheel the bag toward the sound of his voice, Greer in tow. "Look who made it!"

He's seconds from uncorking a bottle of Merlot when he glances up, meeting my sister's steely gaze. I told him she can't help it—she looks at everyone that way. She doesn't trust most people, and she hardly likes anyone. She's slow to warm up, but she *will* warm up . . . one of these days. She just needs to see that what we have is legit and not the premise of a Lifetime Movie of the Week. Regardless, Andrew promised me it didn't matter, that he had thick skin, and that it wouldn't change the way he feels about me. Ever.

"Andrew." Greer forces herself to smile. I can see she's trying to be cordial, so that's a step in the right direction. It suddenly hits me that this is only the third time they've met. Expecting them to be fast friends is unrealistic, so I'll sit back and be patient and let this happen naturally.

My husband takes three crystal wineglasses with platinum-plated stems from the cupboard and pours them to the curve of the chalice.

"Did you have a nice flight?" he asks, sliding our glasses closer. "They were calling for snow. I was worried there'd be a delay."

She takes a small sip. "Guess I lucked out."

"Where's your boyfriend? Harris, was it?" Andrew asks.

"Ex . . . ," I remind him under my breath, twisting the stem of my drink between my fingers.

Greer shoots me a look, and I shoot one back. It's not fair that my love life is always on the table, but hers is a padlocked diary. God forbid we discuss the fact that they broke up years ago but still act like nothing happened. They may not share an apartment anymore and they might have ditched the relationship labels, but nothing else has changed.

"My apologies," he says. "You came to the wedding together . . . I just assumed."

Greer takes another swig, wallowing in silence as her gaze lands on the polished wood floor. For a moment, I think back to our wedding, which was rather elaborate and impersonal, everything taking place in a posh hotel at the top of a snow-covered mountain, no one setting foot in our new home for brunch or to watch us open gifts. We shipped our guests in. We shipped them out. A laundry list of festivities left little time for small talk and catching up.

"I'm going to show her to her room," I say to my husband, leaving my wineglass untouched. My period is a few days late, but I haven't shared that with him—or anyone else—yet. "Thought she could stay in the guest suite down the hall from us if that's okay?"

Andrew chuckles, rounding the kitchen island and slipping his hand around mine. "You don't have to ask for permission. This is your house, too."

Now I feel silly, but I smile through it. I've lived here for months now, but it still feels like *his* place. I don't think I could ever get used to living in a house the size of a megachurch. It's beautiful, but it doesn't feel like home yet, and it sure as hell doesn't feel like it's mine.

"That said, I had Rosita prepare the guesthouse earlier," he adds. "I thought Greer might be more comfortable there." He glances at her. "More privacy. Less noise."

I turn to her. "He has a point. It's his week—*our* week—with Calder and Isabeau. They'll be here tomorrow."

My sister grips her bag, studying him. He can't see it, but I do. Her thoughts may as well be broadcasting across her forehead. If I know my sister, she's fixating on how he's trying to put a wedge between us, how he wants to keep me all to himself and create distance between us. But he isn't like that. He's only thinking of her, of her comfort. Andrew simply wants her to enjoy her stay. Once she gets to know him, she'll see.

"The guesthouse is amazing," I say. "I can show you, if you'd like?"

Her eyes dart to mine. "That's fine."

I wave for her to follow me, and Andrew takes his time releasing my hand. A moment later, we're passing through the sliding door off the back of the house and trekking beyond the covered, heated pool and lighted, bubbling spa toward the entrance of the guest lodge.

The guesthouse is lit like Christmas, the dark siding juxtaposed with the warm light emanating from the professionally styled interior. Everything from the grand, cognac leather sofa and reclaimed wood ceiling beams to the chinchilla-covered throw pillows was hand selected by a designer he flew in from Telluride.

Andrew calls the house quaint, but last I checked, most people wouldn't consider a twenty-seven-hundred-square-foot, four-bedroom cottage "quaint." I imagine there's some perspective dwarfing going on here. Anything placed next to the main house would appear quite "quaint."

Once inside, we pass a table in the entry with an oversize bouquet of fresh flowers in shades of wintry white accented with sprigs of pine. A collection of wickless candles flicker in the fireplace, and Ella Fitzgerald croons from speakers in the ceiling. The faint scent of cedar mixed with spearmint fills the air, and every couch cushion and throw pillow is fluffed and arranged just so. It isn't the holiday season anymore, but it sure feels that way. Andrew says there are two seasons in Glacier Park: Christmas and almost Christmas. I suppose there's no better way to take advantage of the long winters.

"You're going to love it here," I tell her as she stands in the foyer, inspecting her surroundings with her arms tight at her sides, like I've just abducted her and deposited her into a UFO. "The guest *room* is nice, but the guest*house* is nicer. It's basically a private five-star hotel. Housekeeping and everything. And the kitchenette should be stocked. Anything else you need, just dial zero on the phone, and someone will help you."

I roll her suitcase to the bedroom, leaving it at the foot of a downy, king-size bed, but she doesn't follow.

"Greer?" I call for her, stepping back toward the living room. "You can still have the guest room down the hall from us if you'd like. If this is too much, just say so."

"It's fine," she says, lips flat and eyes focused. I'm sure the day of traveling has exhausted her, and it didn't help that the second I picked her up from Salt Lake City International Airport, we hit the ground running. Before dinner at Maesano's, I gave her an hour-long driving tour of Glacier Park, showing off the beautiful French-inspired and Gothic architecture. I fawned over the way the mountains frame the city like a little fortress, and I taught her how to spot tourists. They were always walking at a turtle's pace. Pointing. Wearing North Face and UGGs. If a GP local wore North Face or UGGs, it would be an abomination. Moncler and Bogner are all the rage here, at least among the women, and sometimes I make a game of trying to talk about the latest in skiwear trends without actually having to pronounce those brands.

I'd definitely butcher them if I tried.

Greer sat quietly—or perhaps politely—impressed as I dragged her around the city, but I wasn't trying to show off. I just wanted her to feel at home in my new home. I want her to feel like she can visit anytime.

I haven't made many close friends here yet, and aside from Andrew, I'm embarrassed to admit I don't have much of a life. Seems like there are plenty of women around here who are content to stay home doing nothing, to fill their empty days with facials and manicures and spur-of-the-moment Bunco lunches with their other stay-at-home friends.

I joined them once when one of our neighbors invited me, but the women were all my mother's age, and when they weren't fawning over how "perky my breasts are" and how my "skin glowed like a newborn's bottom," they were treating me like their daughter.

"Meredith, be a lamb and grab me a glass of ice in the kitchen, please?"

"Meredith, you'll have to explain this Instagram thing to me. I have no idea how it works."

"Meredith, I should take you shopping with me. I bet you could pick out some clothes my niece might actually wear for once . . ."

I left the Bunco lunch with a bitter taste in my mouth and the realization that fitting in to Andrew's world wasn't going to be as smooth of a transition as I'd hoped.

The other night, I mentioned maybe looking for a part-time job to Andrew, but he just chuckled and kissed my head, telling me money wasn't an issue for us and that it never would be.

That wasn't my point.

I'm bored.

And lonely.

But it's not like I can come out and tell my husband, *"Sorry to be ungrateful and I love you to death, but this opulent life you've given me is dull and boring, and I kind of hate it."*

"You going to call it a night?" I glance at the clock, mentally calculating what time it would be back in New York.

My sister inhales, nodding, inspecting her surroundings with her feet cemented to the floor.

"I have barre in the morning," I say. I hate barre. I hate exercising in general, at least out here. Leaving the warm gym in sweaty, sticky clothes and walking into an icy cold parking lot always makes me rethink whether or not I want to renew my membership each month. But working out kills time—roughly three hours if I include the time for my preworkout shower, getting dressed (which includes full hair and makeup because that's what women do here), driving to the gym, sweating my ass off in a couple of classes, driving back, showering, dressing, and fixing my hair and makeup all over again. "And then spin class right after. I should be back by ten or so. Let me know what you want to do while you're here."

Greer offers me a reserved half smile. "Sounds good."

Showing myself out, I trek across the backyard, making my way to the house. When I reach the back porch, I stop when I see Andrew seated at the head of the dining room table, a glass of wine to his right and a plate of heated leftovers before him. He's reading the news on his tablet, the little line between his brows deep and pronounced, and my heart feels full.

He's always working, always providing.

The quiet whoosh of the sliding door grabs his attention, and when he looks up at me, his expression ignites. The fact that this powerful, well-to-do man lights up like a firecracker every time I come into the room is enough to make me want to marry him all over again.

Placing his fork aside, he pushes his chair from the table and makes his way to me. Cupping my face in his hand, he kisses my forehead.

"It's going to be really hard not having you all to myself for the next week," he says, a playful tone in his voice. "I'm a selfish man when it comes to you."

CHAPTER 4

GREER

Day Two

The driveway is cluttered with vehicles, marked and unmarked, all of them shiny and black and serious, crammed in one behind another. I climb out of my Yellow Cab and meet the driver near the trunk for my luggage.

My joints ache from sitting so much, and my legs are heavy. I wheel my luggage to the front door, which is open a crack, and I show myself in.

A uniformed officer stands guard by the front door, his fingers hooked on his duty belt. He peers my way, looking me up and down before strutting over like he has all the time in the world.

The lack of urgency with these people concerns me.

He's young, and his eyes are a boring shade of brown that complements the uninterested expression on his baby face. He's skinny, his uniform baggy around his shoulders, and I bet when he's not working, he's hanging out in his mother's basement playing *Battlefield*.

"Ma'am, this is a—" he begins to say, stifling a yawn. His lips press together. His eyes water, quiver. I'm guessing it's nearing the end of his shift, and when he's called to a scene with no blood, no corpse, and no active shooter and told to be a glorified security guard, he finds himself second-guessing his life choices.

I straighten my shoulders and square my jaw. "Greer Ambrose. Meredith's sister."

He stops talking and stands back, pointing me toward the kitchen, and I follow a trail of low voices.

Andrew notices me the second I appear in the doorway. We lock eyes from across the room, but we might as well be locking horns. His gray slacks and navy cashmere sweater are a noticeable departure from his custom three-piece suits, but he still looks as though he woke up this morning, showered as if it were any other day, and put time and effort into his appearance.

"Greer." He comes toward me, wrapping his arms around me and squeezing me tight. He's never hugged me this way before, not even for show when Meredith was around. "I'm glad you could make it."

He pulls away but leaves his hands on my shoulders. I don't like them there. I don't like him touching me. Just because my sister is missing doesn't mean I'm going to forget that he's a pompous egomaniac who plucked my sister from obscurity, all so he could have the shiniest of trophy wives in all this pathetic little ski resort land.

"What's the latest?" I try to ignore the distracting weight of his hands.

"Nothing." He exhales, his eyes drifting over my shoulder and focusing on something behind me as worry lines spread along his forehead. "The forensics team had her phone overnight. They've requested her phone records, but so far nothing unusual. She wasn't texting anyone out of the ordinary . . . making plans with anyone . . ."

"I just don't understand what led up to this. Did the two of you have a fight?" I ask. "Is there any chance she left on her own?"

"Absolutely not." His brows rise. Defensive, perhaps, that I would even suggest such a thing? "It was just an ordinary day. I kissed her goodbye, left for work . . ."

His words trail into silence, and for a moment I think he may be getting choked up.

"So catch me up here." I brace my hand on one hip and exhale. "I need to know everything."

His eyes take their time finding mine. "Like I said, Greer, she went to the grocery store yesterday, and no one's seen her since. There was no fight. No marital discord. We've contacted all the area hospitals, jails, shelters. Everything. No one's seen a woman matching her description."

"What about her car? Any signs . . . ?"

"No signs of foul play, no. Her phone and purse were on the passenger seat. Keys in the ignition."

"So if someone took her, it's someone she knew."

He shrugs, palms in the air. "It's hard to know. Maybe she was held up? I-I don't know. I don't know a damn thing."

My brother-in-law turns, scanning the room, full of strangers who should be doing more than standing around in this ostentatious chef's kitchen, and he points.

"That's Detective McCormack," he says, clearing his throat and pulling his shoulders tight. There's a curious look on his face; his eyes squint as he nods in that direction. "He's leading the investigation."

A man with striking russet hair, a dimpled chin, and broad shoulders nurses a Styrofoam cup of coffee, looking much too young to have accumulated enough work experience to lead a missing persons case.

He's too pretty, too smooth, too green to be here. There are no dark circles under his eyes, no yellow pallor to his skin to suggest he decompresses with a six-pack of Coors Light every evening.

"How many missing persons cases has he solved?" I ask.

"Excuse me?" Andrew takes offense at my question.

"He's standing around sipping coffee. Why isn't he out asking questions?"

"He spent all day yesterday talking to people. Until he has more leads, there's not much he can do." He keeps his voice low, as if me scrutinizing the well-rested detective assigned to my sister's case would reflect poorly on him.

Too bad for him. I don't give a damn what people think.

My jaw tightens. "He needs to go *find* the leads. The leads aren't going to find him. They're not just going to land in his lap. For Christ's sake, this is his *job*."

"Calm down."

I purse my lips until I can trust what's about to come out of them.

"It doesn't bother you that everyone's just standing around like they're waiting for the phone to ring?" I ask, knowing full well I'm overreacting, but I expected to see more bustle, more frenzy. The lack of frenetic energy among the ones who are supposed to be finding my sister only intensifies my anxiety.

Andrew hooks my elbow a little too abruptly, pulling me into an empty hallway off the kitchen, away from the horde of uniformed do-nothings.

"There are people at the station fielding calls on a dedicated tip line." His lips pinch as he exhales, and he keeps his voice low. "Meredith's picture is being broadcast on every local news station in the area, as well as dozens of national programs. They've dusted her car for prints. They've gone through her cell phone. I was at the police station for *hours* yesterday, telling them everything they could possibly want to know about her, right down to the cherry-shape birthmark on her left ass cheek. So if you want to sit here and act like nobody's doing anything, if you think you could do a better job, then be my fucking guest."

Andrew has never sworn at me before. He's never scowled or squinted or grabbed my arm so tight, his hands trembling.

"She disappeared into thin air, Greer," he says, stepping away. His hands lift and fall with a hopeless slap at his sides. "They've got nothing. They've got nothing to work with. We're all just . . . doing the best we can."

Folding my arms across my chest, I study his face, though I'm not sure what I'm looking for. A man with vast wealth and endless resources could make a person disappear without a trace if he wanted to, though last I knew, they were both equally crazy about each other, still trucking along like he wasn't just using her for sex and she wasn't just using him to fill the void of never knowing her father, never knowing what it was like to have a reliable, responsible adult take care of her.

I had finally been starting to accept the fact that he might be good for her, that she needed the stability and adoration he offered, never having experienced those before.

Detective McCormack appears from around the corner, and Andrew follows my gaze in that direction.

"Sorry to interrupt," he says. "We just got a call into the tip line. I'm going to head back to the station, call them back, and ask a few more questions. I'll let you know if anything comes of it."

My ears perk, my focus alternating between the two of them, neither of whom seems particularly hopeful. Maybe it's a man thing, not wanting to invest in hope.

"Of course." Andrew crosses his cashmere-covered arms, his tone sounding more like that of a concerned father accepting responsibility for a runaway teen daughter than a spouse beside himself with grief. "Keep me posted."

"Greer Ambrose." I introduce myself, though I keep my hands tucked tight across my chest. "Meredith's sister."

Detective McCormack studies my face, and I unfairly resent that he looks like the nicest guy in America. I bet he was an Eagle Scout. I bet he can tie impossible knots and light fires with flint, and I bet he can set up a tent in three minutes flat. I bet he had a nice childhood with nice parents, and I'm sure he's a nice guy.

But it's going to take a hell of a lot more than a friendly face to find my sister.

"Ronan," he says, brows lifting. I'm not sure if the first-name-basis thing is an attempt to spark the beginning of some kind of interpersonal relationship or if he does this with everyone. "You have a second?"

I wish he were older, with thick white hair and a bushy mustache. I wish he had a take-no-shit attitude and overflowing cabinets of solved case files, awards plaques on his walls—something to give me hope.

But he's just a regular guy who probably settled for the first job he was offered straight out of college and never left.

I bet he's never known tragedy, never had the one person he loved more than anything else just . . . vanish.

I follow Ronan outside, where we stand beneath a two-story portico that magnifies each shuffle of our feet and every slow, exasperated exhalation.

"When you get a chance, I need you to come down to the station for a DNA swab," he says. "We need a family reference sample—standard procedure."

My head pounds. "Oh, I see. So in case you find a dead body, you can compare the DNA to mine to see if it's her."

He says nothing, but his expression confirms this.

"My sister's not dead," I say.

"Like I said, standard procedure. It doesn't mean anything yet."

I shake my head.

I hate this.

I hate this, I hate this, I hate this.

"Fine." My hands fall to my sides before resting at my hips. "I'll do your little test, but you're giving me a ride, and you're bringing me back here, and when we're finished, you're going to help me find her."

"That's the plan, Ms. Ambrose." His dark eyes flicker—amusement perhaps? "You're nothing like her, you know."

"What are you talking about?"

"I knew her," he says. "Worked with her on a stalker case a couple years back. Very lovely girl. Sweet. Little on the soft-spoken side."

My fingers twist the gold chain around my neck, tugging at the small diamond pendant—a gift from Harris years ago that I've never seemed to be able to part with. He gave it to me on our first anniversary after he'd spent a month working at the Student Union's copy center just to save up for it. It's an ugly little thing with infinitesimal diamonds in dire need of a good scrubbing, but I'll never forget how proud he was when he presented me with the little velvet box over a ramen dinner in my dorm room.

"Meredith never told me she had a stalker." I glance away, my stomach in knots. What else don't I know about?

His lips flatten, and he glances around like he's silently kicking himself for telling me. "Yeah."

"Did you ever figure out who it was? Do you think he could've had something to do with this? Why would she keep that from me?" My voice rises. "She tells me everything. That seems like a pretty big thing to keep from your sister, don't you think?"

"Maybe she didn't want you to worry?" His eyes soften, and in the span of two seconds, he sees me for the neurotic, anxious worrywart I've always been. "Look, I'm sure she had her reasons."

Yes.

I'm sure she did.

CHAPTER 5

MEREDITH

Thirty-Two Months Ago

Blood.

There's blood everywhere: dripping down my thighs, smeared across the marble bathroom floor, streaking down the inside of our pristine toilet bowl.

Resting next to my vanity mirror is a little blue box containing a positive pregnancy test.

I was going to tell Andrew tonight. I had it all planned. A romantic dinner at Sky Port, a starry drive through the mountains, and the big reveal at the end of it all, complete with a heartfelt letter I'd spent all yesterday morning penning.

It was mostly word vomit, talking about how I never met my father and how watching him with Isabeau and Calder makes me grateful to be starting this journey with him. I gushed about how safe he made me feel, how protected and loved. The letter rambled on because, truth be told, I couldn't ask for a better father for my unborn child than Andrew, and I wanted him to know that.

Maybe writing a letter was silly and schoolgirlish, but I figured it'd be nice to tuck away in a baby book to be read years from now.

We hadn't talked about starting a family just yet. The late period last month caught me completely off guard, putting me in a bit of a stunned silence for a while. It didn't feel real, so I waited a month before testing—just to be certain.

The twinges began shortly after lunch today, growing worse with each passing hour. I was in denial at first, Googling "early pregnancy cramping" as fast as my fingers would allow, but when I felt the trickle of blood down my inner thighs and experienced a shock of pain that nearly knocked me to my knees, I placed my phone down.

"Mer, you in there?" Andrew's voice calls from outside our bathroom door. "Reservation's in a half hour. Been looking forward to this all day."

There's excitement in his tone, and I'm leaning against the bathroom door, holding a white towel between my legs, pulling in deep breaths.

I don't want him to see me like this.

"I'll be out in a second," I say, my voice breaking as I summon the strength to clean up and make myself somewhat presentable. I'm not sure if I can walk out of here and sit across from him at dinner like nothing happened, but I'm going to try.

It was early, that much I know.

I hadn't been to the doctor yet. I hadn't had an ultrasound or been given the all clear—that appointment was scheduled in the coming weeks. But tonight marked exactly four months since our wedding, and I thought this would be a special way to ring in an arbitrary anniversary.

I'm on my hands and knees, a bottle of bathroom cleaner in one hand and a roll of paper towels under my arm as I scrub at a splotch of dried blood on the tile—the blood that once filled a now-empty womb.

It isn't fair.

"Meredith." Andrew's voice startles me, and I turn to see him standing in the doorway. I didn't hear the door. "My God, what happened?"

Before I can so much as mutter a single consonant, I'm bawling.

Andrew has never seen me so much as pout, and here I am sobbing uncontrollably, my entire body shaking, my vision blinded with the sting of hot tears.

I feel . . . empty.

Literally empty.

All that love, all that hope, just . . . gone.

He falls to his knees, his hands on my arms, and then he pulls me into his embrace. "Talk to me."

"I was going to tell you," I say, my throat tight, burning.

"Tell me what?" He leans back, though holding me still. His eyes search mine, his words rushed.

"About the pregnancy." I can't bring myself to say the word "baby." Not now.

He's quiet, and his hand that was once rubbing slow circles into my arm stops. A moment later, he pulls himself away, studying my face.

"You were *pregnant*?" he asks, his eyes expressionless, all sympathy gone.

I bite my lip so hard I taste blood, but I don't feel it, and then I nod. "Yeah. I was."

Andrew rises, pinching the bridge of his nose before exhaling, and within seconds he's pacing the little section of bleached floor.

"Andrew . . ." I dry my eyes on the backs of my hands, pulling myself up to standing. This isn't exactly the reaction I expected from him.

"I thought you were on the pill?" His hand drags down his cheek. He won't look at me.

"I am—I was," I say. "Maybe I missed one here or there? I don't know. I just know it happened."

Andrew stops pacing, his hard stare fixed on me. "This can't happen again, Meredith."

I'm speechless. Officially speechless. Staring at the man I married, the man I envisioned spending the rest of my life with—baby carriage, picket fence, and all—and I don't recognize him.

He may as well be a stranger.

A seething, red-faced stranger.

I've never seen that look on his face before: pure, unadulterated rage. He's looking at me as if I've just betrayed him, betrayed his trust, and my first instinct is to get the hell out of here.

So I do.

Ignoring the fiery furnace in my lower belly, I push past Andrew and rifle through my half of the closet, pulling jeans and sweaters from wooden hangers and loading up as much as I can carry. When I turn to leave, he's blocking the door.

"What are you doing?" His expression relaxes, all hint of fury gone—like it was never there in the first place, like I imagined it. "You're not leaving."

I start toward him, searing pain and all. "Of course I am."

Stepping toward me, he gathers the clothes from my arms and drops them on the ground by our feet. They land on the plush carpet with an unsatisfying thud.

"No, no," he says, talking to me the way you would speak to a person about to jump from the top of a skyscraper. "You're not going to do that. It's not a good idea."

A thick tear runs down my cheek.

Andrew wipes it away.

"I'm sorry," he says.

I don't speak.

"I was in shock," he continues, his voice soft, his gaze softer. "I didn't choose my words . . . I shouldn't have reacted that way . . . I didn't mean to upset you." He brushes a light strand of hair from my eyes. "I should've held you, comforted you. You're my wife, Mer. You're the love of my life. You were hurting, and all I could think about was myself. I was wrong . . . forgive me?"

Our eyes hold for what feels like forever, but I can't stop seeing his face from a few minutes ago. His twisted brows. His clenched jaw. His flaring nostrils. The subzero chill in his eyes.

He kisses me, his lips warm and gentle, his hands in my hair, but it doesn't feel the same as before. It's tainted, marred.

Andrew's hands trail down my arms, stopping at my fingers and interlacing them with his. Kissing my forehead, he gives a slow, slight smile.

"We hadn't talked about starting a family yet," he says.

"It wasn't planned."

"I know," he says, his head cocked as he peers down his perfect, straight nose at me. "Just be careful from now on, okay? You're going to make the most beautiful mother . . . *someday*. Until then, I want to enjoy what we have right now. Why rush it? It's absolutely perfect, don't you think?"

He lifts my hand to his mouth, depositing a lingering kiss, and I'm taken back to last night, when he whispered in my ear that his life finally felt perfect, and all I could think about was how much *more* perfect it was going to be with the baby.

How wrong I was.

"I'm not ready to share you yet," he says, maybe teasing, maybe not. "Sorry, but I'm keeping you all to myself for as long as possible."

A week ago, those words would've sent a flutter of butterflies to my stomach and a warm fullness to my chest, but in this moment, I'm numb.

His words, his touch . . . they do nothing for me.

"I'm going to lie down." I pull my hands from his and turn back into the bedroom.

He lets me walk away, and I crawl beneath the mass of downy plush covers on our enormous bed. Rolling to my side, I shut my eyes and breathe in the lavender scent of our freshly washed-and-pressed sheets.

His footsteps are soft on the carpet, and the soft creak of the door is followed by dead silence.

A short while later, my husband whispers in my ear. "Meredith." I don't know how long I've been lying here, and I hadn't heard him come back. The bed dips on my side. "I brought you some water and something for the pain. Sit up."

Opening my eyes, I roll toward him and push myself up. He fluffs the pillows behind me before dropping two matte-brown pills in my palm and handing me a glass of still water.

The light from our bathroom casts shadows on the wall, and I watch as he leaves my side and changes into a silk pajama set before climbing into bed.

"I canceled our reservations," he says, moving close and placing his arm around me. He pulls me into the warm bend of his shoulder before resting his chin on top of my head. "I'm here for you, Mer. Anything you need."

In this moment, I almost forget what happened earlier.

Almost.

CHAPTER 6

GREER

Day Two

A woman with latex gloves runs swab sticks along the inside of my cheeks as I'm seated in a metal folding chair in Ronan's office. From here, I can see past the doorway, where he's fixing himself coffee from a stained machine on a counter next to an almond-colored fridge in a break room.

He takes it black. No cream, no sugar.

My favorite customers back home take their coffee black. They're the ones who don't have time for bullshit. They don't stand at the counter making chitchat about the weather or their upcoming vacation to the Hamptons. They get in line, pay their five bucks, and walk away with their perfect, steaming cup of high-quality caffeine.

I resolve to try to like this detective, as unseasoned as he may be, because he could very well surprise me.

If Harris were here, he'd tell me to stop judging. And I'd remind him that I judge when I'm anxious. When I lose control of my surroundings, I fixate on other people, picking them apart if only for the distraction it provides my frazzled mind. It's a terrible habit, one I've been meaning to break over the years.

"All done, Ms. Ambrose," the woman says, sealing the swabs in a plastic sleeve.

I don't thank her. She doesn't thank me. Gratitude is for happy occasions.

When Ronan returns, he takes a seat at his desk and fires up his computer, which chimes a melancholy jingle, the black screen flickering. The woman leaves a moment later, closing the door behind her, and I watch as he checks his e-mail.

"Were you able to contact that lead?" I ask.

"What's that?" He peers over his screen at me, as if he'd forgotten I was here. I can only hope he's so consumed by this case that he's wrapped up in his own thoughts and unplugged from reality.

"The lead. You got a call . . . the tip line . . ."

"Right," he says, tapping his fingers on the desk and directing his attention to me. Grabbing one of those squishy stress balls, he makes a fist around it before leaning back in his chair and scrutinizing me, like he's trying to figure me out. Maybe it's a detective thing. Maybe they do it to everyone: stare and examine. Only Ronan still looks like a nice guy, and when a nice guy does an assholeish thing, it takes everything I have not to scream. Closing my eyes for a moment, I think of Harris, imagining him taking my hand and telling me to breathe like he used to do, back when we'd opened our third shop and my neuroticism was at its peak. "They didn't answer. I left a message. Gave her my cell."

I couldn't hide my disappointment if I tried.

He squeezes the ball tighter in his hand, his watchful gaze yet to retire. "You don't look like her."

"We're half sisters," I say. "She takes after her father's side; I take after mine."

Neither of us looks like our mother, and I've counted my lucky stars for that every day of my existence. Not that our mother isn't a sight for sore eyes—she's beautiful. I just wouldn't want to look in the mirror every day and see . . . her.

"Born and raised in New York," he states, as if that amuses him, like we're novelties.

"How do you know?"

"I remember when I talked to her a few years back," he says. "Said she was from Queens, and I asked her why she didn't have an accent."

"Not all of us have accents."

"Yeah, but it was what she told me that stood out, I guess." His eyes squint. "She said your mother used to make you watch the nightly news and practice talking like the anchors."

My eyes fall to the ground as I recall all those dinners around the scratched oak table with the news blaring the day's tragedies in the background, our mother dishing out Hamburger Helper and rambling on about the importance of speaking like the educated socialites we were never going to be.

"People hear you talking like you're from Queens and they're going to judge you, make assumptions about you," she would say. "And if they're not judging you, they're going to be annoyed by you."

Meredith was a natural, but she was younger. I had eight years on her, which meant eight years of unlearning everything about the way I spoke and replacing it with what felt like an accent.

"That's Brenda Ambrose for you," I say.

"You guys close? You and Meredith and your mother?"

"I don't see how that's relevant to finding my sister."

"Just trying to examine the case from all angles," he says, tossing the stress ball on his desk. It rolls behind his keyboard, disappearing. "Evidence is everywhere."

"Yeah, well, my sister went grocery shopping and vanished. I highly doubt our mother—or my relationship with her—had anything to do with that." My words slice through the stale office air. "Now, if you'd kindly start looking for my sister and asking important questions to people who might actually know what happened, that'd be great."

He smirks. "You *are* an important person, Greer."

I rise, slinging my bag over my shoulder and tightening my grip on the strap. "My sister and I were separated by thousands of miles and dozens of states. I can assure you, whatever happened . . . I know nothing about it."

"I'm not saying you know what happened," he says, undeterred by my defensiveness. "I'm saying you might be able to provide some information that might lead me in a better direction."

"If I knew *anything*, Detective, believe me, I would tell you."

Ronan rises, his hands splayed on his desk as his back arches. His eyes brush past my shoulder, toward the sliver of window in his closed door.

"Look, I want to find her just as badly as you do," he says. "And I'm going to. I just need you to cooperate. Tell me everything you can about her, even if you think it's not important. You probably know her better than anyone, maybe even better than her husband."

"I'm more than willing to cooperate and I don't mean to sound harsh here, but how is rehashing childhood memories going to help you find my sister?"

His eyes narrow on mine. "We have to look at every possibility." He sighs. "And that includes the possibility that maybe she wasn't taken . . . that maybe she left on her own."

"If my sister wanted out of her life, she would've told me. She wouldn't just abandon her things in a grocery store parking lot," I say.

Turning, I reach for the doorknob, intending to show myself out, but Ronan rushes around the desk and rests his hand on the glass, his stare searching mine.

"Is there any chance your sister was trying to get out of her marriage?" he asks. "For any reason? Is there anything she may have said or done in the past few years to hint at that? Any allusion or inclination? A gut feeling on your part? A strange conversation?"

I sigh. "She loved him. And if she wasn't wanting to be with him anymore, she never said anything to me."

"You never saw any warning signs that maybe they weren't as happy as they seemed . . . anything in the way he spoke to her or treated her?"

"He treats her like a show pony, parades her around, spoils her." I fold my arms across my chest. "He annoys the hell out of me, but he loves her. I can't deny that."

"So there was nothing," he says, as if he needs clarification for the fourteenth time. I get the need to be thorough, but this is overkill.

"If my sister wanted out of her marriage, she'd have left him and moved back to New York. She knew my door was always open. I told her that. Before they were married."

"So you had that conversation once?" he asks. "About what she would do if she wanted out of her marriage?"

"How about this?" I say, my patience suddenly paper-thin. "How about you put down your dog-eared copy of *Gone Girl* and come back to reality so you can find my sister? Maybe you should talk to that stalker. Maybe he had something to do with this?"

Ronan's response is cut short by the piercing ring of his desktop phone. He abandons my side, swerving around his desk and answering in the middle of the second ring.

"Yeah, patch her through," he says a few seconds later before covering the mouthpiece. "It's the tip line."

Ronan motions for me to leave.

"I'm not going anywhere." I stand, feet planted.

"You can't be in here," he says, his words rushed. "Official police business. This is a confidential conversation. Department policy."

Grabbing a small stack of business cards from an open box on the edge of his desk, he pushes them toward me.

"Hand those out to anyone who knew your sister," he says. I hate that he uses the word "knew" . . . as if he thinks she's gone for good. "If they so much as sold her a cup of coffee, I want to talk to them. I've been canvassing, but I could use your help."

My eyes fall to the stack of cards, then back to him.

This could be a good thing, something to keep me busy. I get testy when I'm sitting around doing nothing, stuck inside my own head, drowning in my anxieties and powerlessness.

"Detective McCormack," he says, his eyes meeting mine. He points to the door, and I opt to let him do his job because finding Meredith is the only thing that matters. Covering the mouthpiece once more, he says, "Wait by the front desk. I'll take you back to the Price house as soon as I'm done."

I head to the lobby, which is empty save for myself and a uniformed receptionist, who watches me from the corner of her eye. Maybe she's curious, maybe she's wondering what I'm thinking or how I'm processing this, asking herself how she'd handle something like this. Maybe it's human nature, but I don't care. She can observe all she wants, and she can assume all she wants. I stopped giving a shit about what anyone thinks a long time ago.

Just wish I could say the same for Meredith.

When we were younger, I always used to tell her to ditch the obsession with people pleasing. I'd tell her it was okay if people didn't like her and that it meant she was doing something right.

We're not meant to be best friends with every person who crosses our paths.

Not everyone has our best interests at heart.

Maybe I'm cynical, but those facts I know to be true.

I distinctly remember telling her once that if she continued telling people what they wanted to hear, one of these days it was going to backfire on her.

But my sister was tofu.

Absorbing the characteristics of whoever has managed to capture her attention at that point in her life, assimilating herself and becoming what they want her to become because it makes them like her better. And I can't blame her. It's in our genetics. Our mother is tofu.

I was always better at fighting the urge.

"You ready?" Ronan appears in the lobby doorway, his hands on his hips. There's no pep in his step or life in his eyes that tells me he may have gotten a break in the case.

Glancing at the receptionist, I know better than to grill him on the phone call in front of her, but the second we get in the car, all bets are off.

CHAPTER 7

MEREDITH

Thirty Months Ago

"All packed?" I stand in my stepdaughter Isabeau's doorway as she shoves wrinkled clothes into a monogrammed suitcase. She ignores me, and I ignore the fact that she has entirely too much attitude for a ten-year-old. I blame her mother. "Your mom's going to be here any minute. You know how she gets when you're not ready."

God forbid Erica has to stand in the foyer an extra three minutes. She acts like she's standing at the fiery gates of hell, refusing to move any closer than she has to.

I check my watch. Isabeau sighs. She doesn't want me here. When I first moved in, she wasted no time informing her father that I wasn't allowed in her room, to which he promptly responded by confiscating her cherished iPhone for five days, the worst punishment a parent could possibly inflict on a modern-day child.

She's loathed my presence ever since.

"I know what time my mother arrives," she says. "She comes at the same time every week. You don't have to remind me."

I lift my hands in protest. "Just trying to be helpful, Iz."

She rises, zipping her bag. "I don't like to be called that."

I don't blame her for hating me. One minute her family unit is intact, and the next her parents are divorced and her father's doting over a complete stranger who's suddenly trying to forge an unnatural bond with her.

Andrew tells me it'll take time, that Isabeau doesn't warm up to anyone right away, just like Greer. He's positive that one day we'll be the best of friends. But I don't need to be her best friend—I just need for things not to be so strained and awkward 50 percent of my life.

The doorbell rings, Erica I'm sure, and I wonder how strange it must feel to ring the bell to a house she once shared with her husband. I also wonder if her resentment of me is reinforced each time I answer the door.

"Calder." I yell for him as I traipse across the second-floor gallery, rapping on his door. There's music blaring on the other side, so I knock louder. When he doesn't answer, I open the door to find him zoned out in front of his TV, playing some kind of video game where he shoots at anything and everything. "Calder, your mom's here."

He pauses his game, shoulders slumping, and tosses his controller on the ground. His leather backpack is overflowing, half-unzipped, and he slings it over his shoulder as our eyes meet.

Calder doesn't say much to me, and he hasn't ever since his father found one of my thongs under his mattress and my favorite Agent Provocateur bra in the bottom of his pajama drawer. I regularly catch his eyes lingering in places they don't belong, and he walked in on me in the shower last month—something that felt more intentional than accidental.

Andrew chalks it up to the fact that Calder is fourteen. He's curious about the opposite sex, that's all. It's a phase, and once he bonds with me as a mother figure, all this will hopefully subside.

Never mind that I'm not nearly old enough to be his mother.

Calder pushes past me, not saying a word, and bounces down the curved staircase to the front door. I let him answer this time.

When I emerge from his messy teenage lair, I spot Isabeau making her way downstairs to her mother, tangled hair bouncing and chubby face lit.

The view from the gallery is a straight shot to the foyer, and I watch as Erica ruffles Calder's dark hair before cupping his face.

"You look skinnier and skinnier every time I see you," she says, tongue clucking. "Is Meredith feeding you?"

He jerks his face from her hand, his eyes glued to his phone. "Yeah, Mom."

Isabeau wraps her arms around her mother's whittled waist. If anyone's getting skinnier and skinnier, it's Erica.

Ever since the divorce, she's been sticking to a strict diet of protein shakes and vodka tonics. Or so Andrew says. He finds it amusing, says she's trying to compete with me. Her jealousy makes him laugh, and I'd feel badly about it if I didn't know how awful she was to him for sixteen years—cheating, overspending, never-ending nagging and bickering.

Erica is the embodiment of a typical Glacier Park housewife: entitled, petty, and allergic to kindness.

"When was the last time you combed your hair, darling?" she says to her daughter. "All these tangles. Ugh."

Isabeau tucks a disheveled, cocoa-hued strand behind one ear. "Meredith won't do my hair, Mom. I've asked her, and she always says she's too busy."

My jaw unglues, and I have half a mind to storm down the stairs and call her out on her bold-faced lie, but I won't. I know what she's doing. She wants attention and sympathy from her mother, and if lying about me is the only way to get it, then I'll let it go, and I'll be the bigger person—for now.

The truth always has a way of coming out sooner or later.

Besides, there are far more damaging lies Isabeau could tell.

"Meredith, is that you up there?" Erica calls out. "Are you going to come down and say hello, or are you going to stand there in the shadows, listening to our conversation?"

Bitch.

"Didn't want to intrude," I say. "Was just giving you some space."

"So sweet of you," she says, her voice as fake as the D-cup implants protruding from her chest wall and the luxurious shade of glossed auburn covering her graying mane.

My hand slides down the polished wooden banister as I make my graceful entrance wearing a humble smile, but when I get to the bottom, my phone chimes with a text alert. My mood fades when I read that Andrew won't be home for dinner tonight.

"Trouble in paradise?" Erica doesn't try to fight the pleased smirk claiming her overfilled lips.

"Not at all." I keep my head high, meeting her inquisitive gaze head-on. Shame on her for trying to make me doubt my marriage.

"Let me guess, he canceled on you?" she asks. "Has to work late for the millionth time?"

"I'm not discussing any of this with you."

"Fair enough." Erica's stare is locked on mine as she slips two black leather gloves over her dainty fingers. "Kids. Car. Now."

Calder and Isabeau file out the front door, their designer bags in tow, and Erica comes toward me with folded arms, her heels clicking with each step.

"You remind me so much of myself sixteen years ago," she says. "That brightness in your eyes. The glow on your face. Enjoy it while you can, Meredith. You'll only be the apple of his eye for so long."

"What the hell are you doing?" My nose wrinkles.

"Watching out for you," she says, thin brows arched. "Woman to woman. You know, that kind of thing."

"Bitter and jealous isn't doing you any favors."

Erica laughs. "Sweetheart, you're the last person I'd be jealous of. You think I'm crying myself to sleep every night over losing him? Quite frankly, the only thing I despise about this entire situation is that it's humiliating. My husband of sixteen years dumps me and picks up a wife half his age . . . talk about cliché. You're the equivalent of a middle-aged man's shiny new Porsche. You're nothing but a sex toy. And one of these days, when the newness and excitement wear off, he'll trade you in for something else. That's what Andrew does. Nothing is ever good enough. He's always striving for the next hotter, better, more exhilarating thing."

"How poignant, Erica. Thank you." I stride toward the door, pulling it open for her before I allow her to burrow beneath my skin another inch.

She scoffs, lingering in my space for a moment too long before finally strutting outside, only the second she reaches the crisp Glacier Park air, she turns back to face me.

"One of these days, you'll see I was right. And you probably won't want to admit it, but you'll know. Deep down you'll know. And I won't feel sorry for you because I warned you." Her hazel eyes scan the length of me before crinkling at the corners. "You're nothing but a novelty to him. I promise you that."

"Goodbye, Erica." I shut the door, ensuring it doesn't slam. I wouldn't want her driving off with the satisfaction of knowing that her words had any sort of effect on me, even though they kind of do.

But not for long.

Walking it off, I send Andrew a text, telling him it's fine that he has to work late, and I offer to bring his dinner to the office. If we can't go out on our date tonight, I'll bring the date to him.

My phone rings a minute later. "You're fucking incredible, Mer. I'd love that."

"I'll bring your favorite," I say. "The filet mignon from Centro, medium rare, oven-roasted asparagus, and a house salad, balsamic vinaigrette on the side."

"You know me well," he says, and I can hear the smile in his voice. "Can't wait to see you."

"I'll be there in an hour. And be sure to save room for dessert." I bite my thumbnail, hoping he can read between the lines without seeing the devilish light in my eyes.

"You're making me so fucking hard right now." His voice is a low, grainy whisper into the receiver, and a jolt of anticipation ricochets through my body.

Erica has no idea what she's talking about. I may be his plaything, but he's mine, too. Mix love into that equation, and we're unstoppable.

"Be there soon . . ." I hang up, trotting upstairs to slip on a little something special under my jeans and sweater.

CHAPTER 8

GREER

Day Three

It's odd to think that forty-eight hours ago, my sister was driving these very streets, going about her daily business like any other ordinary Monday. And now here I am, shuffling through the snow-dusted streets, going door-to-door in an attempt to get at least one of her neighbors to answer.

No one appears to be home.

Or if they are home, they don't want to talk to some strange lady dressed in all black who clearly isn't from around here.

Not that I blame them.

Ronan's tip line caller last night turned out to be a dud—or at least that's what he claimed when I asked him on the ride home. Just some woman saying she saw a girl fitting Mer's description riding in the back of a rusted conversion van heading eastbound on I-70. Not much he can do with that besides make a case note and hope he can connect it with something more substantial later.

I'll admit, he seemed just as disappointed as I was last night, and I was tired, so I didn't push or prod. I let him drop me off at Andrew and Meredith's, and he promised to be in touch.

Approaching what appears to be a giant log cabin with stone accents, a red tin roof, and an abundance of evergreens, I remove my right glove and climb the front steps. I only have to knock twice before a woman answers.

With milky skin, platinum-blonde hair cut short, clear blue eyes, and a pointed nose, she positions her lithe body like some sort of barricade between me and the inside of her house.

"Are you Allison Ross?" I ask, neglecting to tell her I found her name on the Glacier County Assessor's website on my walk over here, though I swear Meredith had spoken of her a time or two in passing.

Her brows furrow, and she readjusts her posture. "Who are you? Are you with the press? I'm not giving interviews about Meredith Price."

"I'm her sister."

Allison's tense expression eases, and she licks her rosy lips before glancing over my shoulder. Her eyes are jittery, her movements quick and nimble.

"Come in," she says, waving for me to follow her.

I step inside, removing my snowy boots on a plush wool rug in a dark entryway. Her home is neatly decorated, giving off a vacation-house vibe, and smells like fresh coffee, but its sheer size prevents it from feeling cozy.

"I'm just trying to find someone who maybe knew—knows—my sister," I say. "Someone from around here. Someone she might have talked to on a regular basis?"

It's only now that I see the bags under Allison's eyes, the veins of red clouding the whites around her irises. She looks as though she's been crying. Or not sleeping. Perhaps both.

"Meredith and I were close," she says, voice juddering as she focuses on a landscape portrait on the wall behind me. "We spent a lot of time together."

Allison trembles, her hands running the length of her arms as if that could possibly subdue the shivering taking over her tiny body.

"No one's come to ask me about her, you know?" she says, eyes darting to mine. "I was her closest friend, and not one person has asked me if I know anything."

"Do you know anything?" I lift a brow, my stare concentrated on hers.

"No," she says. "I don't. But don't you think that says something right there? People are talking like she may have left on her own, but the Meredith I know wouldn't have done that."

"So you think someone took her?" I ask.

Allison's shoulders rise and her mouth opens, but she doesn't speak right away. "That's what I'm inclined to think, yes. Or . . ."

"Or what?" I don't have time for hesitation and uncertainty.

"A few months back, I ran out to the store late one night to get some milk," she says, speaking carefully. "I passed this truck on Hanswell Boulevard, and I could have sworn Meredith was in it."

My heart races.

"But the woman in the truck, she was smiling and laughing. I only saw the side of her, and she was wearing a bright red stocking cap with a furry white pom-pom on top—I've never seen her with a hat like that." Allison places her hand up to her face. "And I only saw her for a split second because the light turned green and they were gone, pulled down a side street. I thought maybe I imagined it."

"Did you ever ask her about it?"

Allison shakes her head quickly. "I didn't want to ask because I wasn't completely sure, and if I was wrong, I would've offended her."

"I understand." I bite my lip, wishing Allison Ross would have had enough gumption and brains to frame a simple question in a strategic way.

"I think it's odd," she continues. "Andrew knew how much time Meredith and I spent together . . . You'd think he'd have sent the police here to ask me questions."

"What are you trying to say?" I ask a question to which I already know the answer.

Her eyes squeeze, and she shakes her head. "I don't know . . . I guess I just find it interesting."

"Are you thinking Andrew's trying to hide something?"

She glances up at me, fidgeting with her hair for a second. "I mean, I've known the two of them as a couple for more than two years—ever since we moved to this street—and you'd have thought they were still newlyweds. He was always fawning over her, and she was always gushing about how incredible he was." She stares across the foyer into the living room, focusing on a scenic view of the mountains. "To be honest, I was always kind of jealous of what they had. In a good way, you know? I was happy for her." Allison exhales. "But there was this one time. She came over just before yoga, and I noticed this bruise around her wrist, like someone had put their hand around it and squeezed really hard."

I can't breathe.

If that smug bastard put his hands on my sister, I'll fucking kill him.

"I never asked her about it," she says, her voice dropping. "She was wearing a watch that day, and she never wore watches to yoga, so it was odd. She was clearly trying to hide it."

"Would you be comfortable going on record with this information?" I ask.

Her clear eyes widen, as if I've just asked her to scale Everest in a snowstorm. "I don't know. What if I was imagining things?"

Sighing, I ask, "What if you weren't?"

"I just don't want to implicate the wrong person in any of this, that's all."

"Just talk to them. They can decide what to do with this information," I say, retrieving one of Ronan's cards from my bag. I hand it to her, and she hesitates before accepting it. "Please, Allison."

I don't want to believe my sister may have run off with some random guy without telling a soul, but the fact of the matter is, we don't know the truth. And the truth couldn't care less about what we *want* to believe.

Silence consumes her for a moment, but she finally agrees.

"I've written my number on the back of the card as well," I say. "Call me if you ever want to talk . . . or if you remember anything else."

"Of course." She slips the card into her jeans pocket as I show myself out.

Trekking to the next house, I can't stop thinking about my little sister with a bruise around her wrist.

CHAPTER 9

MEREDITH

Twenty-Nine Months Ago

The bells jingle on the door of Steam Coffee and Tea in Chelsea. Harris is working the register, and his expression hardens when he notices me. I place my pointed finger in front of my lips, a silent plea for him not to say anything, and he nods toward the back office, where my sister is hunched over her laptop next to a mountain of paperwork.

"Knock, knock," I say, rapping on the door.

She turns to face me, squinting until my familiarity registers. I haven't seen her in months, but I know I don't look that different.

"Oh, my God." She rises, still in shock. "Mer. What are you doing here?"

"Andrew's in town for work. I tagged along. Thought I'd surprise you."

Greer's never been a physically affectionate type of person, so her face says it all. She's surprised. And she's thrilled to see me.

"Let's go do stuff," I say. "I have the whole day to myself, and we're leaving tomorrow."

My sister glances at the computer, biting her lip. She's going to put me first, that much I know, but I can almost see her mentally calculating how late she'll be staying up tonight to finish her inventory or accounting or whatever the hell she's doing.

She's always so rational and business minded, which is why she and Harris make the perfect business partnership. He's artsy and creative and forward thinking, and he can make a mean cup of coffee, and she's good at ensuring the bottom line is in check, filing quarterly taxes, interviewing staff, and keeping the paychecks from bouncing.

"I'm stealing her," I say to Harris when I head back to the front. Greer is a few steps behind me, tugging a light jacket over her shoulders.

He pushes his tortoiseshell frames up his nose and stares. He knows he doesn't have a say. Our bond is impenetrable, even by the guy whose name is tattooed on my sister's heart.

"Have fun," he says in a way that doesn't sugarcoat his true feelings. I'm sure he resents the fact that we're frolicking off to pal around the city and have fun while he's stuck behind a register, but it's not like we do this all the time. Besides, the two of them work way too damn much. My sister can take a break. It's not going to kill either of them.

And by now, he should be used to playing second fiddle whenever I'm around. Everything . . . the business . . . Harris . . . takes a back seat when I'm home.

Greer doesn't say goodbye. She doesn't need to. The two of them have been together for something like a decade—almost marrying once. They're well past formalities, niceties, and taking anything personally.

"So I thought we'd get brunch at La Dolce," I start, looping my arm through hers as we hit the pavement outside the shop. "For old times' sake."

Greer tries to diminish her excitement, but her steps grow faster.

"It wouldn't kill you to smile a little more." I nudge her side. "You're always so serious, so . . . controlled."

"Your point?"

"I don't have a point. Just making an observation." Releasing my arm from hers, I step toward the curb and hail an oncoming cab.

"We can take the subway," she says, pointing down the block, where a sign indicates there's a station below the busy sidewalk.

"Cab will be quicker. Less walking, too. These heels are killing me."

Her eyes land at my feet, specifically the red uppers of my shoes. We used to make fun of women who pined after shoes like these. Now I've become one of them. Manolos. Louboutins. Valentinos in every color and heel size. I own them all and for reasons that perplex even myself.

I'm slightly ashamed.

A cab stops, and I motion for her to hurry up when I see a scowling man carrying a briefcase run-walking in our direction, wielding the audacity to try to steal our ride. I miss many things about the city, the least of which are assholes like that.

The ride to La Dolce is quiet, which means my sister is lost in thought.

"What are you going to get?" I ask, a lame attempt to make conversation and bring her into the present moment.

"Not sure."

"You always got the eggs Benedict," I say. "And I always got the French toast. I'm thinking we should probably play it safe and not buck tradition."

I'm teasing, trying my hardest to create a light and casual ambiance between us, but she doesn't respond.

"Why are you so quiet?" I ask. "What are you thinking about?"

Greer exhales, shaking her head as she stares out her window. "It's nothing."

"It's not nothing. You were all about this until you saw my shoes. Is it the shoes?" My voice rises, and the cabdriver checks the rearview mirror. "Greer."

"It's more than the shoes."

"Is it the cab?" I ask.

The driver looks up again.

"I just feel like every time I see you, you're a little less you and a little more someone I hardly recognize," she blurts, her words coming out terse and fast. "Just trying to wrap my head around it is all."

I laugh at the absurdity of my sister's statement. "I'm still me. Always will be."

The cab pulls to a rough stop, and the driver turns off the meter. I swipe Andrew's American Express card to pay for the ride, and Greer climbs out. A moment later, I join her on the curb outside the restaurant.

"It's just that you're doing what Mom used to do," she says, arms crossed.

My eyes widen. "Please tell me you didn't just compare me to her."

"You know I have a point."

Our gazes lock, as if we've reached an impasse, and I don't know what to say to my sister. Our mother had a penchant for morphing into all these different people, sometimes overnight, sometimes over the span of a few weeks or months. She didn't have any kind of personality disorder; she'd just treat her life like an old pair of shoes, changing them out with each turn of the season or each new boyfriend who waltzed into her life.

One year, she went from a free-spirited, gypsy-blouse-and-braid-wearing hippie to an uptight, organic-food-obsessed PTA mom in under eight hours. Most of the time we'd see the changes coming and we could anticipate them, but not that time. I'll never forget her shipping me off to school one morning in her hemp robe with tangled braids spilling down her shoulders, and when she greeted me at the door that afternoon, she was in a pencil skirt with a sheared, sleek bob, getting ready to unload half a dozen brown paper bags from Whole Foods.

Greer says Mom was working as a housekeeper at a private high-rise filled with well-to-do tenants when she met my father. She'd overheard a couple of women talking at the park about how their friend's cousin's sister went from housekeeper to wife of a multimillionaire business mogul. My mother had never met any millionaires, at least none that she knew personally. Cleaning toilets was her way into their world. She was a mouse, and housekeeping was the crack in the wall through which she slipped.

My father's name was Yossi Natan, and he was a real estate developer out of Israel, only in the city for two years. Greer doesn't know how the affair started—just that he was married, with several children back home in Kfar Saba, and my conception was a huge complication. But before he left, he established a trust fund in my name to be accessed on my twenty-sixth birthday and ensured my mother received a modest monthly stipend in exchange for her silence.

I've only ever seen his photo online, and I can never read the captions because they're in Hebrew.

There isn't much I know about Yossi besides the fact that we share the same sandy-colored hair and caramel complexions and our features are an exotic blend of European and Middle Eastern. I have his straight nose, full mouth, and hooded eyes, but other than that, I have nothing else . . . not even his last name.

Or any hope of meeting him in this lifetime, which is still a bitter pill to swallow no matter how many years go by. It's like I'm missing this huge part of me, and there's absolutely no chance I'll ever get it back.

Greer says when I was five, I had an "imaginary dad," which I suppose was like an imaginary friend only more of a father figure? She says she'd hear me through the walls at night, talking to him. And after school, I'd claim he was walking beside us as we navigated the busy Queens sidewalks that led to our apartment.

I have no recollection of any of that, but it makes my heart hurt when I think of five-year-old me, so desperate to know the love of a father.

"I promise, Greer, it's not like that," I say. "I'm not her. Far from it. You have nothing to worry about. I'm me. I just have a better wardrobe these days."

I try to get a smile from her, but I still sense her concern.

"There's nothing wrong with having nice shoes," I say. "They're just shoes for fuck's sake!"

Our eyes lock, and she chews her lower lip. She's always been anxious about things beyond her control, but I don't blame her. She had it rough. Not only did she have to raise me, but she was stuck raising my mother most of the time as well. Greer was always the one making sure our rent was paid on time. Greer was the one who took over grocery shopping when my mother left us with empty cupboards far too many times. Greer was the one who signed me up for school each year and made sure my birthdays were never forgotten.

She always had to stay one step ahead of everything, making sure nothing bad ever happened to either of us. I can't imagine it was easy, always anticipating the worst, living your life waiting for the other shoe to drop.

In fifth grade, my teacher sent me to the school nurse's office because I wouldn't stop scratching my head. The nurse who examined me gasped in horror, freaking out and darting around the room and scrambling for her phone. I overheard her telling the school receptionist that I had the worst case of head lice she'd seen in twenty-eight years on the job. I also heard her say she had half a mind to call Child and Family Services because I was clearly neglected.

But instead they called my mother, who promptly shaved my head that night, tied my hair clippings in a bag, and tossed them down the garbage chute.

I drag my hand along my loose, blonde waves, soft and blown out, the result of Brazilian keratin treatments at salons with months-long wait lists.

"Fine," Greer says. "You can have the nice shoes. Just don't become *her*."

"I won't," I promise her, drawing an X across my heart before lifting my pinky to her. She smirks, resisting my pinky promise, but I persist until she gives in. "Come on. Our reservation is in five minutes."

As soon as we're settled at our table, sipping Italian teas among the clink of flatware on china and the dull lull of conversation in the background, I'm overcome with a wave of contentment, the same warm, gushy feeling I tend to soak up like a dry sponge anytime I'm with her.

"How's Andrew?" she asks.

"Amazing." I can't help but smile when I hear his name. It's a reflex.

I never thought I'd be settled so young, but when I look at some of the girls I went to college with and how they're struggling through their "quarter-life crises" and jumping from jerk boyfriend to jerk boyfriend, it makes me even more appreciative of the way things panned out for me.

Andrew is a real man.

He doesn't play games. He doesn't manipulate or have a wandering eye. He treats me like gold and loves me more than anyone has ever loved me.

Anyway, things could always be worse, and the only problems I have are those of the first-world variety.

My sincerest wish is that my sister could know this feeling, too, one of these days—of being loved, cared for, cherished, whether by Harris . . . or someone new.

"So how are things with you and Mr. Collier?" I ask in an English accent, taking a sip of tea and lifting my pinky finger. When we were little, we'd always pretend to be fancy, thinking it was the funniest thing in the world.

Greer's posture shifts, her back growing straight as she peers out the window to her right. She's not going to play along.

"I've decided to move out," she says, lifting her cup to her mouth.

"That's okay, right? I mean, you guys are broken up now. It's weird that you're living together."

"I guess."

"How do you feel about it?" I don't expect my sister to give me a straight answer. She's still in love with Harris, and I have a feeling she always will be.

Greer shrugs, avoiding eye contact. "It's fine. It was time. No point in treading the same old waters with the intention of going nowhere."

"I've never understood what you see in him anyway. I've never met anyone so pretentious who tries so hard to act like they're not pretentious. He talks down to everyone, and he acts like he knows everything."

"Intelligent, opinionated men are like that." She takes another sip. "He can't help it. He's very passionate about his causes. And he's not pretentious. That's absurd. He's the least pretentious person I know."

Years ago, I used to make fun of Harris for wearing $120 T-shirts declaring his feminist and climate change stances, and he'd make fun of my Tory Burch sandals and overlined Kylie Jenner lips. We never saw eye to eye, but we both loved Greer enough to tolerate each other and keep our razzing to a minimum.

Of course, Greer always opted to believe we were bantering like a couple of squabbling schoolchildren.

I suppose we're always deciding what we want to see in life and choosing how we're going to see it. She never wanted to believe Harris was anything other than perfect, and I blame love. She loved him. Still does.

Sometimes love is wonderful.

Other times it's poison.

"Does he want to see other people?" I ask. Their breakup came out of left field, and from the outside, it seemed amicable and drama-free, but the more I dug into the nitty-gritty of it all, the more I realized how screwed up their situation was. My sister claimed the relationship had grown stale and evolved into a close friendship, but looking back, I can't help but wonder if those were his words.

Greer wastes no time shaking her head. "It's not like that."

"Then what's it like?"

"We're not together anymore. It doesn't make sense to live together. He wants space. So do I. End of story."

"But you'll still be working together every day," I say. "How is that giving each other space?"

"We'll be in different stores."

"You weren't today," I say, tracing the rim of my teacup and watching her squirm. She's trying to act like she was on board with this whole breakup thing, but I know her better than that. This was all Harris's idea. She's just going along with it because she thinks it'll bring him back to her in the end.

That's the curse of us Ambrose women. We're powerless when it comes to our men. I'm just lucky I found a good one. The wrong one could easily be my undoing.

I asked Greer once, "Why Harris?" I wanted to know what she saw in him, why she was willing to place her entire love life on pause in hopes that he'd eventually come around. She was quiet at first, contemplating her response. And then she told me he was her first love. And no matter how hard she tried, she couldn't unlove him. It was only ever going to be him for her.

Then she changed the subject.

Typical.

"You're right, Mer. We *were* in the same store today," she says. "It's end of month, and I was running numbers. My office is there."

"Your office is a computer you carry with you everywhere you go," I say.

"Are we ready to order?" Our server interrupts our conversation with impeccable timing, tossing water on the flames that were starting to shoot a little too high for a midmorning brunch.

Greer orders the eggs Benedict.

I order the French toast.

We talk about the weather.

CHAPTER 10

GREER

Day Three

When I return, Meredith's driveway is crowded with vehicles. I've been gone all afternoon, knocking on doors and visiting local businesses my sister frequented. So far everyone says the same thing.

"She seemed happy, always smiling."

"She had the perfect marriage."

"There were no red flags."

Or the unexpectedly common, *"I never really knew her. Sorry."*

It truly is as though she disappeared into thin air.

I pass through the kitchen and stop when I see a camera crew gathered around the table eating submarine sandwiches and little yellow bags of potato chips. Voices trail from the study down the hall, one of them all too familiar.

"Andrew?" I call.

No answer.

Heading to the study, I stop in the doorway when I see my mother sitting in a makeup chair. Her hair is bleached blonde, just like the photo Meredith sent me, and pressed into beach waves, her skin an unrecognizable shade of bronzed orange. From the looks of it, she's settling into life with her SoCal boyfriend just fine.

"Can you contour this?" She points to her neckline. "And can you fix my eyebrows a little? Make the arch stronger? I just know they're going to disappear under those bright lights. They're so blonde."

Leave it to Brenda Ambrose to be more concerned with her eyebrows than her missing daughter.

A producer with a clipboard and headset takes a seat on Andrew's desk, going over a few things with my mother.

"What's this about?" I make my presence known, eliciting a startled jerk from my mother.

"Oh, goodness. Greer." She fans the makeup artist away, rising to her feet and coming at me. Wrapping her arms around my shoulders when she knows damn well I hate hugs, she buries her face in my neck. "It's so wonderful to see you, sweetheart."

In over three decades on this planet, my mother has yet to refer to me as "sweetheart." "Ungrateful brat?" Yes. "Little bitch." Yes. "Biggest mistake of my life." Yes.

"Sweetheart?" Never.

I almost remind her the cameras aren't rolling yet.

"We just got here a little bit ago," she says. "Wade's in the other room with Andrew."

"I had no idea there was a TV crew coming today."

"Neither did I." She smiles, as if the idea of being on TV makes her feel beautiful and glamorous and special. I wish I were surprised by this behavior. "Connie Mayweather from *Twenty-Four-Seven* on CNN is going to be interviewing Andrew. They asked if we'd make an appearance."

"We?"

"Well, Wade and I. And you."

"Wade met Meredith *once*."

Her smile fades, as if I've burst her bubble with the sharp tip of a little pin made from pure reality. "It's a show of support, Greer."

Showing my face on national television holds zero appeal, but this isn't about me. If Mer is out there somewhere, I want her to know I'm looking for her, too. I refuse to give my spotlight-loving mother all the glory.

"Fine," I say.

My mother flags down the hair-and-makeup crew, telling them they've "got another one to work on" before returning to her chair.

An hour later, my face is contoured and highlighted, my hair has been yanked from its messy bun and curled into something more appropriate for a Sunday-morning church service, and I'm asked if I have another shirt to wear, something less black and faded because it would "depress the viewers at home and appear as though we're prematurely mourning her."

They situate us on the sofa in the formal living room, placing Andrew next to my mother and Wade behind her. The lights are hot, raising the crisp temperature of this room in a matter of minutes, and the caked-on makeup on my face is beginning to melt into my skin.

Connie Mayweather acts like she's a big deal, her blonde bob cut to her sharp jawline, her cheekbones sculpted, her lips painted in a neutral, camera-ready pink. She wears a Chanel suit and sits cross-legged opposite the four of us, her face shaped in sympathy that appears to be genuine, though I imagine years of practice could fool just about anybody.

"Andrew, please walk us through this," she says. "Tell us where you were when you first discovered your wife, Meredith Price, was missing."

He takes his time, and I have to wonder if his pauses are well placed or if he's truly gathering his composure.

"I was at work," he says, exhaling. "In a meeting actually. My receptionist knocked on the door, told me there was a police officer there to talk to me."

Connie's eyes squint as she pays close attention, giving slow, reaffirming nods when he pauses.

"An officer from Glacier Park Police Department met me in my office and asked me when I'd last spoken to my wife." He stops, lifting his hand to his mouth and dragging his fingers down the corners. I try to imagine his lips trembling, but I can't. I've never seen any real emotion coming from this man other than his flagrant, sticky-sweet infatuation with my sister. "I told him we'd spoken that morning, and she mentioned she was going to the grocery store later in the day. That's when he informed me that a store clerk was running some trash out to the dumpster behind the building. He saw a car sitting there, the driver's door wide open. Then he saw her things inside, took down the plate number, and tried to have her paged. No one claimed it, so he called the police to report an abandoned vehicle, and that's when they tracked me down. About the same time, I received a call from the kids' school saying no one had come to pick them up."

His voice breaks. My mother reaches for him, placing her hand over his. Wade, who hadn't taken the time to change out of his Hawaiian button-down and cargo shorts ensemble, rests his hand on my mother's shoulder.

"So they were suspicious," Connie clarifies.

Andrew nods. "It wasn't a normal scene. Nobody leaves their car open like that, their purse and phone and keys inside."

I sit, unmoving, watching this freak show and deducing that these people—my family—have become caricatures of themselves.

Is that what people do when a loved one goes missing? You act the way you think you're supposed to act? And how are you supposed to act? And why would you give two shits when there are bigger fish to fry?

"Tell us what was going through your mind the moment you realized something was wrong," Connie says.

He sits up a little straighter. "Just . . . that I needed to find her. Nothing else mattered. I needed to find my wife. Honestly, everything from that day is kind of a blur at this point."

"He hasn't had much sleep," my mother chimes in, rubbing his knee like he's a small child.

Sick.

"Understandable," Connie says, wincing. "How are you dealing with everything?"

"One day at a time," he replies without pause. "That's all I can do. I stay in contact with the police. My phone is on me at all times in case she calls. We're doing everything we can to find her."

"Do the police have any leads?" she asks.

He hesitates again—a dramatic pause? "No, Connie. They don't. And that's why we agreed to do this interview. Someone out there knows something."

Connie turns to the camera. "I understand there's a dedicated tip line, is that correct? And you're offering a reward? One hundred thousand dollars for the safe return of Meredith?"

Andrew begins to speak, but Mom cuts him off.

"Yes to both," she answers. God forbid she doesn't get equal screen time. "And the tip line is manned day and night. Someone will always answer. And they can call the Glacier Park Police Department as well. They'll put them through to someone immediately."

Andrew squeezes Mom's hand, whispering a quiet, "Thank you."

"Greer," Connie says, somehow knowing my name, "as Meredith's older sister, how are you handling all this?"

I hate her stupid, trite question. What does she expect? How am I supposed to answer this?

"*Greer.*" My mother whips around, visually nudging me to answer.

"How the hell do you think I'm holding up?" I want to reply to Connie's question with one of my own.

"How about instead of asking us *how* we're doing, ask us *what* we're doing to find Meredith?" I ask.

Connie's eyes flit from mine to Andrew's, then to my mother's.

"Greer, you may excuse yourself from this interview," Mom says.

Apparently I'm fourteen, and she's Mother of the Year.

Without saying a word, I leave the living room with the intention of locking myself up in the guest room—not because she told me to, but because I can't stand being a part of this circus.

And I need to think.

I don't need to be sitting on a sofa with millions of eyes on me. I'll leave that to them.

My sister will know I'm trying my hardest to find her. I shouldn't have to shed a forced tear on national television and subject myself to public scrutiny to prove that.

Our heartbreak is not entertainment, and I won't be distraught on national television so Connie Mayweather's show can get ratings.

I utter a silent apology to my sister as I head for the stairs. TV interview or not, I'm still going to find her.

"Greer." Ronan stands in the entryway of the Price manse.

I'd act surprised, but I suspect I'm going to be seeing a lot of him from now on.

"Hey." His lips pull back for a second, revealing his straight pearly teeth. "Been trying to get hold of Andrew for the past hour. He isn't answering."

I huff. So much for Andrew keeping his phone on him at all times in case Meredith calls.

"He's making his national television debut with Connie Mayweather." I nod toward the living room. "Camera makeup, Armani suit, the works."

Ronan doesn't find any of this humorous. His hands on his hips, he watches from the foyer, observing Andrew with quiet tenacity.

"If he wasn't so obsessed with my sister and she wasn't so damn in love with him, I'd be making damn sure your fingers were pointed in his direction right now." I keep my voice low.

Ronan looks to me. "What makes you think they aren't?"

"Do you know something?"

"In any missing persons case, we always look at spouses or partners first," he says, also keeping his voice hushed.

"So you haven't ruled him out?" I ask.

"I haven't. No." Ronan tucks his bottom lip beneath his teeth for a second before giving a quick shake of his head. "Not yet."

I turn back to Andrew, watching as my mother hands him a tissue. Those are real tears, at least in the physical, tangible sense. The influence behind them? Only Andrew knows.

"Why'd you come here?" I ask.

"We got another tip," he says. "Another caller claims to have spotted Meredith in Nebraska with a rough-looking man in a conversion van. They tried following them but lost them after a handful of stoplights during rush hour. We got a description on the driver."

"And?"

"Gray hair, midfifties, goatee," he says. "Van is blue with a rusted bumper. We got a plate, so they're going to ID him. We can question him once they track him down, but for now I wanted to run it past Andrew to see if any of that sounded familiar."

"Right, because Maserati-driving Andrew Price hangs out with conversion-van kidnappers." I tilt my head, rolling my eyes.

Ronan shakes his head. "Amateur."

"Me?" I press my finger against my chest.

"Everything I need to know is going to be in the way he reacts to my question," he says. "What he says won't matter. *How* he acts will."

Connie Mayweather rises from her chair, placing her mic pack on a nearby coffee table as she chats with a producer. Either they're done, or they're taking a break.

"Now's your chance," I tell him.

Ronan cuts through the small crowd, making a beeline for Andrew, who keeps a solemn expression in his presence. From here, I watch Andrew drag his hand along his jaw, furrow his brow, and shake his head. Ronan does most of the talking, never taking his eyes off Andrew, and when a producer approaches them, the conversation ends.

When Ronan returns, I ask, "You find what you were looking for?"

"Not exactly," he says. "But I think I'm getting close."

"So? What'd he say?"

Ronan's mouth forms a straight line as he eyes the nearest door. "Looks like I've got a few things to check into."

"So he knows the guy? The van?" I lift a brow.

He shakes his head.

"So he reacted in a way that makes you suspect something?" I ask.

"Greer, I'll talk to you tomorrow, okay?" He grips my shoulder in passing. And then he's gone.

I get it. This is an active investigation. He can't tell me everything.

Peering across the room, I watch as Andrew speaks to a crew member, nodding, his arms across his chest.

So help me God, if he's remotely involved in this . . .

CHAPTER 11

MEREDITH

Twenty-Seven Months Ago

"There's something on your windshield." Allison points at my car as we walk out of hot yoga on a brisk Monday morning. All I want is a lukewarm shower, clean clothes that don't stick to every crevice of my body, and an iced coffee with Splenda and sugar-free mocha syrup.

"It's probably one of those flyers for that new pizza place on Pike," I say. "Last week I got four of them."

I yank the white paper from beneath my wiper blade, but I don't crumple it yet. There's no pizza logo. Nothing on the outside. Just a white sheet of paper folded into thirds.

Something falls, landing at my shoes, and I swipe it off the ground, finding myself face-to-face with a photo of myself taken just last week. I'm with Andrew, leaving the home of one of his colleagues after a dinner party that ran much too late. This had to have been two in the morning.

"What is it?" Allison comes around the front of my car, peering over my shoulder as I read a handwritten letter.

My Meredith,

Always watching.

X

"Holy shit, that's creepy." Allison covers her chest with an open palm, mouth agape.

My hands tremble. "What do I do? Do I take it to the police? I mean, it's not a threat, but it's . . . I don't know . . . it feels violating. Who the hell takes a picture of me leaving a party with my husband in the middle of the night? Who is this asshole? And how does he know us?"

"Just some lunatic," she says. "Some weirdos get off on this stuff. They do it just for fun. But yes, you should go to the police. This needs to be on record . . . in case anything happens."

My eyes scan the letter again, tracing the small, careful handwriting, noting how he dotted his I's with little circles and that his capital letters are enormous in comparison to their lowercase counterparts.

"Will you go with me?" I ask, an unsettled queasiness resting in my stomach. I'm still so unknown around Glacier Park, and my circle consists of mainly Andrew and Allison. For some crazy person to notice me and follow me . . . it's bone-chilling to say the least.

"Of course. Want me to drive you? You're all shaken up." Allison places her arm around my shoulder, leading me to her parked Audi and helping me in.

Five minutes later, we pull in to the visitor parking lot of the Glacier Park Police Department. Allison leads me inside and does most of the talking once we reach the front desk. We're not seated for more than ten minutes before a detective calls for us.

"Meredith Price?" he asks, his eyes moving between Allison and myself.

I lift a hand, rising. "I'm Meredith."

"Detective Ronan McCormack." His eyes linger on mine. "Come on back."

He leads us down a sterile white hallway covered in posed photos of retired captains, sergeants, and lieutenants. His office is at the end, across from the chief's corner digs.

"Have a seat, ladies." He closes the door behind us. Neither of us speak. "What are we looking at here?"

Retrieving the letter and photograph from my purse, I slide them across the desk. "This was on my windshield this morning."

His face tenses as he reads the words and checks out the photo. "Is this the first time this person has tried to contact you?"

"Yes," I say. "But this picture was from last week. And he knows my name. And the way he signs it? Always watching?"

"And he called her 'My Meredith,'" Allison says.

"That's a fear tactic," he says, his eyes dancing between ours. "Most stalkers, they want their victims to be afraid. Sometimes they'll use possessive phrasing to accomplish that. Can you think of anyone who might want to scare you, Meredith?"

My name is sweet and gentle on his tongue, and he has kind eyes.

I shake my head. "No one. I get along with everyone."

"Except your husband's ex," Allison says, her voice soft as she nudges me.

"Erica wouldn't do this. She's crazy, but she's not this kind of crazy," I say. "Plus, I know her handwriting. This isn't it."

"Maybe she hired someone?" Allison shrugs.

"We find that most victims know their stalkers," Ronan says. "More than likely, this is someone you've interacted with in the past. I mean, it could be someone who saw you once and followed you and figured out who you were, but the odds of that are slim. I won't rule it out, but just so you know. Statistically speaking and all."

"So what happens now?"

"Technically it's not stalking unless there are a series of acts and repeated victimization. A single incident isn't enough to get someone on a stalking charge," he says. "Did you happen to see anyone around your vehicle? Did anyone else see anything unusual?"

"We were at the gym, parked out back," I say. "I can ask if there are cameras . . ."

Detective McCormack's lips flatten as he exhales. "If this person knows what they're doing, they wouldn't have risked being caught on film. It's worth a check, and I'll handle that for you, but I don't want you to get your hopes up."

"I understand," I say.

"Without a description of the suspect, there's not much we can do from here," he says. "For now, you need to be hypervigilant. Pay attention to your surroundings, watch for any strange faces in crowds, anyone watching you—following you. If anything happens again, I want you to call the station, all right?"

He grabs a business card from a holder behind his phone, handing it over and pointing to the number printed along the bottom.

"That's my work cell," he says, sliding it toward me. "I'll have the guys do some patrolling in your area for the next week or so, too. See if we find any unusual activity around your home."

"Thank you."

I know he's doing all he can, but I'm still unsettled, uneasy. My stomach is clenched, my vision blurred from stress. Even here, in the cinderblock-walled office in the local police station, I find my gaze darting around, unable to shake the feeling that someone's watching me.

"We should go." I turn to Allison, gathering my things. I need to try Andrew again. I'd phoned him on the drive here, but his receptionist said he was in a meeting with a new client. She took a message. That was an hour ago.

Detective McCormack shows us out, returning us to the lobby.

"You did the right thing coming here today," he says. "You know, I teach a women's self-defense class at the community center in Ridgewood Heights on Tuesdays. Seven o'clock. You're welcome to join us. Free to the public."

Allison glances my way, brows arched. "Might not be a bad idea."

The detective offers a boyish half smile, though I suspect he's only slightly older than me—late twenties, thirty at most. His presence is calming, the way he takes everything in stride.

My eyes trace over his broad shoulders, and I find myself inappropriately fixated on the way his arms fill the sleeves of his navy button-down, the fabric straining against the outline of his muscles. Self-discipline's written all over him, and I imagine him waking at 5:00 a.m. on the dot each morning, going for a run—rain, snow, or shine—and returning for a protein shake, hard-boiled eggs, and a fistful of vitamins and supplements.

Then I find myself wondering if he has a girlfriend, if she's pretty and sweet or the kind of girl who takes advantage of nice guys like Ronan.

And then I snap out of it, remembering that I'm a married woman. Those kinds of thoughts aren't fair to Andrew. To the sanctity of our marriage.

"Thanks, Detective." I force a smile, warmth blooming in my cheeks as if this man could've possibly read my thoughts. "I appreciate the invitation."

CHAPTER 12

GREER

Day Three

"Is there any chance at all that Meredith left on her own?" Wade asks Andrew that night. He's changed into a different Hawaiian shirt, this one faded and blue, nothing like the cheerful one he wore this morning. A half-eaten, room-temperature pizza sits hardened in a box between us at the kitchen table. My mother's gaze flicks from her untouched slice to her boyfriend, as if he's uttered pure blasphemy.

"At this point, I'm not sure what to think," Mom says, shoving her plate away and clucking her tongue.

"I'm just saying, we have no leads, no evidence, nothing. Is it possible that she orchestrated this in some capacity?" he asks.

I'm fixated on his hair for a moment, the thin, sun-streaked locks hanging limp around his wrinkled face. He's much too old to have hair to his shoulders, and I wonder at what age he stopped surfing. Wade walks with a limp and wears a shark-tooth necklace. Meredith says he drives a vintage Corvette and has three adult children who no longer speak to him.

He's exactly the kind of guy my mom would find on the Internet.

My mother twists the diamond pendant that hangs above her crinkly bronze décolletage. "She has a great life, an amazing husband, a perfect marriage. Maybe someone was jealous of her? Or maybe they wanted her for themselves?"

I lift a brow, biting my tongue as I let Wade's thoughts marinate. My mother walked away from dozens of relationships over her many incarnations. Is it possible she somehow instilled that behavior into my sister over the years?

Deep down, I know anything is possible, but it's as if my mind refuses to believe she would've kept anything from me. I want to believe she would've told me if she were leaving, but after everything that's come to light the last few days, I'm beginning to realize my sister was drowning in an ocean of secrets, and I was inland the entire time, clueless.

Andrew dabs his lips with a napkin, chewing his bite quickly as if he has something to say before anyone else gets a chance. I'm not sure how he can eat at a time like this. My appetite's been nonexistent for days now, my jeans beginning to fall down my hips when I walk.

"She was pregnant." His words suck the air from the room.

My mother cups her hand over her mouth, speechless for the first time ever. This bombshell is cushioned by the ones that dropped before it.

I'm hurt, maybe.

But not surprised.

My attention is glued to him, scrutinizing his concentrated, businesslike mannerisms and wondering where the hell his emotion is hiding right now. Any other "loving husband" would be beside himself, hardly able to function, if his beloved wife was missing. Add an unborn baby to the mix, and that takes things to a whole new level.

But Andrew is as stoic as ever.

Weird.

"She wasn't very far along," he says. "Just found out a few weeks ago. We hadn't shared the news yet. Obviously. But for that reason alone, I know she would never leave on her own. She was excited about the baby, about this next chapter in our life. It was all she could talk about."

The fluffy fur of my sister's black Pomeranian, Maxie, rubs against my feet. Growing up, neither of us had ever had so much as a hamster, but Andrew gifted Meredith with a puppy for Christmas one year, and suddenly she was a dog person, taking Maxie with her everywhere she went in her little Louis Vuitton carrier and joking with me about how much Maxie loved massages and manicures at the local dog spa.

"She is her mother's daughter," she'd said, laughing. Meredith seemed placated by the dog. I never once suspected she was suffering from a bout of baby fever. I suppose in my mind's eye, she was still a baby herself. Forever my helpless, knobby-kneed kid sister.

I asked her once, shortly after she got married, if she wanted a family of her own. She'd had a far-off look in her eyes, hesitating before simply stating, "Someday. Hopefully. Yes. Andrew wants to wait a little longer."

It wasn't long after that, Maxie came into the picture.

My brother-in-law knew what he was doing.

"Do the police know?" I ask. "About the baby?"

Andrew sinks back in his chair, contemplating his answer. "They do. I mentioned it to the detective . . . McCormack."

"I'm surprised the police haven't fed that detail to the media yet. Missing pregnant woman would sell a hell of a lot better than missing woman." My voice is sarcastic and my words sting even myself, yet I speak the truth. The more news outlets discussing this case and sharing my sister's photo, the better.

"Greer." My mother snips my name, and I can't help but wonder if Meredith ever worried about what kind of mother she was going to be. We didn't exactly have a shining example.

"I'm just saying." I turn my focus to Andrew again. "It's odd, don't you think? Wouldn't they want as much publicity on the case as possible?"

"For whatever reason, the police haven't made that public yet," Andrew says, unaffected by the tone I've taken.

Wade blows a breath through his thin lips, his brow wrinkling. "I'm inclined to agree with you on that, Greer. I find that a bit peculiar."

Good old Wade.

He might be the only other person sitting at this table who's worth a damn, and as much as everything about him annoys the ever-loving shit out of me, he just might be one of the more tolerable gentlemen my mother has sidled up to over the past thirty-odd years.

Our conversation ceases, the four of us sharing a round of awkward silence. If the police haven't made this information public, it must mean they're suspecting it could be some kind of motive . . . Andrew's?

The doorbell slices through our nonexistent conversation like a sharp knife, and Andrew wastes no time excusing himself from the table. When he returns with a little blonde thing barely out of college, she offers an awkward wave and takes a seat beside my mother.

"This is Britt," he says. He is *so* the kind of guy who would hire someone like Britt. I bet he uses the excuse "It's easier to train the young ones than to break the bad habits of the experienced ones." Jackass. "She's my executive assistant, and she'll be fielding calls, answering the door, and keeping me from losing my sanity until we figure out where the hell my wife is."

He speaks of Meredith as if she's just run off, like a teenager who's bound to come home eventually. Whether he's fueled by denial or hope, I've yet to figure out.

Britt glances at Andrew with the roundest eyes I've ever seen, like she finds him equal parts fascinating and heroic. Enchanting almost. He has that effect on people, though I've never understood why. I can't help but wonder if he'd hold the same sex appeal if he were donning a plumber's uniform and driving a rusted pickup truck.

I've never been more grateful for my immunity to pompous, Rolex-wearing douchebags with bleached smiles and fast cars.

She lifts the lid of her MacBook, tapping in a password and clicking on an icon when the screen lights.

"I have some e-mails to go over with you when you get a second," she says, her eyes lifting to mine when she feels the weight of my stare. "They're not work related. Your inbox has been blowing up with offers from talk shows and radio shows. Everybody wants to talk to you about Meredith."

Andrew levels his posture, pinching the bridge of his nose. He can act like this annoys him all he wants, but this man loves the attention he's getting. Andrew lives for this shit. He's an attention whore. I knew it from the moment he plucked my beautiful sister out of obscurity and pinned her to his lapel like a prom boutonniere.

"You've also been receiving some, um, inappropriate e-mails," she says, biting her lip. "I'm deleting them, just so you know."

"Inappropriate?" my clueless mother asks. "Like threats? Mean things?"

"Fan mail–type letters . . . offers . . . ," Britt adds. "From women . . ."

"Oh, good God." Mom throws her hands in the air, muttering under her breath. Within seconds, she leaves the table, heading back to the kitchen and plundering the wine cabinet, bottles plinking as she rifles.

Good to see some things haven't changed.

Without saying a word, I exit this circus stage right and head to my room. I can't remember the last time I showered. Or ate a decent meal. Or checked in with Harris. This entire week so far has been a blur, a foggy nightmare where everything feels real and fake all at the same time.

Locking my door, I grab my phone and call my ex.

He answers almost immediately, like he's been on standby. "Greer. Hey."

It's so good to hear his voice, but I don't tell him that.

"How're you holding up? I'm refreshing CNN like crazy, just waiting for some kind of breaking development or something. The whole world's watching right now, you know that? It's crazy. Everyone is looking for her."

"I didn't know that." I yawn, stretching across the foot of the bed, eyelids heavy. "Been trying to stay away from the media. There's nothing they know that I don't already know, and their headlines will just upset me."

"Wise." I hear him walking around in the background, pots and pans clinking like he's just fixed himself dinner. I'll bet he worked late tonight. "You're better off anyway."

Rolling to my side, I reach for a downy pillow and tuck it under my head, wrapping my free arm around it and wishing more than ever that Harris were here. I could use someone warm and something real to cling to. A true sounding board who's not caught up in frivolous emotions. Harris never lets his feelings cloud his judgment, and that's something I've always admired about him.

Ten years ago, I was the girl who was angry at the world, tattooing her resentment on her body and fucking any man who looked like he was a bad idea because it was the only thing that distracted me from the pain of a dysfunctional adolescence.

Then Harris showed up—a cool drink of water to quell the raging inferno inside. What he saw in me I'll never know, but meeting him changed everything. He showed me what it felt like to be loved by a man—a foreign concept to me up to that point. And he showed me that, contrary to my hardened beliefs, I did have a softer side.

It was just buried beneath all the hard.

"You're hanging in there, though?" he asks. "I'm worried about you."

He doesn't elaborate.

He doesn't need to.

He's known from the beginning how protective I am of my little sister. How I've always felt she was my responsibility. When we first met, he told me I had boundary issues and that I wasn't Meredith's mother. I told him he'd never grown up with Brenda Ambrose.

"Don't worry about me," I say, neglecting to tell him how happy it makes me to hear that he's thinking of me and my well-being. He might be the only person I have who gives a rat's ass.

"You want me to come out there? To Utah?" he asks. "I feel so helpless over here. Feels wrong sitting back and doing nothing."

I wish I could reach through the phone, wrap my arms around his shoulders, breathe in his coffee-and-faded-cologne scent, and never let him go.

"You want to help? Stay in the city," I say. "You need to keep the business running so I can afford to be here looking for my sister."

Now that my sister's whereabouts are unknown, I've got no business banking on a good faith loan from her trust to keep us going these next few months.

"Fair enough."

"I'm turning in." I pull the phone from my face, checking the time as if it matters. My body's running the show, and right now I can barely keep my eyes open.

"Call me," he says. "I mean, I know you're busy, but keep me in the loop, okay? I know your sister and I didn't always see eye to eye, but this . . . this is terrifying. And I care about her. Shit, I've known her for ten years now. She's practically family, even if you and I . . ."

"I know." I don't let him finish his thought. The last thing I need is another reminder that we're not together anymore. "I'll call you more. There are actually some things I wanted to run past you, but I'm way too fucking tired to even think straight."

"Oh, yeah?" He sounds disappointed.

"I'll call you tomorrow. Keep your phone on you."

"Of course."

"Night," I say, sliding my thumb across the glass screen.

"Greer?" he asks.

"Yeah?"

"I've been doing a lot of thinking this week," he says. "And I can't stop asking myself what if it were you? What if something happened, and you were ripped out of my life and I had no idea if I was going to see you again? And I've been thinking about how I'd feel if I lost you. If I woke up tomorrow, and I couldn't see you again."

I'm listening.

"It's really just . . . stirring up all of these feelings . . . and I think . . ." He pauses, his silence lasting far too long. "I don't want to be apart anymore."

I release the breath I've been harboring, soaking in his words and replaying them in my mind a handful of times before questioning if I heard him correctly or if I'm dreaming. For all I know, I'm fast asleep, wishing he were saying these words.

It wouldn't be the first time I've had this dream.

"You still there?" he asks.

"Can we talk more about this when I'm home?" I ask. "After I find my sister?"

I know Harris, and though he's a devoted feminist, he's still a man. And I've yet to know a single red-blooded man who doesn't like the thrill of the chase. If I told him I never stopped loving him, that I wanted to be with him again, I'd look pathetic. And I don't want him to think all he has to do is snap his fingers and I'll be back by his side— even if that's true.

I may be hopelessly imprinted on this man, but I'm not stupid.

"Absolutely." He exhales. "Good night, G . . . I love you."

CHAPTER 13

MEREDITH

Twenty-Seven Months Ago

The parking lot of the Ridgewood Heights community center is filled mostly with shiny Lincolns and Buicks, and a group of white-haired, Lululemon-wearing women make their way to the main entrance.

I didn't want to come here, but Allison insisted. And after that note on my car yesterday, I wasn't able to sleep last night. Every little sound, every flash of a headlight outside our windows sent a breath-capturing kick start to my heart while Andrew slept soundly to my left. At one point, I bit my lip and tapped Andrew on the shoulder, whispering in his ear that I thought I heard something, but his face scrunched, and he mumbled for me to go back to sleep.

Taking my gym duffel from my back seat, I fling it over my shoulder and make my way inside.

Ronan is in the front of the room, standing before a wall of mirrors chatting with a couple of the women, while another guy sets up rows upon rows of blue and red wrestling mats. The detective wears charcoal-gray sweats low on his hips and a white T-shirt with GLACIER PARK POLICE printed along the chest in bold black font.

It doesn't take more than a minute before he spots me, though I imagine I'm sticking out like a sore thumb among all these retirees. Ridgewood Heights is a mecca for the nonworking well-to-do, and most of the female residents are former stay-at-home moms who read too many crime books and never miss an episode of *Dateline*. Not to mention that old people with excessive wealth tend to be on the paranoid side. I'm not surprised they insisted on a self-defense class.

"You can never be too prepared anymore," I overhear one of them saying. "Just yesterday, there was a strange man going door-to-door in our neighborhood. Said he was selling pest control services, but Nancy thinks he just wanted to scope out the place, see if we had anything worth stealing. Flat-screen televisions and MP3 players, that sort of thing."

"That's how it happens," her friend says. "Can't trust anyone anymore."

"Meredith." Ronan approaches me, his mouth pulling up at the sides like he's forgotten, momentarily, that we met under less than ideal circumstances. "Glad you could make it."

I let my bag drop. "Figured it couldn't hurt."

"My assistant called in sick tonight," he says. "She pulled a hamstring at kickboxing or something. You mind filling in?"

"I wouldn't even know how—"

"Nah. I just do the moves on you so everyone else can see," he says. "You'll learn as you go. All you have to do is stand there and follow my directives."

Glancing around the room, I realize almost everyone is already paired up.

"Yeah, sure." My shoulders lift and fall, and I try my best not to picture his hands on my body.

He smiles again. "All right, cool. Head up front. We'll be starting in about five minutes."

Ronan leaves, making rounds and chatting with his attendees. They all adore him, telling him he looks like their grandsons and asking if he'd be interested in being "fixed up" with someone when he tells them he's single.

He's single.

When he returns to the front of the room, his gaze finds mine. He speaks to the class, but he's looking at me. And when he reaches out, wrapping his hand around my wrist and pulling me closer, my heart gallops, and my skin tingles.

It's not his fault.

He's doing nothing wrong.

It's all me.

I'm the broken one.

I'm the one who married some big-moneyed older man on a whim despite the warnings of my sister and best friends. They said I was too young, that I needed to find myself first before I settled with the first man who presented me with a blazing, oversize diamond ring.

But I was in love.

I still am—I think.

It's just that that love has lost a bit of luster over the last several months. The newness is wearing off. It was bound to happen—I just didn't expect it to happen this soon.

Anyway, I don't know if it's possible to love my husband *and* feel butterflies when another man looks at me, but it's exactly what's happening, and I haven't the slightest clue how to stop it.

"All right, let's get started, shall we?" Ronan claps his hands, rubbing his palms together as he scans the room. "Tonight we're going to go over six Krav Maga techniques that are going to help you fend off a physical attack." He paces in front of me. "First one. Open hand strike." He slips his hand around mine once more, turning me to face him. "We're going to focus on vulnerable areas. The head. The throat. The neck—front and back. You get the point." His hands mock-strike me, keeping a safe distance. "This is very simple, girls. If you can push, you can punch."

Ronan steps away from me, retrieving a kick pad from a nearby table and asking me to hold it up.

"We're going to strike with the heel of our hand," he says. "And lean in, steady on your feet. Pivot. Drive the energy forward. Like this."

His strikes come at me, and I block them with the pad. He winks, tossing me an approving smirk.

Are we . . . are we having fun?

"Okay, now I want you guys to try." Ronan turns to the class, hooking his hands on his hips as he makes rounds. When he returns a few minutes later, he hands me an ice-cold bottle of water.

"I haven't even broken a sweat," I say, uncapping it.

He's thoughtful. I like that.

"Not yet, you haven't." He turns to the class once more. "Moving on. Groin kicks."

Some of the women in the back chuckle, proving that kicking men in the balls can be humorous at any age.

Good to know for future reference.

"Groin kicks are going to let you keep your distance. If someone's getting too close to you, this allows you to counterattack and leave." Ronan demonstrates on me before taking the kick pad and asking me to do the honors.

Ronan demonstrates a few more moves on me. I try my hardest to pay attention, but I'm so distracted by . . . everything. His voice, his deftness, his confidence, his passion. The way he commands the room.

And when he lets his touch linger a little too long on my hip, I can't be entirely sure if I'm imagining it or not.

When class finishes, I grab my duffel and head for the exit while Ronan's caught up in conversation with a circle of women who make no effort to hide their innocent infatuation.

I'm glad it's not me. Everyone finds him charming.

"Meredith, wait up," he calls in front of the gabbing ladies. "I need to talk to you before you go."

One of the women lifts her brows and nudges her friend. They smile, watching the two of us like it's something special in the making.

Feet planted, I wait for him to approach me. Taking a swig of water and grabbing a small towel to wipe his brow, he maintains eye contact with me, and when he finally makes it over, there's a familiar gleam in his deep chocolate eyes.

I've seen it before.

Men see me, they get this look on their face. It's like a lion stalking a gazelle, planning their approach, clearly interested. It's like I provoke something in them. Something on a primal level.

"You want to grab a coffee?" he asks.

I don't answer right away. Every part of me is screaming, *No, no, no. This is a bad idea. Don't do it. Don't go down this path.*

But there's something about human nature that makes us shameless opportunists. We stumble across a chance, experience the tiniest taste of something we want, and we can't say no.

We literally can't say no.

"Um. Okay." This is bad. This is very, very bad. I'm going to hell.

"There's a place right next door," he says. "Best coffee you'll ever have in your life."

"Is that true?" I fight a smirk.

"I don't know. I've never been there." His mouth pulls wide, and my gaze lands on a perfect row of pearly whites flanked by two of the deepest dimples I've ever seen.

Ronan's dark hair is styled into a fresh crew cut, his skin creamy, clear, and smooth, with a slight flush on his cheeks.

In an irrational flicker of a second, I imagine a life by his side. It's an innocent little daydream. He and I on road trips, backpacking through Europe, hiking with a Bernese mountain dog in tow. In my reverie, I'm not wearing designer dresses and a full face of makeup, and he can't keep his hands off me. And he loves me just the way I am. I don't have to pretend to be someone I'm not because he can't get enough of the person I already am.

I follow him outside, waiting as he hits the lights and locks the door to the community center, and we amble toward a little shop called the Peaceful Bean. The sign is hand-painted in crooked lettering. If Greer ever saw it, she'd have a fit. Such a perfectionist. But from the outside, the place seems defiantly unpretentious—which is shocking in a town like Ridgewood Heights.

Ronan gets the door, following me to the register, and I order myself a London Fog, for which he insists on paying.

We find a quiet corner in the back of the shop, behind a tall bookcase filled with games like *Scrabble*, *Monopoly*, and *Sorry!*

"You doing okay?" he asks after our drinks arrive a minute later. "With the incident and everything? You don't seem as shaken up about it as you were yesterday."

I lift my mug to my lips. "Guess I do a good job of hiding it. See these dark circles?" I point beneath my eyes, where I'm sure my concealer has worn off. "I didn't sleep at all last night. Tossed and turned. Kept hearing things, little noises in the house."

"Your mind was playing tricks on you," he says. "It's common after a traumatic event." Ronan glances around the near-vacant shop before returning his attention to me. "It's good you came to class tonight. If anyone tries to mess with you, you'll be prepared. Peace of mind is priceless."

"You think that stalker guy is going to mess with me?"

He shrugs. "No way of knowing. Violence is either spontaneous or premeditated. If you're prepared, what's it matter?"

I sip my drink once more.

"The thing with stalkers—if that's what we're dealing with here—is that their motivations and how far they take things are usually determined by how they interpret your behavior and reactions," he says. "You just never know, Meredith. You're not dealing with sane people here. They don't think the way we do. They're not driven by the same things we are."

"What do I do if it happens again? If he leaves another note?"

"You call me right away," he says without hesitation. "I'll be there immediately. I want to catch this bastard."

His willingness to serve and protect is refreshing, especially when I compare it to Andrew's immediate reaction yesterday, which was to shrug, sip his wine, and remind me that we have a state-of-the-art security system and an abundance of phones wired in every room of the house should I need to dial 911. It was only after I began obsessing over every little sound, every parked car in the street outside our home, that he began checking on me more, but only ever at his convenience.

He never did call me back after I left a message at his office.

Ronan seems agitated for a second, shaking his head. "Sorry. I get a little worked up when men feel the need to terrorize innocent women. Stalking is about fear. And obsession. And control. He's a fucking coward if you ask me."

"I appreciate you going above and beyond with all this," I say. "My husband doesn't really think anything's going to happen."

His gaze falls to my left hand. "Husband?"

"Yeah," I say, realizing I wasn't wearing my ring yesterday because of yoga, and I made sure to leave it at home again before coming to the self-defense class. It's flashy and sharp and would only get in the way or cut someone. "Been married nine months now."

"Newlyweds."

I trace my finger around the top of my mug, avoiding eye contact as I wallow in shame. Every time I drink a London Fog after this, I'm going to find myself reliving this moment, being here with another man to whom I'm wildly attracted while my husband sits at home.

The tingle in my stomach has no business being there. Neither does the warmth flooding my cheeks.

Now I'm not sure what to say, and wallowing in this awkward silence makes it that much more painful for the both of us.

Staring at my half-empty tea, I push it toward the center of the table. "I'm sorry. I should get going."

He bites his lower lip, wincing a little. He doesn't have to say he's disappointed. It's written all over him.

"Thanks again," I say, rising. I tug my long blonde hair out of my messy ponytail and redo it before gathering my things. "And thanks for the tea."

He stands, his height towering over me as I come almost face-to-face with his muscled chest and broad shoulders. Even after rolling around on the mats, his vetiver-and-bergamot cologne still permeates the air, intensifying from the warmth of his skin.

"Like I said, don't be afraid to call if you need me," he says. "I mean it. I want to catch this guy."

"And I hope you do."

It's a quarter after nine by the time I get home. The house is dark. Andrew mentioned maybe having dinner with a few work colleagues, but that was hours ago, and he was on the fence about it at the time.

He must have chosen to go.

I don't call him—I don't want to be that kind of wife. The nagging, where-the-hell-are-you kind. No man wants to come home to that.

Changing out of my clothes, I climb into our oversize bed, tunnel under a mountain of covers, and zone out in front of a flickering TV while watching *E! News*. My sister's ex always teased me for *caring* about what celebrities are up to, but the real news is too depressing. Missing people. Unsolved murders. Politics.

No thanks. Mom practically force-fed that shit to us when we were younger. To this day, I'm convinced it's why Greer is so cynical and untrusting.

I'm perfectly happy in my little Glacier Park bubble, where nothing bad ever happens and breaking news is when Beyoncé and JAY-Z vacation at the Cerulean Sky Ski Resort up the mountain.

Now that I've had a little bit of distance from Ronan, I feel foolish. A smart woman wouldn't let herself get caught up in daydream affairs all because a handsome man shows a little bit of interest. She wouldn't let herself entertain those kinds of thoughts. And she wouldn't use boredom as a way to justify it either.

I can't let it happen again.

Andrew may not be 100 percent perfect, but he's pretty damn close. And I love him. So much. Even when he frustrates me. Even when this perfect little life makes me so bored I think about hopping a plane to Peru or Grenada and never coming back because an adventure sounds magical right about now.

But I married him in front of all our friends and family.

I took vows.

Till death do us part.

CHAPTER 14

GREER

Day Four

"Oh, Jesus, you scared me." I startle in the middle of the kitchen when Andrew appears out of nowhere. "I came down for some water."

"Can't sleep either?" Andrew asks.

It's odd to see him sitting in the dark, staring blankly ahead. No laptop. No iPad. No *Wall Street Journal.* No chiming cell phone.

I almost consider the fact that he might be sleepwalking.

"Nope," I say, quietly retrieving a crystal glass from the cupboard. Running it under the filtered water dispenser in the fridge door, I turn back toward him and take a swig. *Good Lord, this water tastes like it was sourced from a spring in heaven.* "Can I ask you something?"

Four in the morning might not be the best time to bring up the things that've been burning in my mind the last several days, but I don't know when I'll be able to get Andrew alone again. Could be tomorrow. Could be next month. There are always people here, coming and going, all fucking day.

"Sure." He leans back in his chair, arms folded, already on the defensive.

I do that to people: put them on the defensive. Meredith always said it is because I always look so tense, like I'm in desperate need of a massage and an all-expenses-paid vacation. And she says I talk too fast, but I can't help it. My mind is constantly running, never stopping. It's a wonder I can get my mouth and brain on the same page half the time. When I was little, I used to garble my words together because my little mouth couldn't keep up with my warp-speed thoughts. My mother used to sigh, roll her eyes, and tell me to *"slowwwww downnnn."*

"Why didn't you tell the police to talk to Meredith's best friend?" I ask.

"I wasn't aware she had a best friend."

"Bullshit." My jaw tightens, head tilting. "She's one of your neighbors. They were together all the time."

"If they were, it was during the day, when I was at work. She probably mentioned her a few times, but never in any detail."

"I find that incredibly hard to believe, Andrew." I call his bluff despite the fact that I'm beginning to accept that I didn't know her as well as I thought I did . . . and that maybe none of us truly knew her.

His nostrils flare. "I don't care if you believe me or not. I'm telling you, I had no idea she had any friends, at least not any friends around here. Always took her as more of an introvert, a loner. She was always doing her own thing. We'd see each other in the evening. I never asked how she spent her days, and she never volunteered the information."

"Sorry. Not buying it."

Our eyes lock, and his fist clenches on the table. I've never seen him like this before. Is he upset because I'm pointing out cracks in the case that might paint him in an unflattering light? Is he upset because I'm onto him? Because I'm the only person unafraid to call him out when shit doesn't add up?

"What's her name?" he asks.

"Allison," I say. "Allison Ross. She lives in that cabin-looking place on top of the hill."

"Oh, for fuck's sake. *That* Allison," he says, sighing. "They had a falling-out last year. They hadn't spoken in months."

"That's not the impression I got," I say.

"You talked to her?"

"I've spoken to most of your neighbors," I lie, but it's for the greater good. I want him to know nothing's going to get past me.

Nothing.

"I mean, maybe Mer made up with Allison? If she did, she didn't tell me," he says. "I just know they were close, and then they weren't."

I try to imagine how Andrew is as a father to Isabeau and Calder and how he would be to Meredith's baby. He strikes me as the kind of man who lets his wife do all the worrying and tending to details.

"Allison saw a bruise on Meredith's wrist once." I cut to the chase. "Said she was trying to hide it."

"No idea what you're talking about," he says. "But I know what you're getting at, Greer, and you need to watch yourself."

My jaw hangs, my blood pumping.

"I'm not saying you had anything to do with this. But I'm saying if you did, it's going to come out. The truth always does." I keep my voice low, but I don't soften my brusqueness.

"What reason would I possibly have to hurt my wife?" he asks, dragging his hand through his hair and tugging. "I love her. I love her more than you could possibly begin to understand. And she's carrying my child. Don't you think I want her home safe? With me? There's a reason I'm sitting out here, alone in the dark at four in the morning. Can't get a single goddamn minute to myself during the day. I'm so busy fielding calls and giving interviews that I don't have a spare second to actually miss my fucking wife or worry about her. So I stay up. I don't sleep. I lie in bed and think about her. I think about where she is. Who she's with. If she's cold or hungry or scared. If she's thinking about me. If she knows how badly I want to find her."

Taking a seat across from him, I bury my face in my hands, exhaling. Maybe I've been too hard on him. Maybe I've pointed the finger in his direction because right now, there's no one else to point the finger at.

"I'm sorry." I groan my apology before meeting his misty gaze from the other side of the table.

"You don't think I'm aware that I'm already under a microscope?" he asks. "That the police, the media, the public . . . they're all watching my every move? I'd much rather be out there looking for her, but when Connie Mayweather wants to do a sit-down, do you know how bad that would look if I declined? If I kept to myself, the media would have a field day with that, and you know it. They'd focus on how guilty I look instead of enlisting people to find her."

"No, you're right." I hate that he has a point, but I can't deny it. "This entire thing is so fucked up."

"Our next-door neighbor, Mary Jo Bosma," he says, "the one whose driveway I shoveled all last winter when her husband had hip replacement surgery, went to the police the other day to tell them about a fight she witnessed once. We were yelling, fighting over something stupid I'm sure, but I guess the windows were open. Anyway, she took time out of her day, drove down to the police station, and gave a report about a fight she saw between us a year ago. A goddamn argument. Every couple has their disagreements. Doesn't mean I did something to my wife."

He's right. Technically speaking.

"I'm sorry." I exhale. "That's not fair to you."

"So that's what I'm dealing with, Greer. And when you keep taking these little digs, suggesting that I had anything to do with this, don't think I don't notice." Andrew stands, shoving his chair out. "You're lucky you're her sister, or you'd be sleeping in the street tonight."

It's a little harsh, but I deserve it. Kind of. I resolve to cut him some slack going forward, keeping my suspicions to myself until I have good, hard proof that my worries have merit.

"Good night, Greer," he says, jaw clenched. "Try to get some sleep."

"You, too."

Finishing my water, I place the glass in the dishwasher, moving slowly and quietly so as not to make a sound. When I pass the butler's pantry on my way to the stairs, I stop when the calendar catches my eye.

The last day of the month is circled in red, not once but twice.

Meredith's twenty-sixth birthday.

The day her $5 million trust fund is to be endowed.

The timing of this entire thing is a little too curious for me to believe Andrew's innocent pleas . . . just yet.

CHAPTER 15

MEREDITH

Twenty-Six Months Ago

"Did I tell you we were invited to the—" Andrew stops talking when he glances up from his tablet and sees me hovering over a stack of mail, a single white envelope clutched in my hand. "What is it?"

"This was in the mailbox," I manage to say.

There's no postage stamp.

No return address.

Just my name scribbled in blue ink on the front.

Meredith Gretchen Price.

"I don't want to open it," I say, dropping it on the cold marble counter and stepping back.

Andrew heads toward me, swiping the envelope and ripping it from the side. Blowing a quick breath inside the torn edge, he pours the contents into his other hand: Ronan's business card, a postcard advertisement for the Peaceful Bean, and a folded slip of paper with the words "always watching" scribbled across the front in coordinating script.

"What the hell is this?" Andrew asks, examining each item. My heart stops when he studies Ronan's card.

"He must have seen me go to the police station that day," I say. "He must have figured out I talked to Detective McCormack."

Good save.

"The Peaceful Bean?" He flips the postcard over and back. "Never heard of it."

"I had coffee there last month. With a friend," I say. A half-truth isn't the same as a full lie, but it still feels wrong.

"So the lunatic's still following you." Andrew's mouth presses flat, the way it did when I told him about the note on my car a while back. It seemed to hardly bother him at first, but eventually he took precautions, calling me more and checking on me. But when nothing happened after that, things returned to normal, and Andrew was convinced the only bone-chilling thing about Glacier Park was the north winds in January. He assured me it was probably some teenagers pulling some prank, and when I asked how they knew my name, he said they were probably friends of Calder's.

It made sense at the time.

Or maybe I just wanted to believe his explanation.

It was the least terrifying of them all.

"Should I call the police?" I ask, recalling Ronan's instructions to notify the department right away. Though I have no idea how long this has been sitting in my mailbox. The only things that get delivered anymore are bills and junk catalogs I never read since I do most of my shopping online or in Glacier Park Commons. I'm lucky if I check the box more than once a week.

"It's late." He frowns, glancing at the time on his phone. "I doubt the detective's working right now, and if they dispatch an officer, all we have is this letter that's been sitting in the mailbox for God knows how long. Just go in the morning."

Andrew yawns, coming around the island toward me. Cupping my face in his hands, he presses his lips into my forehead, like I'm a sullen child whose irrational fears can be comforted with a kiss.

"Bed?" he asks, his hands lowering to my waist. I breathe him in, a feeble attempt to soothe myself, but I feel nothing.

No safety.

No security.

"None of this worries you?" I ask, biting the inside of my bottom lip until I taste blood.

"No," he says, his tone uncompromising. "This place is Fort Knox. You're safe here. Nothing's going to happen to you. I promise. Not with me here."

Half the time, I wake up at night and find the security system unarmed. He forgets, and when I bring it up, he laughs because Glacier Park was voted the "safest city in America" nine years in a row in *People* magazine.

"Contrary to what you might assume, I don't sit around all day eating Dove chocolates and watching *The Price Is Right*." I roll my eyes. "I'm probably gone more than I'm home. What if something happens when I'm outside of your impenetrable fortress?"

"Keep your phone on you," he says. "Be aware of your surroundings. Stay away from places you've never been before."

"So that's all I have to do, and nothing will ever happen to me?" I'm being facetious, but he doesn't pick up on it, or if he does, he's not playing along.

Sliding his hand into mine, he tows me behind him, heading to our master suite.

"Let's stop with the worrying, Mer," he says. "It's really getting old. This is some lunatic who probably escaped from the mental hospital in Glen Falls who just wants to mess with you because he gets off on it. No one's going to hurt you."

"You don't know that." The fact that he hasn't suggested Calder's friends this time around concerns me. He has to know this is more than some silly prank.

"You're right. I don't. But I do know I'm never going to let anything happen to you." His expression relaxes and our hands loosen as we climb the stairs. I stay a few steps behind him. "If someone really wanted to hurt you, don't you think they'd do a little more than send you creepy letters that make no sense?"

"The letters *do* make sense. He's trying to let me know he's following me."

"He's just trying to freak you out. Don't let him get to you. Pretty soon he'll get bored with this little game."

"You make it sound so simple."

"I'm just saying, if you ignore him, he'll probably go away," Andrew says. "He wants your attention. He wants to get to you. And so far, it's working."

"And what if he doesn't go away?"

"Then I'll hire a private investigator, and I'll personally see to it that he's dealt with properly." Andrew exhales, cupping my face in his left hand. "You're getting yourself all worked up, Mer, but what you need is some rest."

I refuse to meet his condescending gaze.

Turning to head back downstairs, I resolve to sleep in one of the guest rooms on the main level. For the first time, I can't bear the thought of sleeping next to a man who claims to love me so much yet cares so little about my concerns.

Stopping on the sixth step, I turn back. "If you truly believe nothing bad is going to happen, why can't you at least respect that I'm terrified right now?"

"Meredith." His tone is stern, like the way he speaks to Calder when he forgets to shut off his video game or Isabeau when she doesn't put her dirty clothes in the hamper. "I respect that you're getting yourself worked up. Why can't you respect that I'm not worried because I'm going to do everything in my power to protect you? Besides, what good would it do you if we were both worked up over this?"

Maybe he has a point, but I still feel slighted.

He hears me, but he's not listening.

Raising my hand, I silence him. "Forget it. We'll finish this conversation tomorrow."

He doesn't argue.

When I reach the bottom landing, I listen for the soft creak of our bedroom door, and I watch for the light beneath it to turn to dark.

I can't fight with him tonight.

I don't have the energy.

Fixing myself a cup of decaffeinated Earl Grey, I grab my copy of *Wuthering Heights* and lie on the sofa in the formal living room, spreading a throw across my lap. I'm not a reader, but I could use a distraction. My eyes scan the words on the pages of a book I picked out because I'd overheard some women discussing it at the gym last week. But nothing registers. I can't focus or concentrate.

Even in my own home, I could swear I'm being watched.

For some inexplicable reason, I glance up, toward a small break in the curtains that cover a picture window. Flicking off the lamp on the side table, I pad across the carpet and peek outside.

The moonless sky casts no shadows, and the only light comes from the Gardeners' elaborate solar-powered landscaping display across the street.

But I notice something out of the ordinary.

A black sedan is parked in front of our house.

From here, I can make out the shape of a person positioned in the driver's seat.

The Gardeners have an elegant circle drive leading to a two-story porte cochere, with a fountain taking center stage. Anytime they have company, they insist that their visitors park there and not on the street.

Besides, their house is dark.

They're either gone or asleep.

Within seconds, the taillights on the sedan glow red, and the driver guns the engine. Before I have a chance to get a better look or a single number off the plate, it's gone.

My chest is weighted with each breath, tiny shudders rippling through my body as every nerve ending fires. Standing before the window, paralyzed, I consider dashing up the stairs and waking Andrew, but for what? So he can laugh at me, roll to his side, and go back to sleep?

Pacing the living room, I check the window again and again. This house is vast and its late-night darkness is unsettling in this moment, but if I turn a light on, I won't be able to see outside, and anyone looking in will be able to see my every move, my silhouette behind every curtain.

Tiptoeing to the kitchen, I pull my phone off the charger and scroll through my contacts.

I don't want to bother Ronan this time of night—in fact, I don't want to bother him at all after that silly bout of infatuation last month—but I don't have anyone else.

My thumb hovers over his name.

Detective Ronan McCormack.

Even his name sounds strong, shielding.

Holding my breath, I make the call.

"McCormack." He answers on the third ring, his voice groggy as he sucks a slow breath past the receiver, and I wonder if he always answers his personal phone like that.

"It's Meredith." I keep my voice down, padding across the house to the farthest corner, away from the twenty-foot ceiling in the foyer that makes everything echo. My intentions are innocent this time, but I don't want to wake Andrew. "Meredith Price."

"Right, right." He pulls in another breath, and I hear the rustle of sheets in the background. He's climbing out of bed.

"I'm so sorry to bother you. I know it's late."

"Don't worry about it. What's going on?"

"I found an envelope in my mailbox today." I tell him about the letter, about his business card and the advertisement from the coffee shop.

"Well . . . fuck." The phone swishes. He says something inaudible. It sounds like he's up, walking around, stumbling through the dark and flicking on lights.

"But the reason I'm calling," I say, "is I just saw a parked car outside my house. It was black. Four doors. It sped off before I could see anything else. Maybe it was nothing . . . coincidence or something . . . but it freaked me out. That's why I called."

"You want me to call down to the station? See who's on duty and have them patrol your street?" he asks.

"That'd be nice," I say. Andrew would never know, and the peace of mind just might help me get some sleep tonight.

"I'm on it."

I love that he takes me seriously, that he doesn't laugh or brush my fear off like I'm a child complaining about monsters under the bed.

Monsters are real.

They're real, and they're capable of doing the unspeakable.

And they don't hide under beds or in closets—they hide in plain sight. You just don't always notice them.

"You going to be okay?" he asks.

"Yeah, yeah." I massage the back of my neck, pacing the main floor guest room I've sequestered myself in so I can talk on the phone.

"Get some rest, all right?"

I intended to sleep in here tonight, but the thought of being alone with some creep outside is almost worse than sleeping next to my insensitive husband.

I'm going to have to pick my poison.

And tonight, I choose Andrew.

CHAPTER 16

GREER

Day Four

The cab drops me off outside Glacier Park's hole-in-the-wall police station, and I march toward the front desk like a woman on a mission.

And I am.

"I need to speak to Detective McCormack," I tell the woman peering over the top of her glasses and trying to pretend like she isn't minimizing her game of Spider Solitaire. "Immediately."

She's wearing red librarian frames, perhaps an attempt to be different or kitschy at a job that requires her to dress like everyone else. Her mouth forms a straight line. "I'm sorry. He's not available. He's out of the office. I can have you speak with Detective Bixby if you'd like."

My lips turn down at the corners. "When will he be back?"

She looks away for a moment, pulling in a taut breath before clearing her throat. "He's on paid administrative leave pending the outcome of an internal investigation. I'm not allowed to give out any information beyond that, ma'am. I'm sorry."

Ma'am?

I'm easily ten years younger than this woman.

"Wait, what?" I laugh because this woman has to be joking. "I just talked to him yesterday. I've been working with him every day this week. What the hell happened?"

"Like I said, I'm not at liberty to share that with you, ma'am."

My fists tighten. "I'm Meredith Price's sister, and I've been—"

"Again, I'm sorry. I can't share anything with you at this time." Her compassion, which I'm convinced was nonexistent in the first place, is replaced with impatience the second the phone rings. She swivels her chair away from me, snatching the receiver and cradling it on her shoulder as she plugs her other ear with a finger.

I've been stonewalled.

Storming outside, I order another cab, chewing the inside of my lip as I wait on a nearby park bench next to a weathered bronze statue of a beaming police officer holding hands with two grinning children.

Beneath it is a plaque, engraved with the words CHIEF EDWARD PRICE. THANK YOU FOR 35 YEARS OF DEDICATED SERVICE.

Sneering, I exhale. Meredith told me once that Andrew was Glacier Park born-and-bred and that the Prices were a well-respected family in this area. I'm willing to bet money that Edward Price was Andrew's father and that the Glacier Park police take care of their own.

Small town departments usually do.

The thin blue line isn't reserved only for those with badges and guns; it extends to their loved ones as well. At least that's what one of my regulars told me at the shop one day. A twenty-year veteran of the NYPD, that man had stories for days and little time for bullshit.

My kind of guy.

Scrolling through my seldom-used social media accounts, I see someone's started a website called FindMeredithPrice.com, encouraging followers to use hashtags like #findmeredith and #whereismeredithprice to raise awareness.

I peruse the photos and posts. The outpouring of sympathy is appreciated, but sharing a post from the comfort of your sofa isn't going to find my sister. If these people truly cared, they'd spend less time surfing Facebook and more time actually looking for her. I bet when they lay their heads on their little pillows tonight in their cozy houses with locked doors, my sister will be the last person they're thinking about.

People might care, but only ever for a moment.

Down the road a Yellow Cab barrels this way, coming to a short stop in front of the station.

"Don't they usually give you a bus ticket or something?" the middle-aged driver asks. He's easily fifty pounds overweight, his salt-and-pepper hair in desperate need of a haircut. Clearly not a local.

"I realize I'm dressed in all black and I look like I haven't slept or had a good meal in days, but I assure you I'm not an inmate." I roll my eyes as I climb into the back seat.

He lifts a thick-knuckled hand. "Sorry. Little cabdriver humor. I pick up a lot of folks from here. County jail is just behind the station. Where you headed?"

"Twenty-Two Spring Grove Lane," I say, reciting a cute little address that has no business belonging to an enormous, dark mansion.

"Ah. Nice area." He flicks on his blinker. "Then again, this entire town is nice. Not a rough neighborhood in sight. You know, years ago they had an older part of town, smaller houses and such. The developers, they tore them all down, put up a bunch of fancy McMansions."

I hate that word—*McMansion*. Everyone who uses that word thinks they're being clever and witty when they're really being banal and unoriginal.

I peer out the window, silently wallowing in how much I loathe small talk.

"You're not from around here, are you?" he asks, punching the brakes at the next light. My hands brace against the back of the front seat so I don't end up in his lap. I should probably wear a seat belt.

"What gave it away?"

Checking my phone and debating whether or not to fake a phone call to get out of this painfully stale conversation, I scroll through my Internet history and pull up the Glacier County Assessor page, the one I used to find the names of all Meredith's neighbors.

On a whim, I type in Ronan's name and press enter.

A single listing is presented on the next page. A modest ranch—by GP standards anyway—with cedar shingle siding and a one-car garage. It doesn't look like the typical abodes that are so prevalent in this pretentious city, but the address is local.

"Change of plans," I say to the driver. "Drop me off at Sixty-Four Highland Road."

A red truck is parked in front of the garage, fresh mud on its tires. The house looks just like the one on the assessor page, except maybe some of the bushes have grown. There's a light on, and a dog barks from behind a cedar privacy fence in the backyard.

I ask the cabdriver to keep the meter running, telling him I won't be long.

Rapping on the thin glass storm door, I catch what sounds like footsteps on the other side that come to an abrupt stop. I'm sure he's peering through his peephole, debating whether or not to let me in, but I'm not going to unstick my thorn from his side until I find out why the hell he was placed on leave.

The door opens a few seconds later.

This all-American Boy Scout looks like he's seen better days. His hair is disheveled, his white T-shirt wrinkled, and his once rigid posture slightly slumped, defeated.

"What the hell happened?" I fold my arms across my chest.

He exhales, widening the door and letting me in. His other hand falls, hitting against his side.

"It's a long story," he says.

"I bet."

Taking a seat on the edge of his plaid sofa, I fold my hands in my lap, cross my legs tight, and give him my undivided attention despite the annoyingly distracting dog out back that won't shut the fuck up for two seconds.

He glances outside once more before closing the door and taking a spot on the chair across from me. Resting his elbows on his knees, he drags his hands down his tired face before releasing a hard breath.

"Your sister," he says, "and I . . . we had this thing. On the side. This secret thing. Nobody knew about it."

I'm straddling the line between comprehending what he's saying and trying to imagine my lovestruck sister straying from her "happy" marriage.

This bombshell is heavier than the last one, weighing down my shoulders, slowing my breath, and busying my mind.

I didn't know her.

I didn't know her at all—at least not the person she'd become.

"Forensics was able to analyze her cell phone records and linked her to me. I knew it was going to happen, just didn't know it'd be this soon," he says. "The department's placed me on paid administrative leave. Conflict of interest and all that. And they have to rule me out as a suspect now that they know we were . . . romantically involved."

I study Ronan as if I'm seeing him for the first time all over again, trying to recall little moments, red flags, anything that would so much as hint that he had anything to do with this.

"Why didn't you come forward right away?" I ask. "That alone seems like it might have some insinuations, don't you think?"

"I know how this looks." He buries his face in his hands again. "But there's so much you don't know."

"What do you mean?" I lean forward. "What are you talking about? What haven't you told me?"

My questions launch at him, one after another, and he lifts a hand in protest.

"I'll tell you everything," he says, though now I'm not sure if I can believe anything he says.

"Go on." I wave my hand at him, sitting up straighter.

"I didn't come forward right away because I wanted to be on this case. I wanted to find your sister. I wanted to be as close to all the developments and evidence as possible because I knew her well. I knew who she hung out with and where she went and what she liked to do. I thought that'd give me an advantage, help me find her quicker. And being the lead on the investigation meant I'd be able to keep a close eye on Andrew."

My head cocks. "So you think it was Andrew?"

"There's no solid evidence yet," he says. "But based on what I know? Based on everything Meredith's told me over the last couple of years? He's the only one with a motive."

"And what might that be?"

"For starters, she was pregnant," he says. "And Andrew didn't want her to have kids—not yet. First time she was pregnant, she said he freaked out on her."

"The first time?"

"It was shortly after they were married," he says. "Before I knew her."

The fact that Meredith neglected to tell me that stings, but I bury my hurt and focus on squeezing every last ounce of information out of this man.

"So you were sleeping with her, like, you two were having a full-blown affair?" I ask.

He nods. "Off and on, yeah. It was complicated."

"Did she love you? Were you in love? Were you planning to be together at some point?"

"She was waiting," he says. "Said she had to save up money or something. She had nothing. The house, the cars, the credit cards— everything was in Andrew's name. He had full control over everything. She couldn't leave if she wanted to."

Her trust fund.

She was waiting for her trust fund.

"Did she say how she was going to get this money to leave him?"

"She didn't tell me any details, just that she was possibly coming into some money, and she was going to leave him after that."

"Did he know she was planning to leave?"

Ronan shrugs. "No idea. For all I know, she told him, and he did something to her. Nobody actually saw her at the grocery store that day. All we have is an empty car and an abandoned purse and phone."

"So what are you suggesting?"

"I'm suggesting that anything is possible," he says.

My stomach twists, hardens. When I close my eyes, I can't help but picture Andrew, his hands around her neck, tears streaming down her cheeks. Bile rises, burning my throat, but I swallow it away.

"Her trust fund is going to be endowed later this month," I say. "On her birthday. If she's declared dead . . . it'll go to Andrew. All five million of it."

Ronan pinches the bridge of his nose, his tired eyes squeezing shut. "That son of a bitch."

"Let's not jump to conclusions." I stand because I can't sit still anymore. Pacing his small living room, I tuck my hair behind my ears. "We need proof. We need something we can take to the police."

Ronan scoffs. "The Price family owns the police department. Not literally, but his father was the chief of police for over three decades. His grandfather started that finance firm Andrew runs. Made his first million managing the department's pension accounts. That name is pure gold in Glacier Park, untouchable. The moment I so much as suggested to Chief Rolland that we should do some surveillance on Andrew, he damn near ripped my head off and spat down my throat."

"How can he get away with that?"

"Nothing bad ever happens here. Our crime rate is practically zero. The only reason they have a full-time detective is because the residents complained and city council approved it." He rises, moving toward the window and glancing outside, as if he's being watched. "They're going to try to pin this on me."

My nose wrinkles. "Why would you say that?"

"This is the biggest thing to happen in Glacier Park. This is a chance for the department to shine. To get their fifteen minutes." He shakes his head. "They're desperate to solve this case as soon as possible. Letting it go cold when the rest of the world is watching is the last thing they want to do."

"They can't pin anything on you. There's no evidence, no body, nothing."

"Nothing *yet*," he corrects me. He lingers in silence, lost in thought for a moment. "We have to find her."

"We will."

"I just want to know she's safe," he says. "And then I'm going to destroy the son of a bitch who took her."

Checking my watch, I glance toward the door. "I should go."

Ronan nods.

"I appreciate your being so candid," I add, forcing civility into my tone. I'm not exactly pleased with the way he withheld this detail from me, but blowing up at him would serve no purpose at this point. Besides, with limited resources, I'm not exactly in a place to start burning bridges, and I'd hate to burn the wrong one. "Just wish you'd have come forward earlier."

He doesn't meet my gaze; he simply stands there, his hand dragging across his mouth as he widens his stance. I suppose there's nothing more to be said.

"Anyway, I should go," I say.

I may have given him a pass for now, but that doesn't mean I won't be watching every move he makes, analyzing every word he breathes. I want to believe Ronan's as good a man as he appears to be, but the truth is, all I know is that I know nothing.

And until I know something, everyone's a suspect.

CHAPTER 17

MEREDITH

Twenty-Five Months Ago

"Do you think this is wrong? What we're doing?" I'm seated on the passenger side of Ronan's pickup, sipping gourmet hot cocoa from the Winterbean Café in downtown GP as we drive around the countryside on a lazy Monday morning. I'm supposed to be at yoga. He's supposed to be at work.

"Hanging out?"

I smirk, lifting my cup to my lips. "Is that all this is?"

"Yeah," he says, turning to me and flashing his signature disarming grin. *God, I love his smile.* It's one of my favorite things in the world, I've decided. When I close my eyes at night, it's one of the last things I think about lately. "I haven't so much as touched you. Right now, we're just two friends, hanging out."

"If I wasn't married, would you . . . would you want to be more than friends?" I take a sip, coating my tongue in velvety liquid chocolate. My cheeks heat. Can't remember the last time a man made me blush.

"If you weren't married . . . yes. I'd snatch you up in a heartbeat."
He cruises over a hill, one hand resting at the bottom of his steering
wheel as he turns and winks.

"We're playing with fire."

He doesn't answer, but I know he knows.

It started last month, after I called him in the middle of the night.
Two days after that, I called him again when I saw that same car driving
up and down my street, almost intentionally slow, as if it were menac-
ing me. Andrew was gone that night, out of town for work, and Ronan
came over.

I didn't want to be alone, not with that creep out there again. Of
course, by the time Ronan showed up, the car was long gone. But I
was able to confirm that it was a late model Honda Accord with Utah
plates.

He did a perimeter check, inside and out, and then camped out
in my living room—in the dark—for hours. When I woke up he was
gone, but he left a note saying everything was clear and to call him if I
needed anything.

A few days after that, I bumped into him while gassing up at the
Kwick Starr on Bleu Street. We chatted between pumps eight and nine
for nearly an hour, both of us ignoring the passing time, and when
a waiting car honked at me to move, he asked if I wanted to grab
lunch. Climbing inside my car, I started the engine, contemplated his
invitation, and gave him a quick nod as I moved my car to an empty
parking spot.

I don't have a lot of friends here.

Andrew plucked me out of Denver and planted me here, among his
friends and colleagues and neighbors he'd known for years, neighbors
who treated me like an outsider, a novelty, gossip fodder.

Andrew doesn't see it, but I'll never forget our first dinner party.
I slaved all day in the kitchen, preparing everything myself when I

could've easily had it catered. Two of Andrew's neighbors' wives, Betsy and Luellen, were in the next room, discussing me.

"Poor Erica," Betsy said. "How can she compete with that? The girl looks like . . . who's that model . . . the one that was on that TV show with her mom . . . she hangs out with that Jenner girl . . . she's got blonde hair . . ."

"Gigi Hadid," Luellen said. "My daughter's obsessed with her."

"Yeah. She looks like freaking Gigi Hadid." Betsy sighed, like it was a bad thing. "Erica's beautiful, but she can't compete with Gigi."

Luellen clucked her tongue. "You think they'll ever get back together? Andrew and Erica?"

"Who knows?" Betsy said without hesitation. "I feel like this is just a phase for him. She's pretty and whatever, but there's not much else to her. Honestly, she's kind of boring. Must be the sex because it's definitely not the personality. Men like 'em young these days. What I wouldn't give for an ounce of that energy. And a perky ass."

Luellen laughed. "You're so bad."

"Come on," Betsy told her. "Dinner's about to start. I want to watch her make a fool of herself trying to impress us. It's so cute. She's wearing an apron and everything. I know she's just trying to look the part, but she looks like a little girl playing dress-up."

But then there's Allison. She's the only neighbor who waves when I pass by. Then again, she and her husband only recently moved in. They didn't know Andrew when he was still shackled to Erica.

"My one-year anniversary is next month," I say to Ronan, peering over the dash and wishing he would keep driving.

"Doing anything special?"

"Andrew wants to take me somewhere. Says it's a surprise. Told me to pack a swimsuit," I say, shrugging. I'm guessing it's Fiji or the Virgin Islands. Definitely a place he can brag about to his friends as he shows off pictures from our trip.

I know Andrew loves me, but he also loves to show off his earthly possessions . . . his Maserati, his limited-edition diamond Rolex, me.

"You don't sound too excited."

"I don't?" I hadn't realized. "I am. I just . . . I think I'm in a funk or something."

"How so?"

I've yet to ask myself that question, afraid of what the answer might be if I dig deep enough.

"Are you unhappy?" he asks.

"Not at all," I lie. I lie so hard.

A year ago, I was walking on a breeze, a smile permanently etched on my carefree face, counting down the minutes until my husband walked in the door at the end of the night and barely containing myself the second we crawled into bed.

But then I met Ronan.

And my life took an unexpected detour.

And it's not Ronan. It's not Andrew. It's all me. I know that. I blame no one but myself.

"Actually. I don't know." I sigh, feeling the pressure of the words as they congest in my throat. I've held all this in, not telling a single soul, and I don't know how long I can do it anymore. "When I'm with Andrew, I feel a certain way. Grateful? Fortunate? Loved?"

I pick at a loose thread on his seat.

"But when I'm with you, I feel something else entirely," I say. "And I don't know what that is. I just know it makes me feel alive in a way that Andrew doesn't."

I muster the courage to glance in his direction, watching for his reaction. His brows are angled in, his gaze focused on the road. He's listening. Which is more than Andrew can say lately.

When we first met, Andrew would listen to me drone on and on about everything. He seemed fascinated by my eclectic childhood, my rebellious teenage years, my college shenanigans, and everything in between. He actually listened. We had real conversations with real dialogue that volleyed back and forth.

Now I can't recall the last time we actually conversed for longer than five minutes about anything meaningful. Lately it's "How was your day?" and "What are we having for dinner?" and "Did you want to see that play this weekend?"

"If you're not happy, Meredith, then by all means, get the fuck out," Ronan says. "There's a reason the divorce rate in this country is so high. People make mistakes every day. Love makes us do stupid things."

"Do you know how many people told me not to marry Andrew?" I ask. "All my friends. My coworkers. My sister practically launched an all-out campaign against him. But I loved him. And I didn't want to believe them. I wanted to prove them wrong."

"So you're going to stay miserable just to prove a point?" he scoffs, shaking his head, the first time I've ever seen him annoyed with me.

"I don't know what I'm going to do," I say, resting my forehead against the chilled glass window. "I don't have a single penny to my name. My sister lives in a studio apartment, and living with my mother and her boyfriend-of-the-month is completely out of the question."

"So get a job. Save some money."

I don't tell him about the trust fund. It's none of his business.

"Andrew doesn't want me to work." I place my palm over my mouth. "God, do you hear how I sound right now?"

Ronan turns to me, his lips half frowning. "Yep."

"He'd question it. He'd know something was up." I close my eyes, wishing I'd never agreed to that stupid prenup that ensured that if the marriage couldn't make it past year five, I'd walk away penniless.

I signed the prenup because I loved him. And at the time, I wanted to prove I wasn't marrying him for his money. And it was true. I didn't need his money. I had my own just a few short years away.

Ronan reaches across the cab of the truck, pulling my hand from my knee and holding it in his.

"Life's too damn short to be this damn miserable," he says. "If you want out, we'll figure it out. Together. I'll help you find a way. I'm here for you, Mer."

CHAPTER 18

GREER

Day Four

"How could you not know?" My mother's voice trails through the foyer when I return that afternoon, though I'm not immediately sure who's on the receiving end of her question. "How long has this been going on?"

"They're still looking into the details," Andrew says. "They took him off the case, though. That's the important thing. They assured me they're looking extra closely at him."

I follow the sound.

"What are you guys talking about?" I play dumb when I interrupt, standing between them at the kitchen island. "Who's off the case?"

"Did you know your sister was having . . . *having an affair?*" My mother whispers the last half of her question, as if having an affair is something she deems shameful.

The woman practically wrote the book on the topic, never ditching a boyfriend until she had another lined up and ready to go, and you can't do that without straying, but if you ask her, those weren't "affairs" because she was never married.

Denial is a strange beast, and I'm fortunate to have never known it the way she has.

"I didn't know that," I lie, feigning shock, gasp and all. "With whom?"

"That detective," Mom says, making a gurgling noise in her throat as if she's disgusted. "Can you believe that? Makes me wonder if he was tampering with evidence when he was here."

"Kind of hard to do when there's literally no evidence," I say.

"You know what I mean. Maybe . . . maybe there was a secret notebook or diary or something?" She shrugs.

My fingers tap against the marble counter in quick succession, an old nervous habit. "Nobody writes in diaries, Mom."

"I think Brenda's point is that it was highly unethical for Ronan to work on the case." Andrew's voice grows louder, drowning us out before silencing us altogether. "And I agree. The fact that he didn't come forward about the relationship is a red flag that the police are taking very seriously. And I encourage them to do so."

Great.

Andrew's blaming Ronan.

Ronan's blaming Andrew.

Both of them have valid points.

And we still don't have a goddamn clue what happened to my sister.

"I don't know," I say. "It's dangerous to point fingers before you have all the facts."

"Exactly," Andrew says. "And right now, the fact of the matter is that Ronan McCormack deliberately neglected to inform the police that he was romantically involved with the missing woman whose case he was investigating."

Much to my chagrin, I'm unable to argue with his statement. He might be a smug, old-moneyed know-it-all, but he isn't wrong. Ronan lied by omission, a mistake that could prove to have dire consequences for him if he is, in fact, innocent.

I just hope he was telling *me* the truth.

My mother places her hand over her heart, staring ahead with tired eyes. There's a silver filigree ring on her left ring finger. It's not a typical engagement ring, more like the kind you buy from a beachside gift shop. A gift from Wade, I'm sure. Poor guy. If only I could warn him she's a mere eight months away from getting the urge to move on to the next sad sack.

Mom repositions herself closer to Andrew than to me, which doesn't bother me, but it tells me where I stand with her. It's nothing new. Our relationship has always been strained, distant. Silly me for expecting her to step up to the plate and actually be there for me when tragedy strikes our family.

"Have you eaten yet, Andrew?" my mother asks, her mascara-caked lashes fluttering. She loves this. She loves to feel needed by a man. It's not enough to have Wade's affections; she has to soak up every ounce she can get from any penis-wielding human willing to give it. "Let me fix you a sandwich. Have a seat."

"I'm not hungry, Bren," Andrew says, shortening her name like they're a couple of good pals who go way back. "Thank you, though."

"Nonsense. Sit. Eat." She pulls a chair from the table and points. How she has the energy to wait hand and foot on someone while her daughter is missing is beyond me. She never was good at showing emotions. I'd never seen her so much as shed a single tear at a funeral or get the tiniest bit weepy after a bad breakup. That woman, I'm convinced, is half robot. "Someone's got to take care of you until my daughter is back. Might as well be me. I'm good at taking care of people. It's what I do."

My childhood begs to differ.

"Is turkey all right? Do you take mustard and mayo?" she asks, rifling through the fridge. "And do you want your bread toasted?"

Since the moment Andrew waltzed into Meredith's life, my mother was absolutely taken with him. And I'll admit, at first glance, Andrew

Price is charming and generous and has a way of making you feel like you're the most important person in the room when he talks to you.

The only thing is, I'm not naive enough to fall for it.

I only wish I could say the same for my sister.

◆　◆　◆

"You're up." I climb into bed that night, my phone pressed to my cheek as I check in with Harris. There's a fullness in my chest that wasn't there before, like coming home after a long absence. The last time we spoke, he said he wanted to be together again, and while a week ago I'd have drowned myself in such a sweet sentiment, I only have enough energy now to focus on finding Mer.

"Was wondering if I was going to hear from you today," he says.

Sinking back into the pillow, I press my palm over my forehead and close my eyes. My head is pounding and has been all week. Stress and lack of sleep have done a number on me, and last time I checked my reflection in the mirror, it seemed that my complexion had decided to join in on the fun.

"I have so much to tell you." I exhale. "How much time do you have?"

"For you? All night. Lay it on me."

I tell him about Ronan and Meredith, about the department placing him on administrative leave, and then I bring up the stalker and the pregnancies, laying it all on him and barely taking a breath between stories.

"Shit," he says once I'm done.

"I know." I roll to my side, pulling the blankets up to my chin and settling in for a long talk with my best friend. I realize now that most people lie. Hidden lives are more common than I thought. And Harris is the only person on this earth that I can trust to give me his honest, unabashed opinion.

"I don't know what to say." Harris sighs. "This is all so . . . unexpected."

"It doesn't feel real. None of this does." I gnaw the inside of my lower lip, where it's starting to callous and protrude, rubbing against my teeth when I speak. "Maybe she was too proud to tell me I was right? I gave her such a hard time before the wedding. She knew I hated him. God, I should've just—"

"Don't." He cuts me off.

"Don't what?"

"Don't wallow in the past. Don't beat yourself up for things you did or didn't do years ago," he says. "You do this, and then you reach this point of no return. Not going to let you go down that road. Let's focus on the present."

Exhaling, I say, "You're right. You know me well."

"So what do you think about all of this?" he asks. "Do you think that detective had something to do with it?"

"I don't know what to think. I'm on the fence," I say, eyes growing heavy. "I feel like there are all these crumbs leading to these red flags, but none of them are leading to her."

"Where do we go from here?" he asks. I love that he uses the word "we." He may be thousands of miles from me, but knowing I have his full support is the only shred of comfort I have right now.

"I'm just going to watch them," I say. "Andrew and Ronan. I'll play both sides. What choice do I have?"

"Greer." He says my name in one giant exhalation.

"Yes?"

"Just be careful." He pauses. "If one of those men did something to Meredith, they're capable of doing something to you, too."

CHAPTER 19

MEREDITH

Twenty-Four Months Ago

I tried to enjoy it.

But what began with a hard and fast pull of my zipper and the trail of his fingertips along my inner thigh ended with my husband screwing me like he was on a time crunch, neglecting to so much as look me in the eye or press his lips into mine.

The entire thing was a jarring experience, one that left a lingering soreness between my legs.

He's never fucked me like that.

How everything could flip on its back after a short twelve months is beyond me, but as I lie in the middle of a king-size bed in the presidential suite of a luxury resort in Phuket, I'm at a loss for words.

The door to the bathroom is cracked open a few inches, steam escaping from the shower that Andrew insisted on taking the second he was finished, like he couldn't wait to wash me off him.

Mustering the strength to forge on like everything's fine, I peel myself up and make my way to our hotel en suite to clean up and change into a bikini. Though we landed in Thailand a couple of hours ago, it's late morning here and a balmy eighty-four degrees.

"I'm going to the pool," I tell him a few minutes later, tugging a cover-up over my shoulders.

Andrew's wet, matted head emerges from behind the fogged glass door. "Why are you wearing that?"

"The cover-up?"

"Yeah." He smirks, like everything is normal and he didn't just fuck me like I was a coke-addicted hooker. "That thing."

I get it.

He likes attention. He likes knowing that he has something he thinks everyone else wants. I'm realizing this now.

I can't count how many times I've been hit on at the grocery store or the gym or on my way to the ladies' room at a restaurant, and any time I mentioned it to Andrew, his face would light, proud and gratified, and he'd tell me I should be flattered.

Now I know it was never about me—it was always about him.

Tossing a towel over my shoulder, I leave the bathroom just as he shuts off the water; I grab a paperback, a pair of sunglasses, my phone, and a room key before heading downstairs.

The pool area is moderately packed, but there are no children laughing and splashing about because Andrew selected an adults-only resort. Only tropical music and exotic alcohol.

I find a couple of empty chairs in a sunny corner and situate myself, propping the back of the chair up so I can simultaneously suntan and people-watch while pretending to read.

The kind of people who can afford to vacation at this resort are mostly of the rich, eclectic variety. The kind who spend $14,000 on jewel-encrusted swords emblazoned with their family crest just for the fun of it. The kind who hire entire teams of nannies to look after their bevy of spoiled children. The kind who trade in their Italian luxury sports cars for new models every six months for no other reason besides that they can.

A woman with a face full of fillers and dark hair extensions dripping down to the small of her back saunters past with a younger man. His body is taut and ripped, and he can't keep his hands off her. I imagine she's recently divorced, the recipient of a generous settlement, and he's nothing but a plaything, yet another luxury only afforded to the rich.

I wonder if other people look at the two of us the way I'm looking at the two of them.

Curious. Quietly judgmental.

I don't want to think about that anymore, about the two of us being a spectacle.

Several seats down, a man is being slathered in suntan oil by a girl who appears to be barely one-third his age, her soft hands working his glistening chest hairs. People watch the couple as if they're some kind of entertainment.

A shadow covers me. "There you are."

I shield my eyes, glancing to my left to where my husband stands. A pair of red and white striped swim trunks are tied low on his narrow hips, revealing his washboard abs and smooth chest. A disgustingly expensive pair of sunglasses rests on top of his head, and he slips them over his nose before taking the seat beside me.

We are these people.

Revolting wealth. Unapologetic self-indulgence.

Adjusting my oversize shades, I spread the spine of my book and follow the sentences on the page with my eyes, though I don't read them.

I can't focus right now with all these realizations hurling themselves at me faster than I know how to process them.

Taking five long, deep breaths, I focus on the here and now. The faint scent of chlorine in the air mixed with sunscreen. The trickling sound of the water feature at the end of the pool. Couples laughing. The heat of the sun baking into my skin.

My eyes burn for a moment, a mix of bruised ego and wayward sunblock, but I suck it up and flip to the next page.

A beautiful young woman with thick onyx hair and ruby-red lips strides in our direction, a small notepad in her hand and a drink list beneath her arm.

"Would you like to order a drink?" she asks, her accent thick but her English perfect. She's wearing a bikini, and though her body is covered by a resort-issued sarong, there's surprisingly very little left to the imagination.

Andrew orders a beer, his eyes glazing over as he searches her body. Either he thinks I can't see through his sunglasses, or he doesn't care. When she leaves, he swipes his fingers across his iPad, pretending to check his work e-mail as he stares at the beautiful women across the pool dripping from the arms of potbellied, gold-chain-wearing, new-money types.

A second later, I watch my husband from the corner of my eyes. He's passed out now, his iPad lying on his ripped stomach and his head turned away from me. The faintest snore escapes from his lips.

My hand dips down, retrieving my phone from the cement ground beneath my lounger.

I text Ronan.

Just to say hi.

Just to see what he's up to.

I'm playing with fire, but I don't care.

Match. Strike. Whoosh.

CHAPTER 20

GREER

Day Five

I couldn't sleep last night, which was nothing new or unusual, but the moment the sun came up this morning, I hightailed it to Ronan's so I could hopefully try to put a few of these questions to rest.

"When was the last time you spoke to my sister?" I ask, standing in Ronan's living room. His house smells like breakfast, the air savory and heavy. A small shelf lined with family photos catches my eye. They look like nice people, all of them smiling in matching blue jeans and various shades of blue sweaters and button-downs.

"A couple of days before she went missing," he says without pause. "We ended things. For good that time. She'd found out she was pregnant, and she knew we couldn't keep going. Plus, she always felt guilty . . . about being with me. I did, too. We just couldn't stop, you know? And we'd tried. Many times."

"So her leaving you . . . it didn't send you over the edge?" It's a difficult question, but one that needs to be asked.

He chuffs, his head cocked. "I hated Andrew. I hated that she was with Andrew. But our decision was mutual. We were two good people who did a bad thing, and we were making it right."

I study his face, so earnest, so insisting.

"Is there any chance the baby was yours?" I ask.

He shakes his head, quiet for a second. "It'd be a one-in-a-million chance. I was told I couldn't have kids a while back—sports injury in college. And we were always . . . safe."

"And you're sure Andrew never knew about the two of you?" I ask.

"As far as I know," he says. "Unless she came clean about it when she told him about the baby? I don't know. It's possible. Anything's possible."

A scenario plays in my mind: Meredith confessing to Andrew, telling him she's pregnant and that she strayed from their picture-perfect marriage. Andrew blowing up at her, wanting to hurt her for hurting him. Their future hanging in the balance. Emotions running high.

Meredith wouldn't have wanted to hurt him. She would've wanted to please him because that's who she was. A secret like this would've been one she'd have kept until her dying day.

"Do you think he ever suspected anything? Any . . . infidelity?" I move toward the window facing his front yard, watching a few cars pass by and slow down. Word spreads quickly in these small towns, and everyone loves a scandal, be it fact, fiction, or shameless speculation.

"Like I said, anything is possible," he says, taking a seat in a weathered recliner that's clearly seen better days. Cupping his hands over his mouth, he releases a heavy breath. "I keep asking myself . . . what if he knew? What if he knew all along, and he was waiting for the right moment to . . ."

He doesn't finish his thought.

He doesn't need to.

"He's pointing the finger at you right now," I say. "He thinks you had something to do with all of this."

"And I'm pointing it right back." His words slice through the small space we share, his eyes locked on mine.

"There's also the possibility that neither of you had anything to do with this and you're both wasting your time pointing fingers."

Ronan sighs.

"What did you like about my sister?" I ask.

"What?"

"Just answer the question."

"Everything," he says, sinking back in the chair, his gaze fixed on the darkened TV screen across the room. "I could tell you how kind and thoughtful and funny she was, but I'm sure you know all of that. Guess the thing that drew me to her was how she had this childlike sense of wonder when she was with me. The way she looked at me. The way she touched me. She said I made her feel brand-new. In a weird way, when you boil it down, we had something special. The world kind of stopped when we were together, and that's something you don't find every day."

Any other guy would've focused on her looks, the hot sex, the thrill of sneaking around.

But he dug deeper.

I give him a pass.

For now.

CHAPTER 21

MEREDITH

Twenty-Three Months Ago

I tug my clothes on as Ronan kisses me, my pants unbuttoned and my shirt half-bunched beneath one arm. We step backward, stumbling and giggling in the darkness of his cozy house, his hands returning to all the places they'd known the hour prior.

"I have to go," I say for the tenth time between kisses, my lips pressed against his as I speak.

His hands circle my waist, pulling me closer. "I wish you could stay."

Me, too.

I always wish I could stay.

A month ago, I ran into Ronan at a little café on the corner downtown. He had the day off. And I was running menial errands to fill the void of an empty, rainy day.

We spent the afternoon together, and it was innocent enough until we found ourselves dashing through a puddled parking lot in a torrential downpour.

One moment we were running, the next he was pulling me under an awning, holding me close against him.

And then he kissed me.

Tender. Unrushed. His hands in my hair.

One taste of Ronan on my tongue was all it took.

Now here we are. Me in his living room. His scent covering my body, his eyes claiming every square inch of me.

Ronan scoops me into his arms again, sliding my legs up his sides and teasing like he's going to carry me back to his bedroom again.

I beat on his chest, but I can't stop grinning. "Stop. You know I have to go."

"Maybe one day you won't have to." He lets me go, and I slide down his body until my feet hit the floor, which feels hard and cold, like reality.

"Maybe," I say.

Reaching for his face, I run my fingers through his dark hair and drink him in. Even the dark shadows can't hide his virility or the captivating way he looks at me.

I like him.

So much.

But I don't love him. I mean, I could, but I won't allow myself to.

My life is already complicated enough.

Ronan is my cheap thrill.

My dirty little secret.

He makes me feel alive.

He's the place I flock to when I'm out of my gilded cage.

With him, I am free.

We make it to the front door, and I step into my boots. He's still kissing me, his mouth arched at the ends each time, and not just in a single-bachelor-who-just-got-laid kind of way but in a genuine I'm-falling-hard-for-this-girl kind of way.

"When can I see you again?" he asks.

"I don't know. It's our week with the kids." I glance at the clock on his fireplace mantel. I should've left a half hour ago. We're supposed to get Calder and Isabeau from Erica's by six before heading to Salt Lake City for a weekend of family-oriented fun.

Zoos. Theme parks. Kid-friendly restaurants with screaming babies and exasperated parents chasing after their overly tired offspring, so desperate to enjoy just one dinner out that they'll subject the rest of the world to the fruits of their failed parenting labors.

I'd much rather stay here. With Ronan.

"I'll call you next week," I say, my hand on the doorknob. My gaze lands on his bare chest, and I'm taken back to the image of his body over mine, his arms creating a safe harbor, a refuge of sorts for my dirtiest fantasies.

Ronan, my clean-cut all-American boy, likes his sex dirty, but he's not selfish about it. He may put me in handcuffs, but he doesn't come until I do. He also likes to fuck me in public, knowing the best secret hiding spots and promising me we'll never get caught, that no one will ever find us.

He's my biggest thrill and my biggest weakness.

And there's not a damn thing I can do to keep myself from coming back.

Slipping out the front door, I trek to my car, which is parked a couple of blocks away, along the side of a gravel road the locals rarely venture down because there's nothing pretty to see, no landscape installations, no retaining walls built of eight-ton boulders, no luxury lodges. Only the closer I get, the more I see something strange on my back windshield.

Picking up the pace, I realize someone has drawn a single word into the dusty glass.

WHORE.

My heart races as my eyes dart around, but I'm surrounded with nothingness. Trees. Chirping crickets. A dusky sky.

Someone followed me out here.

Someone saw me go into Ronan's house.

Someone knows about us.

My throat constricts as I fumble for my keys, which seem to have been swallowed by my purse. For a moment, I debate speeding back to his house with the irrational notion that he could possibly do something about this.

But my phone rings. And Andrew's name flashes across the screen.

"Hey," I say, trying to hide the shake in my voice. I rub my hand over the letters on my windshield, erasing them.

"Where are you?"

My jaw hangs loose as I try to clear my head long enough to come up with an answer. "On my way home."

He's quiet.

Does he know?

"Ran to the pharmacy," I say. "Had to pick up a couple of prescriptions before we left for our trip. Spaced it off. I'm so sorry."

I smell like sex and Ronan.

Climbing into my car, I start the engine and fish around in my purse for my travel-size atomizer of Gucci perfume—aptly named *Guilty*—before checking my reflection in the mirror.

When I look into my own mascara-smudged eyes, I'm disgusted.

I'm not this girl—this weak cliché of a woman, throwing herself at another man to spite her affectionless husband and rebel against her boringly privileged little life.

I have to end this.

"I'll be home soon," I tell him, inserting a casual cadence in my tone. "I'm so sorry."

The line goes dead.

CHAPTER 22

GREER

Day Six

I think it's weird that his kids came to stay, but I suppose Andrew's ex couldn't be bothered with adjusting her schedule to accommodate her former husband's missing wife.

Isabeau sits at the head of the kitchen table, shoving spoonful after spoonful of Cocoa Puffs into her mouth as her eyes are focused on the small TV screen under the kitchen cabinets currently blasting an obnoxious cartoon likely meant for children a fraction of her age.

I've only met the children a handful of times . . . the wedding, a couple of visits here and there . . . and Meredith always spoke fondly of them. I know she said it was rough that first year, getting them to warm up to her, but she persisted.

At least that's what she claimed.

I'm feeling like I don't know anything anymore.

"How are you doing, Isabeau?" I ask, wiping down the spilled splash of milk on the counter from when she prepared her cereal lunch. "I know this must be a scary time for you."

Her dead eyes move from the TV screen to me. Her chubby jaw works the crunchy cereal.

"Mom said she's probably dead," she says. "Dad probably paid someone to do it."

I drop the dish towel in my hand. It lands at my feet. "Why would your mother say that?"

"I heard her on the phone with my Aunt Lisa." She takes another spoonful, losing a few cereal pieces as she shovels it into her mouth.

As tempting as it is, I don't pry. She's in junior high. She doesn't know anything about anything, and it's possible she misinterpreted whatever speculative drivel was coming out of her mother's Angelina Jolie–size lips.

"How is your mother, anyway?" I ask, feigning interest.

Isabeau rolls her eyes. "Like you care."

I lift a brow. "I'm just wondering what she thinks about all of this . . . is she sad? Worried?"

Andrew's daughter laughs, her braces covered in chocolate. "Seriously? My mom can't stand Meredith. Nobody likes her. Not even my dad sometimes."

"What are you talking about?"

"They're always fighting," she says. "They think I can't hear them, but my room is right down the hall. I hear everything."

"Fighting about what?" I move from around the island, taking a seat at the table next to her.

"Who knows?" She seems annoyed by my close proximity. Typical thirteen-year-old. "I don't listen. I only hear them yelling and stuff."

My chin juts forward. I can't imagine Meredith yelling. She's the chillest, calmest person in the world. Very seldom has she ever let anything rattle her to the point of throwing a tantrum.

The fridge door opens and slams behind me. I turn and see Calder grab a bottle of Evian and twist the cap.

"You know she's fucking with you, right?" he asks, taking a drink, and I wonder how it is he swears so naturally at such a young age.

Isabeau shoots him a look. I take it they don't get along.

"She's a compulsive liar," he says. "She made all that shit up. Don't ever believe anything she says."

With that, he's gone, disappearing into the bowels of the Price manse, the shrill chime of his phone echoing through the halls when he gets a text message. Turning back to Isabeau, I fully intend to give her a piece of my mind, but she, too, is gone. Nothing but an empty cereal bowl and a milk-spilling spoon resting on the table.

Little shit.

Never has my decision to be child-free felt so reinforced as it does in this moment.

Returning to my room, I lie on the bed. It's midafternoon now, but it feels like the end of the day already. A sleepless night will do that to a person. Exhaustion sinks into my bones, but I don't want to take a nap on the off chance that I might actually have a shot at a decent night's rest this evening.

Scrolling through my phone, I think about Erica and what Isabeau said. Despite the fact that Isabeau had me going for a moment and there's no merit to what she said, I have half a mind to show up at Erica's door and see if she wouldn't mind talking to me for a minute, woman to woman.

My eyes are heavy and my mood is curt and impersonal, but I'm going.

I've got to keep going.

I can't stop.

◆　◆　◆

The exterior of Erica's house is ornate and over the top. It's a bit Gothic, a bit Victorian. I imagine she got a pretty settlement after her divorce from Andrew and purchased a house just as big as the last one simply because she could.

And because a woman like that doesn't settle for anything less than exactly what she wants.

Pressing the doorbell, I hear the faint song of the chime from behind a pair of wooden double doors, and when the door lock clicks a second later, I'm expecting to see a maid or a butler or someone Erica pays to boss around, but it's her.

In the flesh.

Curlers in her hair and a silk floral robe cinched at her tiny waist.

Her eyes narrow when she sees me. She hasn't the slightest clue who I am, and while we've never formally met, I feel like I know her because of all the horror stories Mer used to share.

"Greer," I say. "Meredith's sister."

Her lips form a straight line, and her forehead is smooth as glass. Everything about her is contradictory, from her baby-soft complexion to her pointed glower. I've never understood women who can stand in front of a mirror and obsess over the size of their chin or the width of their nose or their barely-there crow's-feet.

Must be nice to have the time to care about those things and the money to "fix" them.

"Can I help you?" she asks, head tilted.

"I was wondering if you had a minute?" I try my hardest to be cordial.

She exhales, gripping the lapels of her bathrobe. "I'm getting ready for a date."

"It'll just take a sec."

Her nose wrinkles, and she studies my face with a pause.

"I'm not here to accuse you of anything. I just wanted to ask a few questions . . . things that only you'd be able to answer."

"You want to grill me about Andrew." Her lips draw into a sly smirk. "Come on in, honey."

She leads me into the foyer, closing the door behind me before swaying to the bottom of a curved staircase. Erica motions for me to follow her, and we wind up in a master bath the size of my apartment.

"You know I did get a call from some detective a while back wanting to interview me, but when I called back, I got his voice mail and haven't heard anything since," she says, sighing. I don't tell her about the affair. "I suppose I should be used to being an afterthought by now."

A velvet chaise beneath a crystal chandelier centers the space, and Erica points for me to have a seat.

Moving toward a vanity and retrieving a tube of Chanel mascara from a table spread with high-end makeup and face creams, she swipes the wand over her lashes, giving them a little wiggle at the tips, and her eyes intersect with mine in the mirror.

"So what do you want to know?" she asks, a haughty half laugh in her tone. "You want to know if I think he did it?"

I take a deep breath and nod. "Yeah. Basically."

"Andrew is a lot of things," she says. "Materialistic. Conceited. The most insecure bastard you'll ever meet." She turns to face me. "But he's not a killer. Or a kidnapper. He's a smart man with too much to lose. Trust me, if he wanted to be done with your sister, he'd be done with her. He wouldn't do something reprehensible. That would be . . . *beneath* him." Turning back to her reflection, she slicks her lips with a bullet of lipstick in a shade of screw-me red. "I don't care how much he loves her, he loves his money and his freedom more, and no woman is worth losing that. Not to him."

Erica begins removing her curlers, letting her shiny auburn waves fall to her shoulders before combing them with a boar bristle brush. If I squint, she looks like a 1940s film star.

"That said"—her eyes find mine again—"the man has resources for days. And the entire Glacier Park Police Department worships the Price family. If he wanted to make something happen, he could. And he'd get away with it. He's probably the only person who could."

"So what are you saying?" My arms fold, and I sit straight up on the end of the chaise. Her bathroom is glamorous and everything shimmers, but it's not welcoming. I wonder if all these shiny, sparkly things are her way of making up for her dull, unlikable personality. "First you say he wouldn't do it. Then you said he could."

She laughs, her manicured hand tracing her collarbone. "That's exactly what I'm saying. He wouldn't, but he could."

Disappearing into a closet off the bathroom, she returns a few minutes later, a tight black dress hugging her body and a set of diamond earrings in her hands.

"My date's going to be here any minute," she says, head tilted as she places a stud into her earlobe. "Are we done?"

Refusing to have wasted my time, I rise, shoulders tight. "Do you think he had anything to do with this or not?"

Erica brushes a perfect wave off her shoulder. "How the hell should I know? He liked her. That's all I know."

"Did you ever see them interact? Was it ever strained, or was anything ever . . . off?"

"Honey, you're fishing in an empty pond." She returns to her closet, emerging with a set of black stilettos with red bottoms and crystals on the heels, the same style my sister wore in New York a few years ago. I couldn't believe she'd become one of *those* women, the ones we always swore we'd never be. "Every time I was around, the two of them seemed happy and in love—as much as I hate to admit it. Now as far as whether or not it was genuine or for show, I couldn't even begin to tell you. Closed doors and that sort of thing."

The doorbell chimes. I check my watch. "Isn't five o'clock kind of early for a date?"

"Oh, darling." Erica passes me, leaving a lingering cloud of expensive perfume. "He sent a car for me. I'm meeting him at his helipad in Salt Lake City. We're going to Vegas for the weekend."

Her heels click across the glossy tile, her brows arched as she waits for me to follow, and with the flick of a light switch, the chandelier darkens. Erica makes walking in stilettos look natural, and her soft palm slides down the smooth railing of the curled staircase as she descends to the foyer.

She doesn't seem like a woman who gives a flying shit about her ex anymore. And especially not his wife. It's undeniably apparent that she's moved on.

Answering the door, she greets a man in a black suit and points to her luggage, which is placed neatly against a nearby wall. How one woman needs three suitcases for a weekend in Vegas is beyond me, but I'm not surprised.

"It was lovely meeting you . . . ," she begins to say.

"Greer."

"Greer, that's right," she says, her head tilted and her smile frozen. "How did you get a name like that, anyway? I've always had a thing for names. Growing up, there were four other Ericas in my grade. Always swore I'd never give my children a name they'd have to share. If you can find your name on a souvenir shot glass at a drugstore, it's far too common."

She doesn't wait for me to answer her, but that's fine. I don't need to explain the intricacies of my mother's misshapen logic to a woman who's essentially a stranger with a take-it-or-leave-it mentality toward my missing sister.

In the seventies, there was a Manhattan "society girl" named Greer Forbes. She was the talk of the town, a fixture in most gossip columns, and the woman other women whispered about when they weren't busy idolizing her.

My mother always loved the juxtaposition of a harsh, masculine name on a gorgeous woman. She thought it was equal parts classy and interesting. Years later, she went on to admit she should've named me Emily or Elizabeth, something timeless and easy to spell.

I step onto the landing beneath Erica's front porch, realizing I haven't yet called a cab, but rather than lingering like some weirdo, I hit the road and prepare to walk for miles along the snowy pavement until I find a place to grab a hot drink.

When I'm two blocks down, their black limousine crawls to a stop beside me. The back window rolls down, and Erica leans forward.

"There was this one time," she says. "Maybe ten, eleven years ago. Andrew thought I was cheating on him with my personal trainer." Erica's red lips curl at the sides. "Which is hilarious in retrospect because he was gay. Anyway, Andrew about lost it. Had the poor man fired and basically blacklisted from every gym in a sixty-mile radius, which was a big deal because he was one of the most sought-after trainers in the area. But my point, Greer, is that the man has a jealous streak. Do with that information what you will."

And just like that, she gives a little wave, rolls up the window, and speeds away.

CHAPTER 23

MEREDITH

Twenty-Two Months Ago

"Mer." Ronan's lips pull up at the sides, flanked by dimples when he sees me. Pulling me inside, he peers out the door before closing it, catching a glimpse of the taxi parked in his driveway. "Where's your car?"

"I took a cab."

His face twists. "Why?"

I haven't seen him in over a week. A weekend with Andrew and the kids turned into an extra week with them when Erica decided to extend her Jamaican girls' trip by an extra six days.

He takes my hands in his, bringing them to his lips and warming them with his breath. "You're freezing."

"The heat was broken in the cab," I say.

"And you're trembling." He leads me to the sofa, pulling me into his lap. "What's going on?"

The number of times I had sex with this man last month, I can't even begin to count. The number of times I thought of him while lying next to my husband is disgraceful. Sitting here, beside him, my body is tense and electric, wishing I could let him ravish me one more time and knowing that I can't.

"We can't do this anymore." I blurt out the words I came here to say before I lose the strength to say them.

He's quiet, which is exactly the reaction I expected from my even-keeled Ronan.

"Are you happy, Meredith?" he asks, breaking the uncomfortable silence.

"What are you talking about?"

"In your marriage. With Andrew. Are you happy?" His brows meet.

"That's beside the point. This is wrong. And we have to stop."

"You're miserable," he says. "If you weren't, you wouldn't have been coming here."

"You were my escape," I say. "I'm a bored, pathetic woman, and you were exciting."

"You and I both know I'm more than that to you," he says. "And you're not pathetic."

"I'm pathetic for getting caught up in something I had no business being caught up in."

"You're only human." There's compassion in his voice, and I don't deserve it.

I rise from the sofa, pacing his living room and stopping before the picture window, my gaze trained on the waiting cab in the driveway. "You're trying to talk me into staying. Please stop. My mind's made up."

"He doesn't deserve you, Meredith." Ronan sucks in a deep breath, his head in his hands. I've blindsided him. "But you already know that."

"It's not that I don't want to be with you," I say. "It's that I shouldn't be with you. It's wrong. I don't want to be that woman anymore."

I don't say goodbye—I can't.

Instead, I show myself out.

I climb into the back of the cab.

I will go home to my husband, hoping I can forget what I've done, that my marriage is still salvageable.

But as the cab backs out and veers down the familiar, tree-lined street, I find myself missing Ronan already, and I can't help but wonder if I've made the wrong decision . . . if I've chosen the wrong man.

CHAPTER 24

GREER

Day Seven

"You know he has a housekeeper," I say to my mother as she stands over the granite sink in the Price kitchen.

"I'm just trying to help." She's elbows deep in soapy water, washing Calder's and Isabeau's dinner dishes. Her gaze is transfixed on some cable news show on the TV, where a screen full of pundits and crime analysts are discussing my sister on the eve of the one-week anniversary of her disappearance.

"Ugh, turn this off." I reach for the remote, but my mother slaps my hand.

Just this morning the police released a statement about Ronan being a possible suspect and being placed on paid administrative leave, and it seems to have breathed new life into this story, placing it front and center on all the cable talk shows again.

It doesn't help that the tips that were flooding into the tip line the first few days all led to dead ends. I had hopes for the conversion van sightings, but with a license plate number, they were able to track down the driver and determine he was in Missouri the day Meredith went missing.

So now everyone's focused on Andrew and Ronan, scorned lovers, the usual suspects.

"If you ask me"—a man in a gray suit and yellow tie tries to speak over the rest of the crew—"my money's on the ex-boyfriend. The detective. Never in my twenty-five years in law enforcement have I seen anyone pull a stunt like that. You take an oath. You do your job. And if you didn't do anything, you don't have anything to worry about. Not removing himself from the case is the biggest clue we have so far. How you people are ignoring that is beyond me."

"It's got to be the husband," a woman with strawberry-blonde hair, a dusting of freckles, and pale pink lipstick chimes in. The screen says her name is Lindsey Chatham, and she's the president of a not-for-profit domestic abuse center. "It's always the husband. He's the one with the most to gain here. Money, fortune, fame, publicity for his business. His cheating wife goes missing? It's win-win for him."

"Correct me if I'm wrong," Yellow Tie says, "but the husband didn't know the wife was cheating."

Lindsey shrugs. "So he says. We don't know that. Only he does."

"I'd have to agree with Lindsey on this," another man says, identified as Utah criminal defense attorney Vince Barbetti. "With a case like this with nothing to go on but basically zero hard evidence, we have to examine motives. Let's look at the husband. Why would he want her gone? Well, for one, she was cheating on him. Maybe he wanted revenge? Second, money. Was there a life insurance policy? An inheritance? Was she worth more dead than alive? Anything she'd have would go to her spouse. Instant windfall. Third, crime of passion. Maybe something set him off and the husband just snapped?"

"He's a multimillionaire, so you can remove money from your list of motives. Also, he was at work when she was reported missing." Yellow Tie defends Andrew.

"So he says," Lindsey counters. "From what I understand, his receptionist says he was there, but she didn't say if she actually saw him between the hours of ten a.m. and three p.m. He claims he was in his office, working. There are no witnesses to that effect."

"All right, so you want to examine motives?" Yellow Tie asks. "Let's look at the lover. So we know Meredith was pregnant—presumably with Andrew's baby. She'd been seeing Ronan McCormack for years, off and on from what I understand, and she finally has to end it because she's having a kid with her husband. That easily could've been enough to set him off. He's angry because he's losing her. He's jealous because she chose to go back to her husband instead of staying with him. He doesn't want to lose her. You want me to go on here? Because I can."

I wish I could take a side, but they all have valid arguments. At this point, everything's a matter of opinion regardless of their expert backgrounds. We're all just trying to make sense of something that doesn't.

The host, a spitfire with pencil-thin eyebrows named Jeannie Jones, cuts Yellow Tie off midsentence as he rambles on, announcing they're Skyping in a former girlfriend of Ronan McCormack's, and the screen cuts to a woman with mousy-brown hair, dark circles under her eyes, a narrow chin, and slender shoulders. She's seated in what appears to be a living room, with beige walls covered in picture frames and an old piano in the background.

"Okay, coming to us live from Haverford, Utah, is Alana Nash, former girlfriend of person-of-interest Ronan McCormack," the host says. "Alana, what can you tell us about Ronan? When did you know him? How long did you date? Was there ever anything he did that would lead you to believe he was capable of hurting anyone?"

The girl clears her throat, splotches of skin turning red. She's nervous as hell, but clearly something compelled her to speak up and let the world know about Ronan.

"We dated just after high school," she says, her voice as mousy as her hair. "I met him at this store we both worked at, Pitino's Lumber

Supply in Crestwood. Anyway, we dated for about a year. He was really nice. And I thought we were in love. But we got in a fight once. He'd been drinking. We were at a party. He thought I was hitting on some guy, and he got really mad. He pulled me outside and . . ." Her eyes begin to well as she glances down. The host tells her to take her time. "And pushed me up against the side of this house. He put his hand around my neck. I couldn't breathe."

My blood runs cold. I can't so much as picture Ronan touching a woman like that.

"How the hell was this guy able to become an officer of the law?" Jeannie asks, her mouth pulled down in the corners. "Someone explain that to me. Vince?"

Vince Barbetti chimes in, claiming that he'd have to examine the case, but sometimes these charges get dropped and records get scrubbed. It'd be a rare exception, but it was possible. "Alana, did you report this to the police?"

"I didn't. I was too scared at the time," Alana continues. "He had a temper, and I knew if he let it get the best of him one time, it could happen again. I just wanted to be done with him. We broke up after that. I haven't seen him since."

"So what?" Barbetti scoffs. "You can't tell me we're all the same person we were at eighteen. People change. I'm sure that was a wake-up call for him. Clearly he had a respect for the justice system if he cleaned up his act and took an oath."

"Maybe," the host says. "Corruption exists in nearly every department at nearly every level."

"That's a blanket statement," Vince says. "Be careful with that, Jeannie."

"Let's stay on track here," Lindsey says. "We need to find Meredith. Someone out there knows what happened. Someone out there has seen her. We're going to show her photo on the screen again. Johnny, can you pull that up? There we go."

A photo of my sister, which was clearly stolen from her Facebook page, shows her smiling ear to ear on her wedding day, Andrew by her side.

"You've got to be fucking kidding me," I say.

No one looks like themselves on their wedding day. If she's out there, held captive by some lunatic, I highly doubt she's sporting an updo and a full face of Chanel makeup.

Idiots.

"We need to consider the fact that it might not be either of them," a fourth man with curly gray hair and thick glasses chimes in.

"Thank you," I mutter under my breath, throwing my hands in the air.

"Of course," Yellow Tie says. "But right now we're running out of time. This case is about to run out of gas, and we're barely coasting on fumes here. We need to work with what we have if we're going to get anywhere with this."

"But if what you have is useless . . . ," the curly-haired man says.

"This is depressing." I reach for the remote again.

"I want to hear it," Mom says, her lips pursed as she shoots me a look that dares me to touch the remote. "It's interesting to see what they think. You never know, they might actually say something that makes sense one of these times."

Exhaling, I take a seat at the kitchen table. We all seem to gather here most days, like we're all sitting around waiting for a call to drop into our laps, a knock on the door from someone saying they found her safe and sound, or some twist in the case we never saw coming.

When my mother's back is turned, I text Ronan from my phone and tell him to watch Channel 222. I'm testing him. I want to see if he's nervous or worked up now that all his dirty laundry is being aired.

Little busy now, he writes back, sending a picture of the current state of his driveway. The street is lined with news vans, local and national, and anchors with microphones speak into cameras pointed at their faces, framing the shot with Ronan's house.

Jesus Christ.

"Hi, Andrew." My mother's voice pulls me back to reality.

Standing frozen, arms crossed, he listens to the pundits theorize and speculate, arguing why it's Ronan and then countering as to why all signs point to Andrew.

"You shouldn't watch this," Mom says, reaching to shut the TV off, but before she gets the chance, he leaves, misty-eyed and visibly shaken.

I wish I knew if those were tears of a bruised ego.

Or tears of regret.

Or maybe, something else entirely.

CHAPTER 25

MEREDITH

Twenty Months Ago

Andrew kissed me this morning, slow and lingering, and then we made love in the bed of our New York hotel suite. Not once but twice.

We've been doing that a lot lately.

The day I left Ronan's, I came straight home, poured myself a gin and tonic, and waited for Andrew to return from work.

That night I told him about everything—except Ronan—the second he walked in the door. I dropped it all on him. I told him I felt as if I were losing him, that he didn't love me anymore. I told him I wondered if he was just with me because he wanted a trophy wife to go with his collection of sports cars. I told him he was too detached in bed. I told him about the couples in Thailand and how I didn't want to be like them.

Then I told him he was losing me. And if we didn't fix it now, we weren't going to make it.

He dropped his briefcase, came to my side, and took my hands in his. Andrew Price isn't a fearful man. He isn't a gushy, lovey-dovey man. He's a businessman. He's serious and well in control of his emotions.

But I'll be damned if he didn't look absolutely terrified at the thought of losing me in that moment.

"I took you for granted," he said to me. "I've been selfish this past year, and I know that. I'm going to fix this, I promise."

Since that moment, Andrew's been husband of the year. Bringing me coffee in bed before he takes his early morning runs. Whisking me away on kid-free weekends. Taking his time between the sheets, ensuring I'm always left satisfied when we're finished and then some.

So far, so good.

Except for those still, small moments when thoughts of Ronan creep into my mind. It doesn't help that I see him everywhere, always driving his unmarked squad car, dressed in his black suit, his shield hanging from his neck.

I saw him at a stoplight once, felt his stare lingering on me.

I couldn't bring myself to wave or smile or acknowledge him.

Not that I didn't want to, but I've closed that chapter. I've locked that door.

Ronan McCormack was a phase, a reckless decision that spiraled out of control.

And I'm not that girl anymore.

I'm Mrs. Andrew Price, now and forever.

Rolling out of the hotel bed in a posh little boutique hotel in Greenwich Village, I draw the curtains and stare down seventeen stories to a city sidewalk filled with people going about their normal business.

And I'm about to be one of them.

It feels good to be back to normal again.

"Don't you ever call first?" Harris rolls his eyes when I stroll into Steam later that morning. I can never tell if he's joking or actually finds it obnoxious that I show up unannounced every time I'm in the city.

"Where's the fun in that?" I ask.

"You know G hates surprises."

I shrug. "But I love them, and G loves me, so it all works out."

"She's not here." He turns his back to me, making a cappuccino for a foot-tapping woman, and I take a seat at an empty bar with the sole intention of bugging the shit out of him because I can.

"Where'd she go?" I ask.

"Errands," he says, taking the drink to the customer and flashing a charming smile in her direction, the kind of smile that could bring a woman back here time and time again.

I'm not the biggest fan of Harris, but I can't deny how ridiculously attractive he is—but it's not in a Times Square billboard model sort of way; it's more in a hot-nerd, Joseph Gordon-Levitt kind of way. He can talk about any topic with ease, knows his way around the city like he's lived here his whole life, paints the most incredible abstract watercolors, cooks almost any type of cuisine and makes it taste better than takeout, can fix almost anything, and reads a book a day.

How he has time for all that, I haven't a clue, but I see the allure of it.

I can see what my sister sees in him.

He's a fixer. And he's smart. He's her safety net.

She never had a father to call when she needed help with her home-work or when her refrigerator broke down and was leaking fluid all over her floor and she couldn't afford to call a technician.

She never had a father to praise her intelligence over her beauty, to tell her never to settle, and to keep shooting for the top.

She never had a father . . . but she had Harris.

"When are you and Greer getting back together?" I ask, resting my chin on my hands and winking.

"Ship sailed long ago," he says, refusing to meet my curious stare.

"But you don't act like it. You still love her. I know you do," I say. "And she still loves you. She loves the hell out of you. I know you know."

Harris shakes his head, wiping the counter with a red-striped rag. "I don't believe in marriage."

"Oh. One of *those*."

He scoffs. "Marriage is an outdated concept. People aren't meant to be with one person the rest of their lives; we're just not. Nobody belongs to anyone. If we love someone, we can be with them if we want, but we don't need an expensive ring and a flimsy piece of paper that you're going to tuck away in a filing cabinet and never look at again."

Funny he says this because for a while he and Greer were thinking of tying the knot. Guess people change and their opinions follow suit.

"It's romantic, though," I say. "It's a sign of commitment."

"We must have completely different ideas of romance, then."

"Clearly." I rise up, peering over the counter. "Hey, Harris. If you're bored, you want to make me an iced chai?"

I'd request a London Fog, but I can't enjoy one without thinking about Ronan, and I've been doing so well with that lately.

His shoulders sink, and I think he's pretending to be annoyed, but he does it anyway. A moment later, he slides my drink in front of me and greets a Gucci loafer–wearing woman at the register.

At all their other locations, they have baristas and cashiers and the whole setup. But this is their flagship shop, a mere six hundred square feet up front, and he likes to be up close and personal with the patrons.

He's also a control freak who needs to know what's going on at all times and make sure the coffees are brewed at a perfect 205 degrees Fahrenheit and no single cup of tea is steeped longer than three to five minutes.

This may be the smallest store, but it makes the most money, and Harris isn't shy about taking credit for that.

He returns to make the lady at the counter a double mocha frozen coffee, and she tips him a twenty-dollar bill.

"So back to Greer," I say.

Harris's jaw flexes.

"You have to admit, you've been stringing her along for years."

"According to whom?"

"It's not a matter of opinion." I sip my iced chai. It's perfection. Maybe he doesn't hate me after all? Or he's just extremely anal about quality. Probably the latter. "It's fact."

"Not sure what you expect me to do," he says. "We work together. We're always together. And she's my best friend. I can assure you, no one's stringing anyone along. This is just . . . how it is. This is what works for us right now. And need I remind you, she's the one who decided to move out?"

I exhale, contemplating the small lilt in my sister's voice anytime she mentions Harris. She still loves him. She still has hope. And looking at him now, I see he has zero intention of going back to the way they were. If he wanted her back, he would've fought harder for her. If he can fight for climate change initiatives, he can fight for the woman he loves.

"Anyone ever tell you you're kind of an asshole?" I ask. And selfish. Harris smirks. "Never."

"You are." I take a sip. "It's because you're the only boy."

"What?"

"You're the only boy in your family. And the baby," I say. "You think everything's about you. And you've never had to share the spotlight. That's why you're such an asshole."

"Wow." He's quiet for a rare moment. "That's, uh, that's pretty harsh, Meredith."

"I think you could be nicer," I say. "But you're going to have to work at it."

"I *am* nice." One brow lifts.

"Not to me," I say.

"I'm only hard on you because I care. You're like the little sister I never had. And it stresses Greer the fuck out when you do stupid shit like . . . I don't know . . . marrying a man twice your age."

My jaw falls. "Seriously, Harris? You're going to bring my husband into this?"

"Not your husband. Your marriage," he says. "It's kind of a joke, don't you think?"

I shake my head and glance down. My marriage isn't a joke, but his words sting.

The bells on the door jingle. Greer strides across the shop, her phone glued to her ear as she passes me by without looking up. A moment later, she shuts the door to her office.

Climbing down from the stool, I head back, letting myself in. Greer doesn't smile when she sees me. She doesn't seem shocked or fazed. When she ends her call, she buries her head in her hands.

"What? What's wrong?" I ask.

"Just got off the phone with our accountant," she says. "We're going to have to start closing down shops."

"Shops . . . plural . . . as in more than one?" I ask.

Her arms fold across her chest, and she leans back in her chair, eyes glassy. "Yeah. At least three of the five."

"How?"

She shakes her head. "Profits are down. Some of the stores aren't performing."

"Okay, so you just need to trim the fat. Focus on the ones that are making you money," I say.

She's quiet, stewing in her failure.

"Come on. Let's grab drinks. My treat," I say. "I might have a Xanax in my purse that you can have if you want it."

Her pale blue eyes flick onto mine, and I realize I've become one of those pill-toting housewives who are somehow able to get any drug they need from their trusted family doctor with the snap of their manicured fingers.

"I'm kidding," I say. Not really. "But let's go. Let's get out of here. Harris is being a douche anyway."

"I can't deal with you two," she says. "Not today."

"I'm kidding." I lie again. "He's great. We were actually talking about you."

Six words is all it takes to capture her interest and distract her from her despair.

Hooking my arm around hers, I pull her out of her chair and grab her purse. "Come on. Let's get a drink, and I'll tell you all about it."

CHAPTER 26

GREER

Day Eight

The FindMeredithPrice website is particularly buzzing today. Ever since the Ronan development was made public yesterday, every cable news network is recycling and rehashing the same warped theories, and people can't get enough.

According to a poll on CNN, 84 percent of their viewers believe Ronan's behind the disappearance.

I place my phone on the kitchen table when my mom walks in, Wade in tow. It's morning, and they're fixing breakfast. How they can continue to eat so normally at a time like this is beyond me, but my mother's feet are planted more firmly in denial than ever before.

She's compartmentalizing.

We all are.

Shock has stolen my appetite, though. That's what happens when I'm stressed. My body shuts down. It won't sleep or eat. It enters survival mode, sending thirst signals to my brain to remind me to drink water every now and again.

"Greer, would you like some toast?" Mom asks, pulling a loaf of artisan bread from the pantry.

"No thanks."

"You need to eat something," she says, tsk-tsking. "You're skinny as a rail."

"Kind of focused on more important things," I say.

"We all are, Greer," Wade says. I hate how he uses my name like he's trying to be my friend. "But you know your brain functions better on a full stomach. It's proven. Backed by science."

I tried to eat some oatmeal last night after I woke up at two in the morning with a growling stomach, but the second I took my third bite, it all threatened to come up the way it went in, so I stopped.

"I'll fix myself something later," I say just to get them to shut up. I catch Andrew's outline in my periphery vision.

"Good morning, Andrew." My mother presses her lips together, speaking to him the way you would a toy poodle or a two-year-old. "How'd you sleep, sweetheart?"

She rubs his back like a child, despite the fact that they're a mere fifteen years apart in age, give or take.

He mutters a groggy "good morning" before heading to the built-in espresso maker next to the fridge. Fixing himself a small cup, he takes a seat next to me at the table.

"You hear from the new detective lately?" I ask. "What's his name?"

His eyes flick to mine, their dark circles more noticeable than ever.

"Bixby. And yesterday," he says. "They're still working on it."

"That's all they tell you? They're still working on it?" My jaw aches from grinding my teeth lately. "What are they doing? Specifically? What are they doing to find her?"

He takes a sip of his espresso, staring out toward their picturesque backyard. Fog obscures the mountains, save for their frosty peaks, but it's a beautiful scene for such an ugly day.

"They've had search crews combing the woods in the area all week," he says. "Mostly volunteers, working around the clock. People have flown in from all over the world. Search and rescue planes have been using infrared cameras, heat sensing, and all that. They're not sitting around waiting for the phone to ring, I can promise you that."

He seems annoyed with me, but he was the one who offered a vague response, so I don't feel bad.

"They're sending a dog out today," he says.

"A cadaver dog?"

"Something like that."

"So they're looking for a body." My heart sinks, not because I think she's dead, but because they do. They're giving up on her.

"They're looking for anything they can find." He exhales, refusing to meet my cutting stare.

"And why aren't *you* looking?" I ask. "Seems the heat's been taken off you and placed on Ronan. It's safe for you to come out now."

"Greer." My mother's voice scolds, but it has no effect on me, and it rarely did as a child. I could never respect her or take her seriously then. Still don't now.

Andrew's demeanor snaps, and he rises from the table, pounding his fist against the wood. *"Stop."*

My brows lift. "Stop what? Stop pointing out the things that everyone else refuses to acknowledge? Stop looking for my sister? What, Andrew? Stop what?"

He glares. "Stop being such a fucking bitch."

When Andrew moves toward the doorway to the kitchen, he lingers, his fists clenched in the air and his mouth pinched, as if he wants to say more. But he stops himself. His arms fall at his sides, limp.

Isabeau pulls up a seat at the table, her dark hair ruffled from a night of sleeping in her princess canopy bed. She yawns, watching the two of us like we're her personal entertainment.

"Now's not the place," Wade says, nodding toward Andrew's daughter. "Perhaps you two should finish this conversation in private?"

"There's nothing more to be said." Andrew slashes his hand through the air. "My wife is missing, Greer. I'm under an intense amount of pressure and scrutiny. Do you have any idea what that feels like? And for you to sit back and judge me and look at me like I could have possibly had anything to do with this? Why should I let you stay here?"

"Andrew . . ." My mother comes to my defense for the first time in decades. "Let's not say anything we might regret."

"I'm sorry, Brenda." He turns to her. "I can't. I can't do this anymore. She needs to go. At least . . . for a little while."

Fuck.

The hotels in this area are insanely expensive, the cheapest one being $500 a night during off-season last time I checked, and we're in the thick of peak season.

I can't afford to stay here.

I can barely afford the rent on my studio apartment.

But more than that, I can't afford to skip a few days of searching for Meredith.

"Maybe I overstepped my boundaries," I say. "Maybe I came on a little too intense. I'm sorry." I try to look him in the eyes, but he won't return it. "I'll go home for a few days. I'll get out of your hair. And when I come back, we can start fresh. I'll try to be more cognizant of what you're going through."

The thought of leaving here with zero answers to all these questions and not a single step closer to finding my sister makes my stomach twist, but Andrew's heavy breathing and cold stare tell me he needs space. And I need somewhere to crash until we find her.

His lips flatten, and he nods.

Returning to my room, I pack my bag and book my flight home.

My red-eye leaves tonight.

CHAPTER 27

MEREDITH

Eighteen Months Ago

He's home.

Sitting at the kitchen table holding an opened envelope from McCray, Prendergast, and Van Clef PC, I drag my fingertips over the torn paper.

"Hey." Andrew passes by, his briefcase in his left hand, and presses a kiss into the top of my head. "How was your day?"

I say nothing, my blood boiling from my discovery a mere hour ago.

Boredom put me into a cleaning frenzy earlier, and I spent most of the day organizing anything I could find: desks, drawers, closets. But when I headed into Andrew's study and found an opened letter dated six months ago and addressed to me hiding beneath a mountain of paperwork in his bottom left drawer, that's when my world tilted on its axis.

"Why was this in your office?" I ask. "And why the *hell* was it opened?"

I slide the torn envelope across the table, watching as his gaze narrows and his shoulders slump.

Andrew exhales, taking the seat next to me, sliding his hands down his cheeks as he gathers his thoughts.

"You better have a damn good explanation for this." I see red. Nothing but red. I've never felt so betrayed by him. What else has he done that I don't know about?

This envelope contained a letter from my biological father's attorney regarding the trust I was to access on my twenty-sixth birthday.

I'd never told Andrew about the trust.

I'd never told anyone about it.

Greer and my mother were the only two who ever knew, and that's how I intended to keep it.

A woman worth five million could be a dangerous commodity in the wrong hands. I may be young, but I'm not naive.

"I thought it was from a divorce attorney," he said. "I didn't want to be blindsided."

Rolling my eyes, I offer an incredulous laugh. "Seriously, Andrew? That's your excuse?"

"Yes." He looks earnest. And he sounds earnest. But I'm not buying it.

"This is a huge invasion of privacy," I say.

"I'm sorry, Meredith. I am."

He could easily bring up the trust fund, blowing up at me for keeping that from him, but he doesn't, and I'm not sure why. Perhaps five million is a drop in the bucket for him, not worth getting bent out of shape over?

I rise from the table, not in the mood to be within such close proximity to him anymore. But he follows, reaching for my arm. I jerk it away, heading toward the stairs.

"Where are you going?"

"I need to think." I realize the hypocritical nature of my frustration. I'm angry at him for hiding something from me when that's all I've been doing to him this entire time. Still, I feel betrayed. I need to be alone with my thoughts. I need to process this and what it means for the future of our marriage.

Maybe everyone was right. Maybe we have no business being together. A marriage built on a foundation of secrets can't possibly survive.

"I'm sorry." He apologizes again, which is a big deal because Andrew Price rarely mutters apologies. He's following me so closely I feel the warmth of his body, the intensity of his energy along my backside.

Stopping halfway up the stairs, I turn to face him. "Please. I need to be alone."

"No, we're going to talk this out." He reaches for my arm again, his hand gripping my wrist and pulling so tight it almost brings me to my knees.

Jerking my hand back, I rub the throbbing, red skin and hold it close to my chest. "Don't ever touch me like that again."

For the first time, I sense vulnerability in his gaze, and I wonder if he truly is afraid to lose me. He may be richer than sin, but knowing I'm coming into some money of my own means he can't keep me on his leash forever, and that uncertainty rattles him.

Andrew likes taking care of me. He likes that I need him.

And now that he knows I won't, he's losing the upper hand, and that terrifies him.

A year and a half of marriage, and I'm just now beginning to see the extent of this successful, charming, powerful man's insecurities. They run deeper than I ever imagined.

"You should sleep in the guesthouse tonight," I tell him before turning my back. I climb the stairs, head to our suite, and lock the door behind me.

Holding my breath, I press my ear to the door, listening for footsteps, inhalations, anything that tells me he's testing his limits with me.

But the other side is silent.

Peeling off my clothes, I draw the hottest bath I can stand, and when I emerge, I peer out the window facing the back of the house. The guesthouse is lit, his shadow moving behind curtains.

It feels weird to have the upper hand. The control.

Climbing into bed, I hold my phone against my chest, my body sinking into the mattress with the weight of the world.

I need to talk to someone and figure out what to do from here. Do I stay? Do I go? Am I overreacting? If I call my sister, she'll lecture me, pressure me to leave him, and she'll detest him even more than she already does. If I call Allison, she'll think of this moment every time she sees us together, and with her being my only friend, that could get awkward. My mother gives the worst advice and can't keep a secret to save her life.

I need an unbiased opinion, someone who will listen and not tell me what they think I want to hear and not judge me because they're too invested in me to be objective.

I'm tossing and turning when Harris comes to mind.

He doesn't particularly care for me, which means he's not biased, and he's never afraid to be blunt.

I need blunt right now.

I need brutal honesty.

Scrolling through my contacts, I find his name. The number of times I've called him in my life, I can probably count on two hands, but right now he's my best option.

My only option.

It's almost eight o'clock in New York. He may not even be home from work yet since New Yorkers tend to drink coffee all hours of the day, but I'll leave him a message. If he doesn't call me back, that means he doesn't want to talk to me, and that's fine, but I'm going to try.

My thumb presses his name. The phone rings twice. He answers.

"Harris," I say, breath caught in my chest. "Wasn't expecting you to answer."

163

"What's up?" He sounds casual for once. Not like he loathes me.

"Do you have a sec to talk?"

"If this is about Greer, no," he says.

"It's not about Greer."

He's quiet.

"I need some advice," I say.

The clinking of pans in the background layered over jazz music tells me he's at home, probably making himself dinner.

"Are you alone?" I ask, which is my way of asking, "Is she with you?"

"I'm alone." The faucet runs in the background for a few seconds.

"I have all these things I need to get off my chest, and I don't have anyone to talk to," I say.

"Can I be blunt with you for a second?" he asks over the clicking of a gas burner in the background. "You've never been a good judge of character, Meredith. Your relationships have always been superficial at best. There's no depth to them, and that's why they're so short-lived. How many friendships have you made in Glacier Park?"

"One."

"My point exactly. And why aren't you calling that friend right now instead of me?"

"I'm not comfortable talking to her about this."

"Right, right." His condescending tone is nearly impossible to ignore, but I try. "So anyway, what can I help you with? What harsh reality do I have the honor of bestowing upon you tonight?"

Sighing, I lay it on him, thickening my skin and bracing my ego. "I'm having issues in my marriage."

He's quiet. Then, "Continue."

"He's changed," I say. "He's not the same person I married."

"No one ever is, Meredith. He probably feels the same way about you."

"At first it was this hot and cold dynamic that I couldn't wrap my head around," I say. "But earlier today, I found a letter addressed to me, from an attorney, and he had opened it and hid it."

"What did it say?"

I draw in a deep breath, harboring the air as I decide whether or not to share this information with him. As far as I know, Greer's never mentioned a word to Harris about my trust fund. I swore her to secrecy years ago, and I trust her.

But this is relevant.

This is a game changer.

"He found out I'm coming into some money next year," I say. "A decent amount. And I hadn't told him that before we got married because I didn't want him to look at me differently. Plus, he already has money. He doesn't need mine. I didn't think it was relevant."

"Going into a marriage with secrets—especially ones that revolve around money—you're just setting yourself up for failure," he says. "Unless the both of you can be brutally honest and up-front about everything, you have no business being together. You may as well go your separate ways now. Once that trust is gone, you've got nothing."

"I'm angry at him, Harris," I say. "But I don't know if I want to throw in the towel yet. It's not fair for me to be angry at him."

"Why not?" He scoffs. "Opening someone else's mail is a federal offense. Hiding it from them takes it to a whole other level."

"I haven't exactly been the perfect wife myself."

"Explain yourself." The metallic swirl of a whisk against a stainless steel pan fills the background.

"A few months ago, I had a . . . fling."

"Affair, Meredith. You had an affair. Let's not sugarcoat. You won't do yourself any favors if you can't own up to your choices."

"Fine. Affair. I had an affair." I keep my voice down despite the fact that Andrew's an entire house away. I've never said that word . . . "affair."

And I let it settle into my marrow for a second. "I regret it. I got caught up. I made a mistake. But I've never told him."

"You should."

"That would be the end, don't you think? I don't think we can come back from that," I say. "He'd never look at me the same. He'd never trust me again."

"Do you see yourself married to him the rest of your life?" he asks. "I mean, for the love of God, you've been with him, what, a year and a half? And you've already had all these issues? Wake up, Meredith. You married the wrong man. Probably for the wrong reasons. Also, you have some serious daddy issues, and now you have to deal with the consequences of your actions."

Harris speaks to me the way I imagine my father would. Or the idea I have of my father. I've only seen him in pictures, but he seems like the kind of guy who didn't make it to the top by sheer luck. He's intelligent. People don't mess with him. They respect him. They write about his success in articles. He mentors people. He's accomplished so much, at least from what I can tell. People respect the hell out of him in Israel.

I've always wondered how he treats my half siblings. Whether he's father of the year, there for them more than just financially.

He didn't have to take care of me in the monetary sense, but he did.

He may not have wanted to meet me, to acknowledge my existence, but the fact that he set me up with a trust fund shows that on some level, he cares, and in a weird way, it sort of breaks my heart every time I think about it.

"And let's face it, you're young. Some might even call you a typical millennial. You refuse to accept that you don't know anything about anything, and every decision you make revolves around your fragile little ego," Harris continues, "so let's start there. Accept that you made a mistake. Accept that there are going to be consequences."

"Should I come clean about everything?" I ask.

"Yes. He's your husband. He has the right to know if you've recently had the pleasure of another man's cock inside you."

"No need to be vulgar."

"How do you think he'll react? Is he going to make your life a living hell and go crazy on you?" he asks. "I've seen men do that before. They seem totally fine, and then they . . . snap. The ones with the biggest egos snap the hardest."

I glance at my wrist. It's red, and it's going to bruise. The throbbing has mostly subsided.

"I have no idea," I say. "I don't know him as well as I thought. I've seen him get upset about things, but this . . . this is big."

"Just be careful," he says. "Anyway, I'm going to eat my dinner now. Is this all you needed?"

Pulling the covers up to my chin, I lie back. "Yeah."

For now.

"Thanks for talking to me," I add.

"Of course."

"And Harris?" I ask before he hangs up. "Please don't tell Greer we talked. She's going to know something's up."

"Your secret's safe with me."

CHAPTER 28

GREER

Day Eight

I stop at the police department on my way out of town to meet Bixby, the detective who replaced Ronan as the lead investigator on the case, and I'm surprised to find him standing in the lobby, shooting the breeze with a female dispatcher who appears to be on a coffee break.

"Bixby," I say, my attention trained on his name tag before rising to his smug, double-chinned smirk.

"Yeah? Why?" he asks.

"I'm Meredith Price's sister," I say, extending my hand in an effort to make a good first impression. I want him to trust me, to be able to confide in me the way Ronan did. "Greer Ambrose."

His expression falls, and the dispatcher mutters a quick goodbye before disappearing down the hallway.

He shakes my hand. "Harold Bixby."

His belly hangs over his belt slightly, and the fabric of his uniform top is pulled taut, held together by small, shiny buttons.

"Andrew said you're bringing a cadaver dog out today?" I ask.

He studies me. "We're exhausting all options. This is standard operation. Doesn't necessarily mean—"

"Okay." I cut him off before he can finish. "I just didn't know if maybe there was something you knew that you weren't necessarily sharing just yet?"

"We've shared everything we can with Mr. Price," he says.

"Is there anything you're *not* sharing?" I offer a benign smile, like my question isn't annoyingly persistent.

"If there is, ma'am, I couldn't tell you. We share everything as it becomes available to be shared."

"Yes or no, Detective?" I say, smiling so hard it makes my cheeks hurt. I probably look like a crazy person.

"Like I said, we share what we can," he says. "Anything that could possibly jeopardize the investigation is unable to be shared with the public."

"But Andrew's not the public. He's her husband."

"Either way. We have a job to do, and we have to do it in such a way that it won't jeopardize the case." He drags his thumb and middle finger down the sides of his mouth, cocking his head. "That said, I'm not saying that we have any additional information."

"It's just that the last detective was willing to keep us in the loop about everything," I say.

"And that detective is currently on leave for his unethical handling of a case that was entrusted to him."

Fair enough. "We're looking for her just as hard as you are. If there's anything that can help us, we'd like to know."

"I'm sure you would."

Ignoring his sighs and folded arms, I add, "Anyway, I'm leaving for a few days, going back home to New York. If anything develops while I'm gone, I was wondering if you could call me? I'll give you my number. My phone's always on. I can be on the next flight back here."

My mind plays a devastating scenario . . . the cadaver dog finding human remains . . . me hearing about it on some cable news show before I so much as get a phone call from anyone here.

He motions toward the reception desk, and the woman behind the counter hands him a pen and sticky note. I scribble my number, write my name in full, and thank him profusely for what an *amazing* job he's doing on the case.

He folds the sticky note in half, placing it in the pocket covering his left breast. A million dollars says he forgets all about it until he finds it in the washing machine, soggy and illegible.

"Thank you," I say again, extending my hand one last time. "I appreciate your help with everything."

Turning to leave, I make my way outside toward the waiting cab.

With everything going on today, I haven't had the chance to tell Harris I'm coming back. He hates surprises just as much as I do, but he'll just have to deal.

Besides, I want to see the look on his face when I show up.

That just might be the only thing that's going to get me through this red-eye.

CHAPTER 29

MEREDITH

Seventeen Months Ago

New York sans Andrew is . . . different. But ever since the trust fund letter came to light, he's been loosening his tether on me, giving me space like he's afraid he'll lose me if he holds on too tight. He hasn't come out and said it, but he knows I could walk out the door at any time if I wanted to, and I think that's made him reevaluate everything.

Last week over dinner, I casually mentioned that I wanted to visit my sister for a week. The next morning his assistant booked my flight, and Andrew put me up in the presidential suite of our favorite hotel.

When I arrived in the city yesterday, there was a package on my bed with a note from him. He'd had my favorite local treats delivered, as well as a Chanel handbag to mark the occasion, an advance copy of the newest Diane Chamberlain novel—autographed—as well as a list of reservations he'd made for me at various wait-listed restaurants and high-end day spas.

He's almost trying too hard now. The pendulum has swung in the opposite direction.

I just want to pal around the city with Greer, eating hot dogs and pretzels from carts near Central Park. Popping into our favorite little shops. Grabbing frozen hot chocolate from Serendipity if the mood strikes. Riding the subway for hours with the sole intention of people watching, just like we did when we were younger.

The bells on the door of Steam jangle when I pass through them that morning, and Harris glances up from a noisy cappuccino maker. For the first time in forever, he doesn't groan or sulk or sigh or furrow his brow when he sees me.

We've been talking on the phone almost nightly for the past month. Most of the time I wait until Andrew's in bed, and I sneak out to sit in the car or tiptoe to the guesthouse under the veil of night.

I'm not cheating.

I'm not emotionally attached to Harris or fantasizing about him in any way.

He's 100 percent just a friend.

Andrew wouldn't understand. And despite our differences, I trust Harris. I trust his brutal honesty because he has no skin in the game.

"Hi," I say, stopping short in the middle of the crowded coffeehouse while some indie rock band plays from the ceiling speakers. This feels like a scene from a movie.

I smile. He smiles.

"Hi," he says.

This is . . . new.

"Where's Greer?" I ask. For the first time in forever, I'm not actually surprising her. Being in town for an entire week, I had no choice but to fill her in so she could make time for all the things we were going to do together.

I take a seat at the edge of the bar, watching as Harris whips up drinks with the help of a part-time barista whom I've never seen before—some guy with dyed black hair, a nose ring, and tattoos covering both arms. He's young enough to still have the bane of dealing with acne, and he keeps his head down and works his ass off, probably because he knows Harris is watching him like a hawk.

"Who's the new guy?" I ask.

"Oh, him? That's my protégé," he says. "Little Harris."

I smirk, rolling my eyes. "What's his real name?"

"Jake. But Little Harris has a nice ring to it, don't you think?"

"You're so full of yourself." I pull my phone from my bag, checking my e-mail out of sheer boredom. The only e-mails I get these days are when Nordstrom has a sale or Net-a-Porter has free shipping on orders over $500. "Make me an iced chai, will you?"

He places a mug in front of me.

It was already made.

"Whoa." My eyes meet his. "When did you . . . ? I didn't even notice . . . Wow. Thank you."

"Don't act so surprised. I'm not always a giant fucking asshole." He returns to Little Harris, instructing him on the best way to make a foam leaf on the top of a cappuccino, and when he comes back, he rests his elbows on the counter. "I just want to apologize."

"What for?"

"For always being so hard on you."

"That's an understatement."

He glances down for a second. "Talking to you this past month, getting to know you . . . I realize that you were just lost, doing the best you could with what you were given. A flaky mother. An absent father. A control freak sister."

He smirks. So do I.

"I don't know what the hell I'm doing," I say, my hands around my sweating cup.

"Neither do I," he says. "No one does. We're all just . . . doing the best we can. Trying to make sense of things that probably never will."

"Do you have regrets?" I ask when Ronan comes to mind. He's been playing like a loop lately, and I haven't the slightest clue why. Sometimes I can go days, weeks, without thinking of him. Other times I can't get him out of my head . . . wondering how he's doing . . . if he's thinking of me, missing me and what we had. Wondering why after all these months it still matters . . .

He shrugs. "Life's too short to fixate on that shit. Suck it up. Move on. And try to do better next time."

"Have you ever cheated on Greer?" I place my hand over my heart. "Swear to God, I won't say anything."

His nose wrinkles, as if my question has insulted him, and he tucks his chin against his chest. "Never."

I don't think he's lying, but then, I've never been the best judge of that.

"What Greer and I had was messy and complicated. But I never strayed," he says. "I never strayed because I loved her. I truly loved her. When I was hers, I was hers completely."

"I loved Andrew," I say, wondering why I'm using the past tense. "*Love* . . . Andrew."

"No, you don't." He shakes his head. "You only think you do. You don't even know what love is because no one's ever showed you before."

"How do you know?"

"I've known you a long time, Mer," he says. "I've seen the guys you've brought home, the ones in your social media news feed. I've seen the men who hit on you, who want you for reasons you can't see because you choose not to."

"What do you mean?"

"Come on," he says. "Do I really have to spell it out for you? Andrew."

"Andrew loves me."

"No." He swipes a hand through his hair. "Andrew loves the way you make him feel about himself. That's what Andrew loves."

Shaking my head, I say, "You've met him all of one time. I don't think you're qualified to make that call."

"Oh, I'm making that call. I'm calling it," he says, half teasing, half clearly frustrated with me for not buying what he's selling. "He's a wealthy, insecure man. You're a young, beautiful woman. Nothing good can come from a combination like that."

I blush. Harris has never called me beautiful. I don't even think I've heard him call Greer beautiful.

"What do you have in common with him?" he asks. "What drew you to him in the first place?"

I start to answer, but he cuts me off.

"He's older. Wiser. More experienced. He has money, which means security and safety," he says. "He looked at you like you were the hottest thing he'd ever seen, and he made you feel sexy in a way the younger guys never could."

Harris sums up the first six months of my relationship with Andrew in under ten seconds.

"Like I said, you have daddy issues." His hands lift in the air. "So does Greer, but you didn't hear it from me."

I vaguely recall a wild phase in my sister's early college years, hearing stories of her sexual recklessness and finding new tattoos and piercings on her body each time she'd come home for a break.

All that changed when she met Harris.

He grounded her, balanced her out, gave her the kind of stability she'd never known before.

"Anyway, where is G?" I ask, tapping the counter and glancing around. "I thought she came in at nine?"

"She comes in when she wants to come in," he says. "I don't keep track anymore. My guess is she stayed up late last night trying to get ahead on work. Taking the week off is really stressing her out, but don't tell her I told you that."

I feel like this is a common thing between us now . . . *"Don't tell Greer."*

"Now I feel bad," I say.

"Don't. She needs this. She needs a break from here. And I need a break from her." He laughs, and I get it. She can be intense. And last I checked, she's still not over him. I bet she hangs around him every chance she gets, her codependence a trait that evolved over the course of their relationship.

"Stop talking about me." Greer's voice fills my ear, her warm palms on my shoulders. I don't know when she walked in or if she heard anything we said, but judging by the smirk on her mouth, she's teasing. Shooting Harris a look, she says, "You done ragging on my sister now?"

Harris and I exchange looks.

"Yeah," he says, leaving it at that.

Sliding off my seat, I follow my sister back to her office. She promised me she'd only work for a half hour today, an hour max, and then we could bounce.

"I should stay with you in your fancy suite. I bet it's twice the size of my apartment, maybe more," she says a moment later, firing up her computer. "It's not every day I'll have a chance to see how the one percent live."

Rolling my eyes, I shake my head. "Whatever. But yes, you can if you want. I think there's a pullout sofa."

Perusing the oddities in her crammed office, I settle on a photo of the two of us kids on a Ferris wheel at a seaside amusement park in New Jersey that I'm pretty sure no longer exists.

Her arm is around my shoulders, and we're grinning ear to ear.

Mom's boyfriend at the time took the photo with his fancy camera in an attempt, I think, to impress her. He was always talking about his photography business and how talented he was, but I never saw him actually go out and do any work. The guy was a permanent fixture on our living room sofa, watching sports all day while Mom was at work.

"I remember this day," I say, plucking the silver frame and holding the picture closer.

"You remember the corn dog?" Greer asks, fighting a smirk.

"Yes, I remember the corn dog," I moan, rolling my eyes. She's never going to let me live that down. We'll be old and gray, sitting in a nursing home, and she's still going to ask if I remember the freaking corn dog.

"God, it was so disgusting," she says, sticking her tongue out the side of her mouth. "I'll never forget that smell."

With a belly full of processed meat and fried corn bread, I had climbed into the fastest roller coaster in the park, which I was barely tall enough to ride. When we were finished, Greer told me my face was green, and before I could reply, I threw up all over her white Chuck Taylors. But instead of freaking out the way most teenage sisters would, she walked me to the bathroom, held my hair as I emptied the remaining contents of my stomach, and told me we could leave if I still wasn't feeling well.

My mother threw a fit, complaining about how much money she'd spent and how we'd taken a subway, a train, and a bus, and wasted most of the morning to get out here.

But Greer stood up for me, snapping back at my mother the way she always did and insisting that we leave.

It was a humid ninety-degree afternoon, but I was shivering and sweating, my stomach in knots. Turns out it wasn't the corn dog. It was the flu.

My mother insisted I toughen up and force myself to enjoy it. She said we were never coming back if we left after only two hours.

Greer took my hand and led me to the gated exit, leaving my mother and her camera-toting boyfriend with no choice but to follow.

"You've always taken such good care of me," I say.

Greer shrugs like it's no big deal. "You're my favorite person."

Placing the photo back on her desk, I move around to her chair, flinging my arms around her shoulders and burying my face into her neck.

"What's this for?" she asks, playing it cool.

"For always looking out for me," I say. "Worrying about me when no one else does."

"Like I have a choice," she says. "You're my sister. Worrying about you is my job."

"Love you, G."

"Love you more."

CHAPTER 30

GREER

Day Nine

"Jake, where's Harris?" I fully expected to walk into Steam this morning and find Harris posted behind the cash register, shooting the shit with one of our regulars, but instead it's only Jake, the tattooed college kid he's been grooming for the last year and a half after I told him he needed either a clone or an assistant because he was working way too damn much.

Jake grabs a ten-dollar bill from a man in a leather fedora, counting out his change in a whispered hush before turning his attention to me. "What do you mean?"

"Is he in the back?"

Jake's nose scrunches. "I'm confused."

"No, *I'm* confused." I press my pointer finger into my chest, eyes squinting.

"Assumed he was with you? Looking for your sister?"

I shake my head slowly. "No . . . he was staying back, manning the stores."

Jake tends to another customer, and my impatience almost eats a hole through me. He moves closer, whipping up a tea latte, and glances up at me.

"He left, like, four days ago, I think?" Jake stops what he's doing, his head tilting. "Called me early that morning, put me in charge, said he wasn't sure when he'd be back, but he'd keep me posted."

"Has he checked in with you at all?"

"Nope." He takes the tea latte to the man in the hat, who promptly deposits a handful of change in the tip jar. Cheap ass. "I've been watching the news, though, trying to keep up on everything. Sorry about your sister."

"She's not dead." I don't mean to snap, but everyone assumes that "missing" equals "dead," and until there's proof of life or death, I don't want to jump to any conclusions. "I mean, we don't know anything yet."

"I just meant I'm sorry you're going through this."

Now I feel bad. "Thank you."

He attends to two more customers, a pair of gossip queen–types with platinum-blonde extensions, matching Karen Walker sunglasses, and overdrawn Kylie Jenner lips. They're not our usual customer, but whatever. They each order huge iced macchiatos and cinnamon scones before asking if Jake can break a hundred-dollar bill.

"Okay, so help me understand exactly what happened," I say. "Harris told you he was going to Utah to look for my sister? And you haven't seen or heard from him since?"

Jake rests his hands at his hips, glancing at the ceiling, exhaling. "He didn't say where he was going. I just assumed, but yeah, he left and didn't say when he'd be back. Figured he'd at least call and check in or something, but nothing."

"It doesn't make any sense," I say, though Jake doesn't seem to comprehend the gravity of this situation. I don't blame him. He's just a barista barely making enough to afford the bottom bunk of the bed he rents in a shitty studio apartment in the Lower East Side. He doesn't understand the delicate complexities of my relationship with Harris. He doesn't know that Harris told me he loved me for the first time in years last week, all the while leading me to believe he was still in New York running the stores. "He'd have told me if he wasn't going to be here."

I think back to that morning standing outside his apartment door. The sympathy in his tired eyes. His apology. His hug. The promise that he'd be there for me.

The entire time I've been in Utah, he's answered each time I've called, never rushed to get me off the phone. Let me vent. Let me whine. Let me wallow in the tragedy of this situation, offering his poignant words of support.

I don't want to believe it was all a ruse, but . . .

Leaving the store, I try his phone.

It doesn't ring.

His voice greeting plays, but I hang up.

Hailing a cab to his apartment, I scale the stairs to the third floor as soon as I arrive, not having the time or patience to wait for the slow-as-molasses elevator, and when I get to apartment 3F, I pound on the door with both palms.

"Harris! Harris, are you home?" I ask a question to which my intuition already knows the answer, but I have to try.

I think back to the last time we spoke on the phone, if anything seemed different, if I missed any red flags, but I've been so focused on Meredith this entire time that I wasn't paying attention to anything that didn't directly pertain to her.

An older man exits the door down the hall, eyeing me with intense scrutiny, like I'm up to no good. I don't recognize him, which means he probably moved in after I moved out.

"Have you seen Harris Collier?" I ask. "It's an emergency. I'm a friend."

There's a slight limp in the way he walks, and his lips are twisted into a permanent scowl.

"Nope," he says as he passes. "Never heard of him."

Typical New York ass.

Before I can press him for any additional information, he disappears around the corner, headed toward the elevator bay.

I need access to his place.

Dashing toward the stairwell, I make my descent two steps at a time until I get to the landlord's apartment at the end of the hall. I may have moved out, but my name is still on the lease because Harris insisted on signing a thirty-six-month agreement to lock in the ridiculous discount they were offering at the time.

Pounding on the door, I hear the sound of her TV, the squawk of her prized cockatiels, and the sound of her husband yelling at her that he thought he heard someone knocking on the door.

It takes a minute, but she finally answers.

"Mrs. Conway," I say, breathless. "Greer Ambrose. Apartment 3F."

She looks me up and down, the scent of stale cigarettes and bird shit encircling me like an invisible fog. "You still live here? Thought you and that boy broke up."

"We did," I say. "And I don't live here, but my name is still on the lease. I need in the apartment."

Her head leans to the side, like she can't decide if I'm lying.

"I can't get hold of Harris," I say. "His phone is off, and no one's seen him at the shop for over a week."

"Have the police been notified?"

"That's my next step," I lie. Kind of. I don't know what my next step is; I just know I need to get inside his apartment as soon as possible, and only then will I be able to figure out my next move. "Do you have a master key or anything? I just need to take a peek inside, see if anything looks amiss. I don't want to bother the police if it's for nothing. Maybe he left a note?"

Her eyes squint, and she exhales.

"Legally, I'm allowed into that apartment, Mrs. Conway." I try to be as polite as possible, though I know I'm speaking too fast and my eyes are twitching. I don't blame her for being skeptical. After everything I've been through in the past week and now this, I'm not in a good place, and there's nothing I can do to mask that.

"It's true, Edith," her husband chimes in from his sunken-in spot on the living room sectional. "Give her a key so we can finish this damn show and clear it off the DVR."

Mrs. Conway places a finger in the air before closing the door. When she returns, she places a shiny gold key in my hand.

"Here," she says. "Bring it back to me as soon as you're done, you got that? And don't steal anything."

"Yes, ma'am."

With that, I'm gone. Heart pumping, cheeks flushed, vision dizzy and blurred, I run back to the apartment and jam the key in the lock so hard I worry I might have broken it off, but with a quick twist the lock pops.

I'm in.

A stale scent fills my lungs, like the place is void of fresh oxygen. The counters are clear of clutter and recently wiped down at some point, and the pillows on the sofa are fluffed. Whenever he left, it doesn't appear that he did it in a hurry.

His family photos still line the fireplace mantel.

His shoes are neatly placed on a rug by the door, save for his favorite pair of leather Chucks and his black Doc Marten combat boots.

The way he left the place makes it look like he's out running errands, due back at any moment.

Moving into the kitchen, I open a few cupboards, finding cans of Wolfgang Puck soups and unopened boxes of his favorite organic version of Frosted Flakes. I check the fridge next.

It's empty.

No milk. No eggs. No butter.

Nothing perishable. Nothing that would start to smell over a long period of time.

In fact, the fridge isn't even cold.

He turned it off before he left, which tells me he planned to be gone for some time.

Slamming the door, I check his bedroom next. His bed is made, the corners neatly tucked and the pillows standing upright against the headboard, and his laundry hamper is empty.

Opening the closet doors with a clean jerk, I find it in a state of haphazard disarray.

My heart sinks.

A significant portion of his clothes is missing.

Jeans, T-shirts—all the casual stuff is gone. Nothing hangs but a few old suits he never wore except for special occasions, a collection of skinny ties, and a bunch of old, pilling sweaters from college he's been meaning to donate for years.

I check his bathroom next.

His cinnamon toothpaste. His argan oil shampoo. His triple-blade razors.

All of it . . . gone.

CHAPTER 31

MEREDITH

Eight Months Ago

"You're making a huge mistake." Harris sounds particularly annoyed with me tonight.

I've spent the better part of the last few months venting to him about Andrew, and tonight I've dropped a handful of bombshells.

Couples counseling is going exceedingly well.

I still love Andrew.

And now he wants a baby.

"This is your fork in the road," he says. "This is your chance to get out while you still can. I don't get it, Mer. What the fuck changed?"

Over the past few months, Harris has been steering me in the direction of divorce despite my insistence that Andrew's been treating me better than he ever has.

When I first solicited Harris's advice, it was because I knew he would be unbiased. Somewhere along the line, I guess he decided he liked me as a human after all, and he wouldn't stop pushing for me to leave my husband. He's just like Greer, and now I don't even know if I want to talk to Harris anymore. All we do is have the same conversations fifty different ways because he refuses to accept the fact that things between Andrew and myself have improved.

"Maybe I don't want to get out anymore," I say.

"That's not what you said a week ago." His tone is terse, and I imagine his jaw is clenched tight. "God, every other week it's something else. Make up your fucking mind, Meredith. Stop waffling."

After a while, I got tired of Harris's lectures, so I'd let him yammer on while saying, "Yeah" and "Mm, hm" and "Okay" to show I was still listening, which in retrospect wasn't a good idea because he actually thought I was agreeing to do all the things he said . . . which in a nutshell was leave Andrew, move back to the city, and start fresh as soon as I could access my trust fund.

"Why are you being like this?" I ask. "We're friends. Support me. Support my decision. Be happy for me."

"We're not friends." His words sting. "I'm your voice of reason. Nothing more, nothing less."

"Look, I don't expect you to understand," I say. "But I still love him. And neither of us is perfect. And I'm not ready to throw in the towel yet."

"But a week ago you were," he says. "You caught him flirting with your waitress when you came back from the bathroom."

"Yes, and we discussed that in couples counseling," I say. "It turns out he knew her. She was the daughter of one of his clients. They were laughing because he'd made a joke about her father. When I saw them, I just assumed they were flirting."

"I can't fucking believe this." In other words, he thinks I'm an idiot.

"I don't know why you care so much. The only reason I started talking to you about any of this was because I thought you *didn't* care." I pace my living room. Andrew's going to be home any minute. "I wanted your objective opinion, but it seems like you can't even give me that anymore."

He's quiet.

I've struck a nerve.

He knows I'm right.

He *knows* it.

"My objective opinion has nothing to do with this," he says. "I'm trying to guide you in the right direction. Prevent you from making the second biggest mistake of your life."

"Second biggest? What was the first?"

"Marrying him."

Rolling my eyes, I check the street, watching for his car. I need to wrap this up.

"Don't call me again," he says.

"You don't mean that."

"I do. I'm tired of the hemming and hawing," he says. "Get a fucking diary. I'm done."

"Harris."

"You know what, Mer? You're just as flaky as your mother. But at least she had enough sense to get out before she was up to her elbows in someone else's bullshit."

"Now that's just mean. I'm *nothing* like her."

"You're *exactly* like her." His voice is a low sneer laced with revulsion and darkness.

My skin is hot, my heart firing away. Comparing me to my mother is a line Harris knows better than to cross.

Before I have a chance to offer my rebuttal, the line goes dead.

Sliding my phone across a nearby table, I head to the kitchen to pour myself a glass of wine.

It's Friday. It's almost five o'clock. It's Andrew's weekend, and we're supposed to pick up the kids from Erica's later.

I need to unwind, but the second I uncork my favorite dry red, the doorbell chimes. Abandoning my liquid Xanax, I get the door, only the person standing on the other side is the last person I expect to see on my steps.

"Ronan." My face wants to smile, my heart dropping to my fluttering stomach when I see him.

He looks good, even better than the last time I saw him.

His hair's a bit longer, his skin a bit tanner. Recent vacation maybe? And he's dressed in plain clothes, though his shield hangs on a chain around his neck. Over his shoulder, I notice his unmarked car parked in the street.

"Was on my way home," he said. "Wanted to stop by and let you know we finally caught that stalker."

The stalker.

God, that seems like forever ago, and now it's all coming full circle, bringing Ronan into my life all over again.

"Come in." I pull the door wide.

"It's okay. I'm not staying long." There's a bittersweet longing in his eyes, and his hands are shoved in his pockets. He looks at me the way you look at the flickering glow of a candle, knowing it's beautiful and tempting but it'll hurt if you touch it.

The stalker hasn't messed with me in forever, well over a year. In the back of my mind, I always assumed maybe Erica hired someone to have me followed just to mess with me. That's something she'd do out of sheer spite.

"Apparently this guy was targeting random women in Glacier Park," he says. "Just some mentally unstable local. Lived in a log cabin outside the city limits. Bit of a recluse. Anyway, someone caught him in the act, and we got a description of him as he fled, along with his plates. That's how we nailed him. He confessed to following you, and he claims he picked you at random. Just thought you'd like to know."

It's sweet of him to come all this way to give me peace of mind when he owes me nothing. What we had may have been a fling, but I still hurt him. There's pain in his eyes when he looks at me, sending a sympathetic ache to my chest.

How I wish we could've met under different circumstances, in another lifetime.

"Thank you," I say, resting my hand over my heart, wishing I could hug him but knowing it'd be completely inappropriate in our current states. "How have you been? I think about you often . . ."

His face lights. He doesn't say it, but I know he thinks of me, too. "Good. I've been good."

"Anything new?" I wish he could come in. I wish we could catch up. I could talk to him for hours, always could.

"Just been working," he says. "Going on some dates."

His gaze softens, and he smiles. I think he wants me to be happy for him. Deep down, it feels as though I've been punched in the gut.

"Really? Dates?" I lift my brows, forcing a smile, though I'm sure my voice gives away my disappointment. Despite the fact that Ronan's not mine and never will be, I'm jealous of those faceless girls who get to ride shotgun in his truck, bask in his perfect, brilliant smile, and experience the toe-curling kisses I'll never have the pleasure of knowing again.

"Yeah." He smiles.

"Anything promising?"

He shrugs. "Maybe."

"Anyone I'd know?" I doubt it, but I'm dying to hear a name, something, anything. Is this what jealousy feels like? Nausea, stinging eyes, a crushing heaviness like I'm staring at the one who got away, knowing he can never be mine again?

Silently scolding myself, I shake it off. I have no right to care about who he dates. I have no right to miss him, to envy the woman he'll someday fall in love with and marry and start a family with. He'll take one look at her, and he'll know it was always supposed to be her, and in that moment, he won't be thinking of me.

I bet he'll be a good dad.

He'll be home for dinner each night, teach his kids how to throw a football, carry them on his shoulders at theme parks, and hop in the pool with them in the summer, teaching them how to dive and letting them ride on his back.

Andrew's a good father to Isabeau and Calder, but in his own way. It's not fair to compare the two.

The flash of headlights veering into the driveway steals my attention. My husband's home.

"So what was the stalker's name?" I ask. "Just so I know."

And so I can tell Andrew, so he doesn't grow suspicious of this unexpected house call.

"Perry Davis," he says without missing a beat.

My lips jut forward. "Oh, okay. Never heard of him."

"He's currently awaiting sentencing. Rest assured we'll be watching his every move," he says. "He won't be able to so much as fill up his gas tank without one of us knowing."

I imagine the old-moneyed husbands of Glacier Park would have a conniption if their little police department did nothing to thwart some deranged lunatic harassing their pampered wives.

The chink of keys on the counter and the beeping of the security system echo through the foyer, and our eyes meet.

"Mer?" Andrew calls. "I phoned you six times on my way home. Why didn't you answer?"

He's been doing this more and more lately, getting worried if I don't answer, if I don't text him back within minutes. Ever since I mentioned in one of our counseling sessions that it bothers me how he never seems to worry about my safety, he's been going overboard trying to make up for it.

"Ringer was off," I call out. "Sorry."

Ronan forces a breath through his flared nostrils, his lips flat as he bites his tongue. He doesn't have to say anything. He knows I know exactly what he's thinking.

"Had me worried. Thought something happened to—" Andrew appears from around the corner, stopping short the second he sees Ronan. "What's this?"

"Detective McCormack stopped by to tell me they found my stalker," I say.

"About damn time," Andrew says, resting his hands on my hips and kissing the side of my neck, just below my ear. He lingers, his grip laying claim to my body as if he feels threatened by the sheer presence of Ronan.

Does he know?

The two of them loiter, all hard stares and broad shoulders, a couple of bucks fighting over a prized doe. Ronan studies us, his gaze fixated on Andrew's hands at my hips.

"I should go," he says after a moment. "Just wanted to let you know."

"Thank you so much," I say, wishing I could walk him to the car, dying for just a few more innocent moments with him.

Just being in his company gives me the tiniest hint of a rush—a sliver of what I felt with him before.

I miss the rush.

I miss him.

But I made my bed. I married Andrew for better or for worse. This is the life I chose.

Giving him a small wave and ignoring the upsurges of melancholy washing over me, I stand, watching as he leaves, until Andrew slams the door shut.

"That was random," he says. "You haven't been bothered by that stalker in a couple of years, right?"

"Apparently he was messing with other women in the area," I say. "He must have moved on from me. Ronan—Detective McCormack—was just following up with me as a courtesy."

"Ronan?"

Shit.

I'd hoped he wouldn't notice.

"First-name basis, eh?" Andrew's expression darkens as he pushes past me and heads to the kitchen. I follow him, watching as he helps himself to the bottle I'd uncorked, taking my glass for himself.

Folding my arms, I shoot him a look. "What are you getting at?"

His gaze skims to mine. "You tell me."

"Remember what Dr. Connelly said about confronting each other like adults and being clear and direct in our communication? If you need to ask me a question, just ask me," I say, trying to de-escalate this conversation before it reaches the point of no return. "Playing these little games is detrimental to our relationship."

My husband clears his throat.

"Fine." Andrew tosses back the remainder of the wine. "I know you were fucking him."

I can't breathe. The wind has been knocked from my lungs, but I muster the courage to present myself with unruffled feathers.

"How did you find out?" No sense in denying anything at this point. I'm a big girl. I can own this. Harris says there are consequences to every decision, and I'm seconds from finally discovering what my foolishness is going to cost me.

"I have my ways," he says with an arrogant snort, topping off his wineglass.

"How long have you known?"

"Long enough." He makes his way around the island. "Remember when I fucked you like the whore you are?"

I swallow the hard knot lodged in my throat, but it's still there.

I knew it.

That morning in the hotel . . . he was punishing me.

"You wrote on my windshield, didn't you? It wasn't the stalker that time." I squint in his direction, recalling the giant, ugly letters spelling out the word "Whore" when I'd come out of Ronan's the night I ended things.

I hadn't mentioned that to him. I didn't want him to suggest we track down parking lot surveillance footage from the pharmacy I'd claimed to have been at.

His lips pull into a knowing smirk, and the dangerous glint in his eyes is one I've never seen before.

"I don't understand. Why would you not tell me? Why would you act like you didn't know? Weren't you angry?"

"Of course I was angry. Still am," he says, taking a slow sip of Merlot. "But you came home to me, and when you stopped spending time with him, I figured you finally came to your senses and realized this is where you belong. Here. With me."

"You had me followed," I state, not asking. My mouth runs dry. He nods.

"Anyway, after that I was willing to turn a blind eye to your little . . . indiscretion. Lord knows *I'm* not perfect." He takes me in, watching for my reaction. He wants to see me in pain—the same pain I caused him.

"So you cheated, too?" I deserve this gut punch, and I know it.

"Almost." He chuckles, gazing away, but his smile fades. "I tried once. Got to the hotel, started taking off her clothes, but then I stopped. I thought it would make me feel vindicated. Thought I'd feel better. But it only made me feel worse because, Meredith, you're the only one I want to be with. Such a fucking shame you didn't feel the same."

"I'm sorry, Andrew." I rise, going to him, but he recoils when I reach for his arm.

This is bad.

Beyond bad.

But we can fix this. He still loves me—he wouldn't be so angry if he didn't.

The weight of what I've done sinks into my bones. My eyes mist, clouding my vision.

"You need to make this right," he says, as if the solution to our problem lies solely in my hands. His tone is ugly. Just like that my tears cease, and our eyes lock. His lips almost draw into a hint of a snarl. I see now that I disgust him. "I've worshipped the fucking ground you walked on since the moment we met. But you? You're the one who couldn't keep your clothes on the second some jackass with a badge paid you a little attention. Really, Meredith? Are you that insecure? Who *are* you? Because you're sure as hell not the woman I married."

He's right.

He's absolutely right.

And I don't even have an answer for him, though I wish I did.

I'd be lying if I said there weren't days I avoided my reflection in the mirror after returning from Ronan. The first few times, the girl staring back was ripe with shame and guilt and shameless sex hair, and I hardly recognized her.

"And do you have any idea what this would do to my reputation if this got around?" he asks. "People entrust me with managing their money, their millions. Do you know how incompetent and clueless this would make me look? My beautiful wife running around on me? Finding pleasure in the arms of some blue-collar Cub Scout? I'll be damned if my marriage to you turns me into gossip fodder."

"What do you want me to do?" I ask, falling to my knees in a last-ditch effort to physically show him I am willing to do what it takes to earn that look in his eyes again—the one he had the first time he told me he loved me. This may be melodramatic—it's a desperate gesture—but I have to show him how sorry I am. "How can I make it up to you?"

"I don't know if you can." He removes himself from my presence, his footsteps heavy.

"So that's it? You're just going to walk off? End of discussion?" My voice is raised, broken.

"I need some space," he says from the stairs. "The fact that that fucking detective had the nerve to show up at *my* house and look me in the eyes after fucking *my* goddamned wife . . . has got me a little on edge."

Andrew leaves out the back door, marching toward the guesthouse, and I give him the distance he needs.

Everything makes sense now.

The hot and cold. The rough sex. The extremes our relationship has endured. He was hurt. He was in pain. And *I* did that to him.

All this time, he *knew*.

All this time, he still loved me.

All this time, never once did he want to let me go.

Harris was wrong. Andrew genuinely loves me. And if I'm lucky, our marriage can survive this.

I can survive this.

CHAPTER 32

GREER

Day Nine

I try Harris's phone for the fiftieth time, each attempt more in vain than the one before, and I hang up the second his greeting starts. The voice that once brought me comfort, made me feel loved and worthy, now makes me sick to my stomach.

Sitting in the middle of his noiseless living room, I rifle through my contacts, trying to determine if anyone else might possibly know where to find him.

I stop scrolling when I find his mother's number. I haven't seen or spoken with her in years, but I always kept her in my phone just in case. A retired professor, she lives in northern California now, and as far as I know, the two of them still speak on the phone at least once a day.

Harris is a total mama's boy—a quality I'd always found endearing over the years, ignoring the fact that she was oddly possessive of her only son and viewed his relationship with me as some kind of threat for the first several years. At some point, she came to accept the fact that I wasn't going anywhere, and things were cordial after that.

Pressing her name, I lift the phone to my ear, my heartbeat whooshing as it rings.

"Hello?" Her familiar lilt answers. "Deborah Collier speaking."

She must have deleted my number after Harris and I called it quits.

"Deborah, it's Greer," I say.

I'm met with momentary silence before she clears her throat. "Oh, yes. Greer. Hi. It's been a long time."

"Yes," I say, picking at a loose thread on Harris's sofa. "It has."

"I'm so sorry to hear about the situation with your sister," Deborah says. "I've been watching the news every day, trying to stay on top of the story, but unfortunately there doesn't seem to be much to stay on top of lately."

Thanks for the reminder.

"Do you know where Harris is?" I cut to the chase.

I'm met with silence. She knows something; I know she does.

"I need to find him," I say. "He's not answering his phone, and Jake at Steam says he hasn't heard from him in days. I'd been speaking to him on the phone almost every day while I was gone, and he led me to believe he was still in New York running the stores . . . but he lied to me, Deborah. And I need to find him. I need to know why he lied."

She exhales. "Oh, Greer. I . . . I don't want to get involved."

"Deborah." I say her name with force and grit. "I know you talk every day. Where is he?"

"Yes," she says. "We speak often, but not every day. We spoke a few days ago, matter of fact. I guess I just assumed he was at home."

Massaging my temple, I draw in a breath of stale apartment air and let it go. "Do you have any idea where he might be? Any idea at all?"

"I wouldn't even begin to know where he'd run off to." She speaks of him like he's some playful, elfin child.

"If he did something . . . ," I say, voice trembling. Heat creeps up my neck, blooming to my ears. Never once did the notion that Harris had anything to do with Meredith's disappearance cross my mind. Until now it had been an absolute impossibility. Anyway, I don't know if he's with my sister. All I know is he's gone and she's gone, and there are no such things as coincidences. "If he had anything to do with my sister's disappearance and you're withholding information that could lead to her, you're going—"

"My son would *never* cause harm to a woman." Deborah's voice is raised, drenched in a shrill tone she's never taken with me. "To even suggest that, Greer, is just . . ."

"Fine," I say. "If you're so convinced he didn't do anything wrong, then tell me where to look for him."

She pauses, mulling over her answer, perhaps, and then she exhales. "There's our family cabin in Vermont."

I remember.

The first year we dated, he was trying to impress me with his survivalist skills, and we road-tripped it to Rushing, Vermont, where his family owned a basic cabin that had been in the family for generations. It had running water and indoor plumbing, a fireplace, but no AC. The house was seldom used, smelled like mildew, and was nestled on a mosquito-infested lake, but we had a blast.

Then again, we were in love. We would've had the time of our lives anywhere.

"You think he went there?" I ask.

"A few months ago, he was asking if anyone was going to be using the cabin this month. He was itching for a vacation, said he'd been working too much and wanted to disconnect," she says. "Now that I think about it, I told him it was all his, and he said he'd get back to me, but he never did. I just assumed he changed his mind."

"If you hear from him, Deborah, you need to let me know," I say. "It's very important."

"Will do," she says, but I don't trust her.

I'd tell her my sister's life is on the line, but she'd probably laugh. Her perfect, God's-gift son, a born and bred feminist, would never so much as lay a hand on the finer sex, she'd say.

"What's the address to the cabin?" I ask before I let her go.

She hesitates before exhaling. "Seventy-three Goodwin Road in Rossford Township, but I can assure you he isn't there."

"Then where is he?"

"Like I said, Greer, I don't know. But I doubt he's at the cabin. He would've said something."

"Please let me know if you hear from him." Ending the call, I type the address into my phone before I forget it; I save it before dialing Ronan. Ronan and Harris are complete strangers. If Harris is involved in this, if he ran off with my sister, I need someone to help track them down, someone as desperate as I am to find her. Someone who can make sense of all this because I'm sick with confusion.

"So what do you think?" I ask Ronan after word vomiting every minute detail of the last two hours of my life.

"Don't jump to conclusions," he says, breaking his silence. "And for the love of God, don't go out there alone. Wait for me."

"I don't have time to wait for you. You're on the other goddamned side of the country."

"I'll get on the next flight, meet you in Vermont," he says. "Promise you'll wait for me, Greer."

"I will."

"And whatever you do, do *not* call the police," he says. "If Harris was clever enough to organize this entire thing, he's probably listening to local scanners. He'll know if anyone's been dispatched or if the police there have been told to look for a man matching his description. We want him to think he's under the radar. Last thing we need is a moving target. He doesn't know you came home, right?"

He's on it. He's a pit bull, spouting directives and trying to stay two steps ahead of this entire situation in real time. He wouldn't do this if he were guilty, if he had something to do with this.

I have no proof that Harris is with my sister. All I know is he's gone, his stuff is gone, and he clearly didn't want me to know.

"No," I answer.

"He doesn't know you're looking for him?"

"No." I palm my forehead. "Shit."

"What?"

"His mom. If she talks to him, she's going to tell him I'm looking for him."

"Call her back. Tell her it's absolutely imperative that she not share that with him," he says. "That could jeopardize everything."

"I'll try," I say, exhaling. Her loyalty isn't exactly to me these days.

"I'll text once I book my flight, Greer," he says, breathy almost, like he's scrambling around packing a bag. "We're going to find her. We're going to bring her home safe, I promise."

And I believe him.

If he didn't love my sister, didn't want to save her, he wouldn't be hopping on the next plane to Vermont to try to find her with me.

CHAPTER 33

MEREDITH

Three Months Ago

Three times last week.

Four times in the last two days.

"I'm beginning to think you're following me," I say to Ronan as I pass him in the cereal aisle at Hawthorne Food Market at two o'clock on a Wednesday.

It's like he's everywhere I go lately. Every stoplight. Every gas station. Every random side street. And maybe I'm exaggerating, but when you go from hardly seeing a man to seeing him every other day, it's tough to disregard.

Ronan smirks, grabbing a box of peanut butter Cap'n Crunch from a middle shelf. I tell myself I'm making this worse than it really is. Anyone who wears a badge around his neck and eats children's cereal for breakfast is harmless.

"Was about to say the same thing to you," he says, pushing his cart closer and eyeing the bags of Halloween candy in mine. "You're everywhere I go lately."

Checking my watch, I realize I have to leave soon to get Calder and Isabeau from school. "Guess I'll see you around?"

I chuckle, trying to make light of a bizarre series of events and ignore the strange lump in my throat.

Ronan's eyes flash, and his smirk fades. "Oh."

He must realize I'm slighting him.

"I have to get the kids," I say, pointing toward the checkouts. "Need to get in line early. You know how crazy pickup can be if you don't get there at a certain time."

No, he doesn't know. He doesn't have kids. And the fact that I'm being all awkward with this conversation isn't helping the situation. He knows he's making me nervous.

"How have you been, Meredith?" he asks, ignoring my attempt to exit this exchange.

My brows rise. "Good. You?"

His lips tighten. "I hate this."

Glancing around to ensure we're alone in this colorful aisle, I step closer. "You hate what, Ronan?"

"How awkward this is," he says. "It's like we're a couple of strangers now."

"Ronan."

"I want to be able to say hi to you without making you all flustered," he says. "Without making you scramble in the opposite direction."

"I really do have to get the kids," I say, eyeing the checkout once more.

"It's two o'clock," he says. "You have plenty of time. Just . . . do me a favor."

"What's that?"

"When we see each other around, don't ignore me. Don't make it a thing. Just wave. Say hi. We can be adults about this." His thumb hooks his belt loop, and he hasn't taken his eyes off me once.

"This really isn't the time or place." I scan the aisle again, thanking my lucky stars when a woman from the gym glances down and keeps walking. She didn't see me. Didn't see *us*.

"Shit." He covers his face with his hands. "I'm sorry. You're right. I forget you've got more skin in the game than I do."

"I really should go."

"Can we talk sometime?" he asks as I push my cart away.

"About?" Not that I'd say yes. Curiosity has gotten the best of me.

Ronan follows me, the wheels of his cart clicking against the tile floor. "There's something I think you should know. About your husband."

My heart falls like a dead weight. "What about my husband?"

"I'd rather tell you in private."

I refuse to go anywhere with him. I've been doing so well lately, working on my marriage, focusing on Andrew and renewing my commitment to him. I'm not proud of what I did. It was selfish and wrong, and I'm not about to tiptoe off for some secret meeting with an ex-lover.

"Meet me in the parking lot after I check out," I tell him. "I'll give you five minutes, and then I have to go."

He follows me toward the front of the store, and I hold my breath until he chooses a different lane. A few minutes later, I'm wheeling my groceries to the fifth parking spot in the last row, and he's strutting out the automatic doors, two bags in his muscled arms.

I watch as he heads to his truck, dropping them in the back, and then comes my way.

"So?" I ask, slamming the lid of the trunk. "What's this thing you think I should know about my husband?"

With folded arms, he widens his stance, studying me. "I have reason to suspect he's been cheating on you."

"Do you have evidence?" I ask.

He shakes his head. "Nothing hard. Nothing tangible that I can present to you. But I'm working on it."

"Stop." I push past him, heading toward the driver's door. "Please just . . . stop meddling. Stay out of my marriage. I know we have issues. Neither of us is perfect. We're just trying to make this work."

I don't believe him.

Or maybe I just don't want to.

Either way, I know one thing's for sure: I don't want Ronan involving himself in any of this.

Andrew's been a dream lately. I think he'd say the same for me.

We've come too far, worked way too hard.

And now we're trying to start a family. Officially. Both of us on the same page, both of us equally excited about this next chapter.

"So that's it?" he asks.

My grip pauses on the door handle. "What do you mean?"

"I tell you your husband's cheating, and you walk off like *I'm* the asshole in this situation?" Ronan scoffs, his finger digging into his chest, trembling almost.

My gaze flicks into his, and I gather that this was never really over . . . not for him. How long has he been pining for me? Silently waiting in the wings? Wishing for another opportunity?

"You picked the wrong guy," he says, voice cracking.

"It was never you against him," I say, keeping my voice low and moving closer. "I married him. My choice was always going to be him."

Ronan's expression darkens, jaw flexing and stare hardening.

"I *love* Andrew," I say. "You were my escape. My little cheap thrill. But he's my *husband*."

"Convenient how little that mattered when you were fucking me." He spits his words at me, lingers for a moment, towering over me.

"I'm pregnant." I hate to lie to him, but clearly, he's hurting for closure. And I might as well be expecting. We've been trying like crazy. It's bound to happen sooner or later.

Ronan's eyes water, and his hands lift to the back of his head. He steps backward, away. And then he's gone. Climbing into his truck, he peels away, and I exhale, watching his taillights grow dim in the distance.

I didn't mean to hurt him. That was never my intention. But he needs to move on.

We all need to move on.

CHAPTER 34

GREER

Day Ten

The Burlington airport is quaint and easy to navigate, which is much appreciated given my current condition.

I find Ronan by the baggage claim, thumbing through his phone and periodically glancing up to check the crowd for my face. His flight landed an hour before mine. I'm sure the wait was hell.

"Hey," I say.

He dangles a set of keys, peering around again, not meeting my gaze. "I've got the car."

Within minutes we're loading our carry-on bags in the trunk of a rented Dodge, barreling down the highway toward Harris's cabin, which is a good three hours from here according to the GPS on my phone.

Road noise layered over silence does nothing to quell the anxious twist in my middle. Legs crossed, my ankle bounces, and I nip at my nails, biting them to the quick one by one.

"So tell me about the dynamic between Meredith and Harris," Ronan says, his fists gripping the steering wheel so tight his knuckles whiten. "Help me understand how this possibly could've evolved."

I shake my head, my eyes unfocused on the road before us. "They couldn't stand each other. From the moment they met, they butted heads. She thought he was an opinionated jerk. He thought she was everything that was wrong with her generation. They were constantly giving each other shit, sometimes joking, sometimes not."

"Is it possible it was all a ploy?" he asks, checking his rearview mirror. "Maybe something was going on between them, and this was their way of covering it up?"

I laugh at his ridiculous suggestion. "My sister would never hook up with my ex. And I was with Harris all day, every day, at the shop, morning till close. There's no way he had some secret relationship going with her."

"Okay." He rubs his fingers along his lips, squinting into the late-afternoon sun. "This doesn't make sense. Where's the motive? Harris was in New York the day Meredith went missing, right?"

Exhaling, I nod. "Yes."

"And we know she didn't leave willingly because why would she leave her things in her car and make it look like she was taken?"

"I know. It doesn't make sense. Nothing makes sense." I tug on the strap of my seat belt, uncomfortable under its restraint. Cars make me feel claustrophobic, and road trips put me on edge the moment boredom and anxiety marry impatience.

For a moment, I wonder if perhaps these two things are unrelated. If Harris ran off to be with another woman while I was gone . . . but that doesn't add up either. He was free to be with anyone he wanted, and he wouldn't have told me he wanted to get back together if he were seeing someone else.

My mind spins, but the thoughts are old and tired. It's like I keep considering the same plausible scenarios over and over, trying to piece together a puzzle that doesn't fit.

Perhaps she and Harris had something going on the side all along? Maybe that's why he didn't want to be with me anymore? Maybe that's why she ran off with him—she couldn't bear to come forward with this?

Exhaling, I concentrate on counting the number of blue cars passing us. I need a distraction, a momentary reprieve. My mind is screaming for a break from this nightmare.

Seventeen miles and two blue cars later, my thoughts return to Meredith and Harris.

I try to imagine them touching, kissing, and then my stomach churns. Rolling down the passenger window, I gasp for fresh air until the sensation subsides.

"All right. Let's think." Ronan forces a rugged breath between his lips, his jaw flexing. Everything about him is on edge today, like he's ready for a confrontation. Before we hit the road, I watched as he pulled his gun case from his bag, assembled and loaded it, and then slid it into a pocket holster.

If this nightmare didn't already feel real, it came to life in that very moment.

"We have to examine this from every angle," Ronan says, brows furrowed.

Pulling my phone out, I bring up CNN's website and nearly choke on my spit when I see a flashing red banner across the top of the screen with the scrolling words BREAKING NEWS. "Oh, my God."

"What?" Ronan springs to life, whipping his attention toward me.

Pressing the flashing banner, I'm redirected to an article that takes forever to load, and I'm finding it impossible to breathe.

"Breaking news," I manage to say, reaching for the air and cranking it up. Surely if something happened, my mother would call. I wouldn't expect to hear from Andrew, but I can't imagine anyone would let me find out about it this way.

The white page finally loads, filling with text, and the photo of a blonde, pigtailed toddler fills the top of the screen. The headline reads ALABAMA TODDLER KIDNAPPED IN BROAD DAYLIGHT.

I exhale, eyes scanning the article about a little two-year-old who was kidnapped while playing at a park. Her mother was there, but apparently she was chatting with another parent. When she turned back, her daughter was gone. There was a witness who claimed they saw a gray minivan speed away about that time.

I stop reading.

The article already has 3,782 comments, and it's been up all of twenty-nine minutes.

Tapping back to the front page, I scroll down. The headline with my sister's name in it is at the very bottom, like it's old and stale and a few news stories away from being pushed into oblivion.

This is what's wrong with our society.

We treat tragedies like entertainment, the American public priding ourselves on being armchair detectives trying to solve these crimes, but the second the sensationalism dies down and the case grows cold, we move on to the next exciting thing.

And the media. That's another thing. They need headlines that sell. Stories that stir up emotions and garner web traffic and ad clicks.

I hope to God they find that Alabama baby, but watching the public forget about my sister is a stab in the heart.

"Have you heard anything lately?" I ask. "From the department?"

Ronan's hand grips the wheel, and his mouth purses. "Nope. Heard they sent out a cadaver dog the other day, but they found nothing. That's a good thing, though. For now. The volunteer searchers have combed as much as they can. They're starting to go home. There are a few that'll stay a while longer, but they can't stay forever. They've got lives to go home to. Jobs. Families."

"I know." I rest my head against the window. "That Bixby's an ass by the way."

Ronan chuckles. "Isn't he?"

"Ugh. He's a walking, talking cliché. A pompous good ol' boy." I shudder when I think of his bulbous belly, that smug smirk, and that untouchable attitude. "Is he any good?"

Ronan lifts one shoulder. "Blew out his back years ago and took a desk job. He's been around forever. Kind of does the bare minimum."

"Great."

He switches lanes, checking his mirror and readjusting his posture. I'm not sure how long we've been driving yet, but I don't want to think about how many more arduous minutes we have to spend staring at long stretches of gray highway.

"Bixby's worthless." There's a slight rasp in his throat when he says the name. "But you've got me."

CHAPTER 35

MEREDITH

Ten Days Ago

Two pink lines, the promise of parenthood, and a mile-wide smile on my husband's face—that's what makes this ordinary Monday extraordinary.

I spent the morning on the phone, making doctors' appointments and dinner reservations for a celebratory date night this Friday, and when I wasn't daydreaming about baby names and nursery colors, I managed to put together a grocery list.

It's our week with the kids, which means I'm picking them up from school today, and they're going to expect a full pantry's worth of assorted snacking options. Erica also requests that the children not eat takeout more than once per week; I suspect she's becoming preoccupied with Isabeau's inability to shed the baby fat she's been hanging on to since childhood.

There's an eating disorder waiting to happen there, but God forbid I chime in with my two cents.

Tearing a sheet of paper from my notebook, I scribble a few names just for fun.

Jameson Andrew Price.

Poppy Wren Price.

Serena Greer Price.

Emmett Ambrose Price.

Crumpling the paper, I toss it in the trash, buried at the bottom, where Andrew won't find it. I don't want him to think I'm being silly, and it's still so early. Getting my hopes up is dangerous.

Rising, I fold my grocery list and slip it in my purse before grabbing my keys and tugging my suede boots over my jeans. Seems like an hour ago I was staring at a positive pregnancy test and kissing my husband goodbye, and now suddenly it's early afternoon. Somehow I've lost several hours today, though I'm not sure what I did with them.

Daydreams do that, I suppose.

Climbing into my car a minute later, I head toward the grocery store and park in the back of the lot. Andrew is a stickler about door dings, and despite the rest of the Glacier Park population sharing the same sentiments, he still prefers that I park "away from everyone else."

Killing the engine, I check my texts and almost call my sister to share the news, but something gives me pause. She's been a little more distant lately, ever since I offered to bail out her business. It killed her to accept the help, but she wasn't in a position to say no, and I'm going to be coming into all this money that I'll have no use for—at least not in the short term.

Darkening my phone screen, I decide to wait until we at least have a heartbeat and a due date. Maybe I'll text her a picture of the sonogram when the time comes. Or surprise her in the city with a cheesy T-shirt she'll never wear that says WORLD'S COOLEST AUNT.

My mouth draws into a curve when I think about the kind of aunt Greer will be. She's never been baby crazy or one to so much as talk about wanting a family someday, but what people don't realize is she's nothing but fluff on the inside. It's why she's so hard on the outside. Greer's personality is her armor. Inside she's nothing but love, and she's got an enormous amount to give. Someone just needs to crack her impossibly hard shell so we can pour it out of her.

I'm about to put my phone away when a tap on my window followed by a dark shadow sends my heart into my throat. Glancing up, I exhale when I see the familiar face; I place a palm over my chest to throttle the errant beats. Opening my door, I climb out and straighten my jacket.

"You scared me," I say. "You shouldn't sneak up on people like that."

And then everything goes dark.

CHAPTER 36

GREER

Day Ten

"There it is." I unbuckle my seat belt and point across the dash, my mouth running dry at the sight of the little dark cabin nestled in a thicket of green. It's unnerving now, sitting here all by itself. The pond to the north is dark and daunting, and the sky is beginning to dim.

Ronan pulls off the road and follows a set of tire tracks worn into the grass and covered in pea gravel.

The closer we get, the more I see the hint of light shining through one of the windows, the kitchen perhaps?

As badly as I want my sister to be in there, I almost hope she isn't. If she's hiding in that cabin, willingly tucked away with Harris . . . it'll kill me. It'll break my heart in two.

"What now?" I ask when Ronan slows to a stop. He doesn't stop the engine; he just sits in silence, staring at the house, maybe contemplating his entrance strategy.

"Wait here," he says.

"I'm not waiting here." I reach for the door handle, but he places his hand across my lap.

"It's safer if you do." He removes his seat belt and slides out, keeping the noise to a minimum. Retrieving his concealed gun, he clasps both hands around it and keeps it trained on the door of the cabin as he treks through an overgrown lawn and over a stone path sidewalk.

Maybe the gun is overkill.

I don't even think Harris has held a gun in his life. If he's hiding out on the other side of the door, the harshest weapon in his arsenal would probably be an old can of pepper spray.

Then again, anything is possible, and if Harris did run off with my sister, that means I don't know him like I thought I did.

Chewing my thumbnail, I cross my legs, my ankle bouncing as I watch him try the door. It's locked. Of course.

He moves around the cabin, checking windows and disappearing behind the building for a heart-stopping minute. When he reappears, he returns to the front door.

One hard kick is all it takes. The door swings open. Ronan disappears inside.

My heart races. I can't sit still, can't breathe.

I imagine him carrying her out, bringing her to the car, peeling out of the weedy driveway and careening to the nearest hospital.

Only he emerges a short time later, holstering his sidearm and keeping his gaze low. When he climbs back into the car, he exhales.

"She's not in there." I state the obvious.

"Nope." He shifts into reverse. "By the looks of it, no one's been there in a long time. At least from what I could tell. Light's probably left on to make it look like someone lives here."

Sinking back into my seat, I bite my trembling lip and blink away the mist clouding my vision.

I will not cry.

Crying won't find my sister.

◆ ◆ ◆

The hotel air conditioner hums way too loud, and I'm halfway to becoming a human ice cube, but I'm too exhausted to get up and do anything about it.

The flight back to Utah leaves first thing in the morning. I'm not sure where I'll be staying when I get back. Ronan hasn't offered, and I haven't asked, but I'm not beneath groveling to Andrew.

Lifting my phone, I swallow my pride and call my brother-in-law.

"Greer," he answers on the third ring, his tone indifferent.

"Hi." I'm defeated, desperate, and too tired to pretend I'm anything but. "Look, I'm sorry about the way I've been treating you."

"I shouldn't have kicked you out," he says next, his tone softening.

My entire speech flies out the window. Andrew's never apologized for anything, ever. At least not to me.

"I'm under a tremendous amount of pressure and scrutiny," he says. "I didn't want to deal with it under my own roof, from my own family."

He's never referred to me as "family" either.

"Completely understand," I say. "I was actually planning to come back tomorrow, but I wasn't sure where I was going to stay . . ."

"You're welcome to the guest room again," he says.

"Are you sure?" I can't hide the breathy relief in my voice. Drawing my legs close to my chest, I tuck my body under the thin hotel sheets.

"You're her sister," he says, as if his reason for forgiveness boils down to that single, solitary reason.

Not wanting to dwell in sentimentalities, I change the subject. "Any developments since I've been gone?"

Andrew chuffs. "I wish. Sounds like they're still focusing on Ronan."

Rolling my eyes, I shake my head. "They're wasting their time."

"And how would you know?"

I wish I could tell him. I wish I could come clean and tell him about Harris being gone, about Ronan hopping on the next flight to help me rescue her from an empty cabin in the woods, but the truth is, I feel stupid, and without an ounce of real evidence to justify everything we did, he's going to think I'm insane. He'll never take me seriously again.

As of now, all I'm going off of are my instincts and the fact that Harris is MIA. I have to believe that if Ronan took my sister, he wouldn't have flown to Vermont the way he did, a man with a gun on a mission to save the woman he still loves.

"I don't know," I say. "Just a gut feeling. I think he really wants to find her."

"So you've been keeping in contact with him?" Andrew asks. "Since he was removed from the case?"

Pausing, I finally answer. "Yes. Here and there. Someone needs to keep an eye on him."

He's not going to understand. I had to stay in contact with him. I had to keep him close on the off chance that he might slip up and I might find a hole in his story that could lead me to Meredith.

"Greer." Andrew groans into the phone.

"What?" I sit up in bed, my back resting against a wooden headboard.

"You need to stay away from him." Andrew's direct tone and the clear, succinct delivery of his words send a chill down my spine. "The department did some checking into that stalker case he'd been handling for her a few years back. Turns out there was never a stalker. Never any paperwork filed. Nothing. He made it all up. Everything he ever told her."

My blood turns to ice, and I can't feel my lips.

"Are you sure?" I ask.

The only thing separating me from Ronan right now is a slim hotel wall and a door that adjoins our rooms.

"Positive," Andrew says. "We think he's been following her for years, obsessed with her."

"This doesn't make sense," I say, my thoughts moving from a still very much MIA Harris to the bombshell Andrew just dropped.

"What doesn't make sense?"

"I came back to New York," I say. "Found out Harris has been gone for days. He never told me he left town. All those times I spoke with him, he made it sound like he was running the shops."

Andrew's silence concerns me, but I suspect he's just as baffled as I am. Finally he says, "I'm not sure how Harris would figure into any of this."

"Me neither." I whisper more than I speak now, fearful Ronan's got his ear pressed against the paper-thin walls.

"Just come back to Utah," Andrew says. "And whatever you do, stay away from that detective, you understand?"

I swallow the hard ball lodged in the base of my throat. "Yes."

CHAPTER 37

MEREDITH

Eight Days Ago

I wake with a start, my entire body jerking, my consciousness pouring over me like a bucket of ice water, only I can't move. Plastic cuts into my ankles, securing me to the legs of a metal chair in a small rustic kitchen.

It's dark in here, save for the light above the stove. The heady scent of mildew mingles with the sooty odor of burning logs in the next room.

A spot on the back of my head throbs in time with my quickening pulse.

My arms are asleep from the elbows down. I pull as hard as I can, but they're tied tight with what I imagine to be a zip tie.

The last thing I remember is sitting in my car behind the grocery store, being startled by a tap at my window, and then climbing out when I saw Ronan standing there.

I told him he scared me, that he shouldn't sneak up on people like that.

Everything went dark after that.

"You're awake." Ronan stands in the doorway of the kitchen, looking like a grim shadow in the dark. "For a second I was worried I hit you too hard."

My vision moves in and out of focus. He steps closer, and my body tenses.

"Why?" I manage to ask. "I don't understand."

The man standing before me is a stranger. A stranger with a twisted smile, his once kind eyes replaced with something darker, something unstoppable.

"What are you going to do with me?" I ask, my words jumbling into one. My own words are barely audible, forced air leaving my lips in an uncertain gasp. The whoosh of my pounding heart fills my ears, a reminder that this moment is real, that I'm not in the midst of a nightmare.

Ronan stands before me now, lowering his gaze to mine and cupping my chin in his hand. "Do you honestly think I'm going to hurt you, Meredith?"

He laughs through his nose.

"I *love* you," he says. "I just want to be with you." Ronan rests his hands on the tops of my thighs. "That's all I've *ever* wanted."

Kissing my trembling mouth, he breathes me in.

My stomach rolls, my body recoiling at his touch.

"You'll learn to love me again," he says, wrongfully assuming I loved him once. "I promise, Meredith. It's you and me forever now."

CHAPTER 38

GREER

Day Eleven

Harris's phone is still off. The seats at our gate are beginning to fill. I can't stop twitching.

"Do you want a coffee?" I ask Ronan. Feigning normalcy is proving to be more challenging than I expected. "I think we're boarding in ten minutes, but I can grab—"

"No." Ronan cuts me off. All morning he's barely looked my way, barely said more than a handful of words.

"I'm going to grab myself one." I rise.

"Line's probably too long," he says. "And it's five gates over. You won't make it back in time."

I know he's right, but I also don't want to give him the satisfaction of thinking I'm a malleable woman.

"I can at least check," I say, rising and slipping my bag over my shoulder.

"Sit. Down." His jaw clenches.

"What's with you today?" I ask, forcing myself to chuckle.

Ronan shoots me a look before shaking his head. "I'm tired. You had me fly across the country—literally fly across the country—to search an empty cabin."

Exhaling, I nod. "I'm sorry. I really thought—"

"It's fine." His jaw hollows. "Just want to get home so I can keep looking for her."

For a second, I bask in the genuine concern on his face and the logical explanation that he's just as tired and frustrated as I am. But Andrew's words echo in my mind, and I'm forced to remove my rose-tinted glasses.

"Hey, what was the name of that stalker?" I ask. I realize my question is out of the blue, but if I can maybe gauge his reaction, I can get an idea of whether or not Andrew's bombshell has any merit.

Ronan's gaze snaps onto mine. "Why would you ask me that?"

I shrug. "I was just thinking, when we get back, I really want to look into the stalker. Maybe he had something to do with this?"

"You don't think they've already checked into that?" He huffs, shaking his head like I'm some kind of idiot.

"I'm sure they have," I say. "But you never know. It doesn't hurt to double-check. Do you remember his name?"

His lips press together, and he leans forward, his elbows resting on his knees and his fingers forming a peak as he stares ahead. "That was a really long time ago. I'd have to look it up."

"Were there charges? It'd be a matter of public record, right?" I grab my phone. "I could check online."

A woman's voice plays over the speaker, indicating the commencement of the boarding process. Ronan stands, his back toward me. His section is called first, and he disappears into a line of travelers.

He's supposed to be my ride back to Glacier Park, but if he's guilty, if he did this, he's got the next several hours to figure out that I'm beginning to suspect him now more than ever.

I shouldn't have pushed so much about the stalker case. I can't tip him off if I want to find Meredith. If I do, he'll move her. And then we'll truly never find her. She'll be gone. Forever.

But maybe she's already gone.

If Ronan took her . . .

If he flew to Vermont and left her alone . . .

Who's taking care of her?

CHAPTER 39

MEREDITH

Seven Days Ago

The pillowcase beneath my damp head has turned cold from my wet hair, and the distinct scent of Ivory soap emanates from my skin. My body is covered in a white nightgown, my wrists and ankles secured to bedposts. He must have bathed me while I was unconscious. The thought of his hands touching my body, exploring every piece of me while I lie helpless, sends a rush of bile up my throat.

The room is dark, with only the crack of light shining around a door to offer a shadowy depiction of my surroundings.

Andrew's face fills my mind. I think of him warm in our bed, wondering how he's holding up. He's always so stoic, so serious. I bet he's keeping up a front, and I'll bet people are going to suspect him for it, blame him for not caring, but he's never been good with handling negative emotions. He prefers to skirt around them when at all possible, focus on the good, the things he can control. His image. His reputation. The success of his business.

The door swings open with a soft creak, as if Ronan didn't want to wake me. I watch with bated breath as he stands at the foot of the bed, his stare weighing heavy on my body. A moment later, he takes a seat beside me, peeling back my covers. The nightgown is thin and damp from my skin, sending a chill when it meets the cold night air.

I realize then that I don't know if it's night. I don't know what day it is or what time of day it is for that matter.

Everything's dark.

Everything blurs together.

Everything's one infinite, endless nightmare.

"I'm leaving in a little bit so you need to eat," he says. "I'll untie one of your hands, but I need to know you're not going to try anything."

Ronan's eyes shine in the dark. I nod.

"Trust me," he says, his voice gentle and sweet. "I don't want to hurt you, Meredith, but I will restrain you if I have to."

A few seconds later, he heads toward the hall, leaving the door open. Light spills in from a vintage globe, illuminating an iron bed frame and an old pine dresser. The walls are covered in decorative maps, and an empty gun rack is mounted next to the door.

The sound of silverware clinking and a faucet running fills the silent cabin, and a few minutes later, Ronan returns with a tray.

"Chicken soup," he says. "And a London Fog."

His eyes smile, as if he's proud of himself for remembering my favorite drink.

Placing the tray on the nightstand beside me, he retrieves a knife from his back pocket and clips the zip tie on my left, nondominant hand. When he positions the food over my lap, he places the spoon between my fingers and takes a seat beside me.

"They're going through your phone right now," he says with an amused huff. "As soon as they link you to me, they're going to place me on administrative leave. Lucky for us, there's no body, not a shred of evidence. They won't be able to pin any of this on me, but they'll probably fire me for misconduct. The case'll go cold. I'll go on my way. Eventually you'll be a forgotten headline, maybe a cold case people bring up on Reddit every now and then."

Ronan shakes his head, smirking ear to ear, like he can't get over how well his little plan seems to be playing out.

"You're not eating." His expression fades. "You haven't eaten in days, Meredith. I don't need you getting dehydrated. We're hours from the nearest hospital. We're hours from anyone, really."

I lift the spoon to my mouth. It tastes like salt water, the noodles soggy, as if the can had been sitting in the cabinet for decades. My appetite is nonexistent, but my baby needs to eat, so I choke it down.

"You'll like it up here," he says. "It's really quiet. Peaceful. You know how I told you once I like to hunt? And I'm an avid survivalist?"

I nod, vaguely recalling a conversation we'd had over hot chocolates on one of our many late-night drives together. I hadn't given it another thought. In fact, when he told me, I thought it was cute. And fitting. My all-American Boy Scout, I'd teased him.

"Figured we could live off the land," he says. "Off the grid."

My body begins to tremble. The more I try to still the tremors, the worse they get.

"You're shaking." Ronan places his hand over mine. "You're going to spill. Here." He takes the spoon from my hand, feeding me like an infant. "See, I can take care of you. And I don't need a Maserati and a giant bank account to do it."

We're swallowed by silence for a moment, each spoonful of soup followed by the clink of the silverware against the bowl. The liquid has long since grown lukewarm, but Ronan seems intent on making sure I get every last bite.

"If this baby happens," he says, his words stopping my heart cold, "we'll have to figure something out. Find it a decent home. Something like that."

"*Ronan.*" My teeth grit when I speak his name.

He sniffs, his mouth pulled up at one side. "You can't expect me to raise *his* child as my own. That's just insane. Besides, we'll have a bunch of our own. You'll forget all about this one eventually. Anyway, I'm trying to get my hands on one of those pills."

A thick tear slides down my cheek.

He removes the soup and places a mug of tea in my hands. It's barely warm, but my throat is parched, my tongue like sandpaper. Lifting it to my lips, I swallow the milky liquid, downing the entire cup in one go.

Ronan takes it from me when I'm finished, inspecting the bottom to ensure it's empty.

"You drugged me, didn't you?" I ask.

He laughs, reaching for my face, tilting my chin up until our eyes hold. "I'm not a bad person, Meredith. I may do bad things, but I'm a good man with good intentions. My means always justify my ends."

"It was you, wasn't it?" I ask. "There was never a stalker. It was always you."

He releases my face from his grasp, gathering the dishes and lifting the tray, his back toward me. I find my answer in what he doesn't say.

Thinking back to one of our very first conversations, I distinctly recall Ronan telling me stalkers were mentally unstable, unpredictable. He told me some of them got off on fear, while others were simply obsessed.

If I want to survive, I'm going to have to play along. I'm going to have to convince him that he did the right thing, that I should've chosen him all along.

"Thank you for dinner," I say when he reaches the doorway. A hazy fog begins to wash over me, my eyelids thick, weighted.

He stops. "You're welcome."

Ronan disappears for a minute, returning with a fresh zip tie.

Clutching my fist against my chest, I gaze into his eyes. "Do we have to? My hands are falling asleep."

Bending over me, he reaches for my free hand, sliding his fingers around my wrist and lifting it to an iron rail in the headboard.

He kisses the top of my head, soft and gentle. "Yes, Meredith. We have to."

CHAPTER 40

GREER

Day Eleven

He answers.

Harris answers.

"Oh, my God." I clasp my hand over my mouth. "Harris, what the hell is going on? Where are you?"

I glance around the airport, searching for Ronan. We left the baggage claim a few minutes ago, and he headed to the restroom, his gun case in tow.

"Gre . . ." His voice cuts out. "I'm . . . my way to . . . don't . . . Ronan . . ."

My phone beeps. The call ends.

A warm hand clasps my shoulder. Ronan. "You ready?"

The buzzing of my phone in my hand startles me, and Ronan glances down only to find Harris's name flashing across the screen. Before I have a chance to slide my thumb across the glass, Ronan snatches it from me.

Leaning into my ear, he presses something hard into my back. It was only for a split second, hardly long enough for anyone around us to notice, but I know exactly what it is.

"I highly recommend you not make a scene." His voice is low, reverberating off my eardrum. *"Walk."*

We head toward the pickup lane, pass a line of waiting taxis, and enter the long-term parking garage. His hand hooks into my elbow, leading me toward the elevator, and as soon as we round a corner on the third floor, he ditches my phone in a nearby trash can.

"I don't understand," I say as he jerks me along. Maybe if I play dumb, he won't perceive me as a threat despite the fact that I have every intention of tearing him limb from limb the first chance I get.

His truck is a few paces ahead. "I think you do. I think you under-stand perfectly."

Glancing around, I realize we're alone. And even if we weren't, I couldn't make a scene. Not here. And not yet.

He has my sister.

And that means he has all the power.

At least for now.

CHAPTER 41

MEREDITH

Six Days Ago

"Wake up." Ronan's voice in my ear pulls me out of a deep sleep, and when I open my eyes, I'm surrounded by darkness.

"What time is it?" Not that it matters. I don't know how long I've been gone. How many hours I've slept. But I think if I ask normal questions and not the kind of panicked questions a victim might ask, it might help in the grand scheme of things. "I'm so hungry."

Yet another attempt at normalcy.

Ronan strokes his hand through my hair, his fingertips tangling in the matted strands. "I bet you are. Anyway, I brought you something."

I begin to sit up before realizing I'm still tied, spread eagle. He chuckles.

"You're going to eat at the table," he says. "You need to move, or your muscles will atrophy."

He snips the zip ties, keeping a watchful eye on me, and then he takes my hands in his, pulling me out of bed. There's an ache in my low back that radiates down the backs of my legs, and my muscles stiffen with each step, but I suffer through it, determined not to lose my strength because it's the only thing I have right now.

Ronan's fingers interlace mine, our palms fused, and he leads me to the kitchen, one slow step at a time. My head is light, the floor beneath my feet seeming slanted. I must be dehydrated.

"Sit here." He kicks a chair out before lowering me, and without hesitation, he retrieves more zip ties from his pockets, slipping them around my ankles.

A cardboard box rests on the stove. The overwhelming aroma of garlic and greasy pizza floods my senses, followed by a wave of nausea, but I'm starving. Ronan places a piece before me on a bed of recycled paper napkins and grabs a bottle of water next.

I inhale everything.

My stomach twists, gurgles, but I want more.

"I'll try not to be gone so long next time," he says. "Your sister, she's something else. Stopping by unannounced, asking stupid questions."

I pretend not to care, staring ahead at a photo of mountains buried in snow mounted on the kitchen wall in a cheap, crooked frame.

"She's really looking for you, like relentlessly. Probably even more than your husband." He sniffs, chuckling. "It's cute, really. Let's just hope she doesn't become a problem."

"You won't hurt her," I manage to say, shooting him a narrowed glance. "If you love me, you won't hurt her."

He places his hand over mine, leaning toward me. "I do love you. And that's why I'm willing to do whatever I have to do so we can be together."

My eyes water, and I swallow the roughly chewed bite of pizza in the back of my mouth. It's tasteless, threatening to come up if I don't get myself under control.

If he's crazy enough to snatch me from a grocery store parking lot in broad daylight, he's crazy enough to hurt my sister.

Greer's persistence has always been a great strength. I imagine it's stronger now than ever before. If I know my sister, she'll stop at nothing to find me.

She once fought off a group of four men who tried to mug us in Brooklyn on our walk home from the park. She couldn't have been more than fifteen. They swiped at her purse. The next thing I knew, fists were flying, feet were kicking, and Greer was screaming at the top of her lungs.

She looked insane. Clinically insane. It was enough to scare them away.

Ronan won't scare her.

But unfortunately, I don't think Greer will scare him either.

"You know, I was thinking," I say, attempting to iron out the rough kinks in my trembling voice. "I'm coming into some money at the end of the month, on my birthday. Maybe we could use it to start over? Start a new life together? I just, you know, wouldn't be able to collect it if I'm missing . . ."

Leaning back in his seat, he rests his chin on his hand, observing in silence, breathing hard.

"We don't need money, Meredith," he says a minute later. "I've got it all handled."

"Everybody needs money."

His mouth presses into a straight line. "Money only makes good people do bad things and bad people do worse things."

"We're talking millions, Ronan." The name that used to give me butterflies now makes my blood heat. "We'd be set for life."

Exhaling, he leans close again, lifting his hand to my cheek. "I don't need millions, Meredith. I only need you."

I'm hitting brick wall after brick wall with him, treading water.

"You're right," I lie. "I've always kind of wanted a simple life anyway. I'm going to look at this as an adventure."

"That's the spirit." He rises, grabbing a slice of pizza from the box and leaning against the kitchen counter as he takes a bite. Dabbing his mouth with a crumpled napkin a moment later, he points at me. "Attitude is everything, Meredith. Energy follows thought. If you believe everything's going to work out, eventually it will. It's like the first day I saw you . . . I knew I had to have you. Those thoughts consumed me, woke me up in the middle of the night. I couldn't get you out of my head no matter how hard I tried."

My skin tingles, stippled with gooseflesh, but I smile through it, pretending I find it endearing.

"When was the first time you saw me?" I ask.

His full mouth draws into a slow curl, his gaze lifting toward the ceiling. "You were leaving a restaurant—Blanca's on Locust, I believe it was. Your husband was at the valet stand, and you were waiting next to him in a little blue dress, a satin clutch under your arm. There was something strange and beautiful about you, and I couldn't stop staring. I was walking by, and we locked eyes. You smiled. And I swear, Meredith, in that moment, an entire lifetime with you flashed before me."

I don't recall any of this.

Lifting my brows, I dab a falling tear with the back of my hand. I'm not touched.

I'm disgusted.

And he's delusional.

"I could see right away that you weren't happy," he continues. "You were just some pretty little thing on his arm. An accessory."

I nod, biting my lip. "You're right, Ronan. You're absolutely right. He never loved me. It was all for show."

"A woman like you deserves to be happy, Meredith. And I'm going to spend the rest of my days making sure of that."

"That's really sweet, Ronan. I want to be happy. And I want to be happy with *you*," I say, hoping he buys what I'm selling. "We were destined to meet, I suppose."

"I looked and looked and looked for you after that." Shaking his head, he says, "Never saw you again. Not until a few months later. You were going into yoga with your friend. That's when I ran your plates and got your name so I could leave the note on your car. It was the only way I could bring us together, face-to-face. I knew you'd come into the station and report it."

I force a laugh. "That's . . . really sweet, Ronan. I can't believe you went to all that trouble."

His expression darkens, his thick brows centering. "No, Meredith. It wasn't sweet. It's a fucked-up story."

Glancing away, I brace myself as he charges toward me. Moving my chair so I'm facing him again, he lowers his stare to mine.

"If you want to convince me you're on board with all of this, you're doing one hell of a shitty job." There's a slight clench in his perfect teeth when he speaks. A second later, his eyes soften, and he rises, drawing in a slow breath. "This is going to take time. I don't expect to pluck you out of that fantasyland you were living in and have you immediately on board with this."

Ronan takes a seat across from me, crossing his arms, head tilted as he studies me.

"It's going to be a process. Maybe painful at times," he continues. "But one of these days, you're going to thank me."

Glancing into my lap so he doesn't see the dampness filling my eyes, I say a silent prayer, willing anyone who's listening to help me.

"You need a hot drink," he says. I realize I'm shivering, but I'm not cold. "I'll add some logs to the fire before I go."

With his back to me, he fills a kettle with water and places it on a burner. He's making me another London Fog. The soft shake of a pill bottle follows the shrill whistle of the teapot a few minutes later.

Bringing the finished product toward me, he places it in my hands, wrapping my palms around the mug.

"Drink this," he says. "When you're done, I'll take you back to bed."

"I'm not tired." I lift the mug to my lips, pretending to take a sip.

"It's safer for you this way." Ronan's hands hook at his hips. He won't leave until every last drop of this cup resides in my belly. "I don't want you . . . getting yourself hurt while I'm gone."

"What did you put in here?" I ask.

"Nothing your doctor wouldn't give you." He reaches for the mug, bringing it back to my mouth and tilting up the bottom. "I need to get going, Meredith. I need to get back home before anyone notices I was gone." He presses a kiss into my forehead. "It won't always be like this. I promise. This is only temporary."

I finish the drink, not that I have a choice, and Ronan clips my zip ties before escorting me back to the room at the end of the hall. Within seconds, my restraints are in place, and he pulls the blankets up to my neck.

"Warm?" he asks.

I nod.

"I'll be back soon," he says, running his palm down the outline of my left arm. "I love you, Meredith."

My mouth trembles. I have to say it back. "I love you, too."

"No." His mouth draws down. "You don't. Not yet. But you will."

CHAPTER 42

GREER

Day Eleven

We drive for hours.

Windy roads that dip between mountains.

Signs pointing toward towns I've never heard of before, all of which we pass, all of which grow tiny in the distance.

I try to remember every last detail, every passing farm, every highway diner. But after a while, it all jumbles together, and I'm back to fixating on the present moment.

I've plotted my escape half a dozen times so far, each time imagining something different, each time predicting his reaction. In my mind, I've kicked his steering wheel, kicked his face, mouthed "help" to a passing car, and flung my body out the window while we're barreling down the road at sixty-five miles per hour.

But I have to remind myself this isn't the movies. I have no idea what I'm doing, and my usual strategy of go-fucking-crazy-until-it-scares-them isn't going to work when the perp is already as cracked as they come.

Besides, I suspect he's leading me to my sister because wherever he put her, it's clean out of sight—which is exactly where he seems to be taking me.

Ronan's foot presses the brake, and he checks his rearview mirror, taking a sharp left without signaling. The truck bumps down a rutted, gravel road before winding down a hill and passing through a wall of pine trees several stories tall.

Watching the clock, I note the time.

One minute passes, then another, and another.

Eleven minutes later, he pulls to a stop outside a weed-covered driveway I'd have missed had we passed it. A No Trespassing sign hangs from a nearby tree.

Ronan shifts into park before climbing out and sliding a key into the padlock that secures a rusted iron gate. This sort of setup won't keep the police out, but it sure as hell would keep locals out—too bad there don't seem to be any.

No one's going to know I'm here.

I could scream until my lungs bleed, and no one would hear me.

He slides back into the cab of the truck, gunning the engine through the opened gate. We bounce over each groove and channel, each hardened gravel pocket, and come to a hard stop in front of a small white house.

My heart thrums against my chest wall at the thought that my sister might be inside. As long as she's safe and alive, we're getting out of here. I don't care what we have to do to get free, and I'm not above murdering this demented son of a bitch.

Ronan steps out, circling the truck before retrieving me. His movements are casual, oddly unrushed, and he whistles a cheerful tune as he yanks me toward the front door.

Ronan kicks an old silver storm door open, and his right hand digs into my arm as his left works the key in the lock. A second later, we're in, greeted with a cloud of stale, frigid air and dust.

I glance around, checking every corner for a sign of another human, but the place looks like it hasn't so much as experienced fresh oxygen in years.

"She's not here," he says, jerking me toward a back room. "If that's what you're wondering."

My fingertips are frozen, and I lift them to my lips in an attempt to breathe warmth onto them, but he shoves me along. Stopping in front of a tapestry hanging from a wall in the center of a dim hallway, he pushes it aside to reveal a hidden door.

He twists the knob, and my stomach drops.

A moment later, I'm staring at a metal folding chair resting in the middle of an empty, windowless room, a single naked lightbulb hanging on a chain from the ceiling. He pushes me backward, and the chair breaks my fall.

Crouching, he retrieves a handful of clear plastic flex-cuffs, taking his time looping them through one another and around the legs of the chair before connecting them with the one around my wrists. It's an elaborate setup, one designed to keep me from moving, let alone leaving.

"There." He exhales, admiring his work with a proud glint in his dark eyes.

Pulling against the restraints, I check to see how much wiggle room I have, refusing to believe this is the end. I'll figure something out. The second he leaves me alone, it's on.

The human spirit is inherently resilient, as is the will to live.

"I'm amazed at how calm you are, Greer," he says. "Your sister, she cried a bit, but you . . . you're this steely beast of a woman, from that impenetrable stare to your inability to show an ounce of emotion when you're seconds from the end of your life."

He's trying to scare me.

He wants me to think he's about to kill me so I'll give up, but I refuse to let him rattle me. I won't give him that privilege. I won't give him what he wants.

Reaching behind himself, he retrieves his gun from his concealed-carry holster, watching me with an amused glint as he takes his time drawing it out. With both hands clasped around the grip and one finger steady on the trigger, he smirks.

Oh, shit.

My breath quickens, the skin beneath my arms growing clammy and damp. The knots in my stomach twist, and my vision blurs.

In my final moment, the only thing I think of is my sister. And how I failed her.

"You couldn't let it go, could you?" he asks. "All you had to do was shut the fuck up about the stalker, but you kept pushing and pushing. All those stupid questions. It never fucking ends with you." Ronan winces. "I'm not a murderer, Greer. I've never hurt anyone in my life. I want you to know, this is all your doing. I have to do this because if I don't, you'll ruin everything, and this would all be for nothing."

"Ronan," I say, knowing full well I can't reason with crazy, but I'll be damned if I die without trying. "You're a handsome guy. You're successful and nice and charming. You can have any woman you want—"

"Well aware." He sighs, dropping the gun to his side and releasing a steady breath. "You're not going to talk me out of this, so I guess . . . if you have anything you'd like me to pass along to your sister . . . say it now."

A million memories float to the surface of my mind before scattering like leaves in the wind.

Meredith is my best friend. My sister. My soul mate. We've been through hell and back. I'd do anything for her and she for me. There's nothing I can say in this moment to do any of that justice.

A thick tear slides down my cheek, settling between my lips. The salty taste of defeat is one I've never known until this moment.

"You'll take care of her," I say, my stare as cold and hardened as my bitter soul. I'm not asking. "You'll make sure she's safe and happy."

Ronan scoffs. "Don't fucking insult me, Greer. I'm not a monster."

"You can justify this all you want, but you couldn't be more wrong," I say. "You are a monster. You're selfish. And crazy. And she's never going to love you the way you want her to."

He squints at me, lifting and pointing his gun. "Enough. Stop talking."

Ronan racks the slide.

My world is suspended.

Closing my eyes tight, I savor my final breath.

CHAPTER 43

MEREDITH

Five Days Ago

Ronan strips my urine-soaked panties off me as I stand in a moldy shower. "I meant to come back sooner. Media's been swarming my house lately, trying to get a statement."

"A statement?"

He smirks, flicking the water on. It's icy on my skin at first, morphing to a somewhat tolerable lukewarm seconds later before transitioning to a near-scalding temperature that my freezing body welcomes. This cabin gets so cold, sometimes I can see my breath. I'd linger in this boiling shower for hours if I could.

"Ever since they caught wind of my link to you and the department putting me on leave, they all want to pin it on me."

"And you're not worried?" I ask.

Shaking his head, he massages a bar of soap into a damp washcloth.

"There's no body, no evidence, no proof. Just an angry mob wanting answers." He glances up at me, sliding the ragged, sudsy cloth between my thighs. His touch is gentle, his stare all-pervading. "Like I said before, as soon as the case goes cold, no one's going to even remember your name. We'll be free to move on."

"Did this make national news?" I ask, wondering why the thought had never occurred to me before.

He chuffs, brows angled. "Um, yeah. A wealthy white woman goes missing from a ski town? The media's eating this alive right now. It's a fucking feeding frenzy. Andrew's been giving interviews left and right. You should see him. All dressed up like he's some kind of celebrity, designer sweaters, his hair all combed nice and neat. Don't think for one minute he's not trying to figure out how to profit from this. Guarantee you he's got publishers knocking on his door offering seven-figure advances."

I try to take Ronan's words with a grain of salt; for all I know, he's trying to manipulate me.

All this time I've been wrapping my hope around the fact that Andrew loves me, that he'll do everything in his power to find me. But maybe I'm wrong? I've been wrong about him before, misjudged him. Assumed things I shouldn't have assumed. But that was then. I thought we were better now.

"So I guess you could say this whole thing is win-win for everyone." Ronan slides the rag higher, washing, stroking. I'm surprised he hasn't forced himself on me yet, though something tells me it won't be long. "Andrew gets fame. You get a chance at a normal, happy life with a man truly deserving of your affections. And I get you."

Bracing my hand against the shower, it takes all the strength I have to keep from falling. The room begins to darken, and my lungs gasp for air. The steam must be getting to me, the hot air aggravating my dehydration.

"I think I'm going to pass out," I say, breathless.

Ronan jerks the shower lever before wrapping me in a towel and scooping me up in his arms. The chilled air clings to my damp skin as he carries me back to bed. Once there, he situates me on the edge while he grabs a T-shirt from a nearby drawer.

I wish I had the energy to run.

I wish I had the strength to kick him between the legs, drive the heel of my palm into his nose and eyes, and run the hell out of here.

But the room hasn't stopped spinning yet, I'm still struggling to breathe, and my body is mush. I imagine his underfeeding me is somewhat deliberate, an attempt to keep me weak and reliant on him, unable to fend him off or run away should I get the chance.

Tugging the shirt over my head and shoulders, he crawls into bed beside me, hooking his arm over my stomach.

In this moment, I'm free of restraints. But I'm still his prisoner.

Nuzzling his nose into the bend of my neck, he exhales. "God, I wish I could stay here with you all night." Ronan's hand slides down my damp T-shirt, past my caving stomach until he tugs at the hem, drawing it up. "I've missed this, Meredith."

My breath suspends.

He stops.

"Soon," he says. "You need to get your strength. I won't fuck you like this, when you're shaking and tired. I wouldn't enjoy that. You wouldn't either. I'll wait until you're better, when you can give yourself completely to me. Just like you used to do."

The warm graze of his lips against my neck sends a sting of hot tears to my eyes, and for the first time, I'm grateful for the dark.

Closing my eyes, I lie in silence, sensing his breath on me as he watches me. The bed shifts with his weight as he climbs out.

If he thinks I'm asleep, maybe he won't drug me tonight?

I'm statue-still, refusing to so much as turn my head or lick my lips or make any other move that might indicate I'm not in the early stages of a sleep coma.

Ronan's feet shuffle across the hardwood floor, followed by the creak of the door. He returns, kneeling beside me, the mattress dipping with his weight. The quiet rustle beside me tells me he's getting ready to restrain me for the night.

His hand circles my wrist, lifting it above my head and securing it to an iron rail. He does the same with my left. Keeping up appearances, I don't move. And just when I'm expecting him to move toward my ankles next, the bed gives, and the door closes.

He's gone.

I'm afraid to open my eyes, afraid my instincts are wrong . . . that he's standing over me, testing me.

So I keep them closed awhile longer.

The clinking of pots and pans in the kitchen a few minutes later confirms my suspicions. He left me alone, my feet untied. I can't begin to imagine how I'm going to free myself at this point, my hands still bound and useless. But I'm sure as hell going to try.

Seconds turn into minutes, all of which I count in a feeble attempt to keep myself busy and awake, and when the cabin rattles and the front door slams, I listen for the sound of his truck.

One, two, three, four . . . I continue to count, hoping I'm right. Praying he didn't run outside to grab something.

The cabin is cloaked in cool silence.

Until it isn't.

The gentle rumble of his truck engine clatters through the boarded windows above the bed. My throat burns, squelching a happy cry. I'd be crying tears of joy if I weren't so desiccated. I wait for the sound to grow distant, farther away, before opening my eyes.

Rolling to my side, I slide one foot on the floor, followed by the other. The soles of my feet tingle, and I bump into a tin bucket I hadn't realized was there. He must have left my feet unrestrained so I wouldn't piss myself again. I imagine he wants to keep the bodily-fluids mess to a minimum. Insanity and intelligence aren't mutually exclusive.

Yanking my wrists from the headboard, I twist my body, contorting it any way I can and trying half a dozen different positions before realizing none of them is going to be viable.

Stepping off the bed, my body bent over the mattress, I manage to squeeze myself between the wall and the back of the iron bedposts. Sucking in a deep breath and fueled by adrenaline, I begin to kick.

My bare feet ache with each kick, but eventually I feel nothing. I'm a caged animal, clawing my way out of here. I'll die trying if I have to. It's freedom or death. Life with this deranged psychopath isn't an option.

I'm not sure how long I've been kicking when one of the iron spindles loosens. There's a small gap between the top of the spindle and the top of the headboard, an exposed sliver of sharp metal almost glimmering in the dark. Sliding my right wrist to the top of that rod, I hold my breath until I manage to pass the plastic cuff through.

Moving on to my left wrist, there's no time to bask in this tease of freedom. Kicking harder, faster, I manage to nick the bottom of my heel, but the spindle refuses to budge.

Resting, I realize my vision has adjusted to the blackness, and I'm able to make out the outline of a desk lamp. Stretching my body as far as it'll reach, I search for a string and give it a tug.

The room is illuminated.

My eyes sting at first, squeezing tight until the sensitivity subsides, but when I'm finally able to take a look around, I find myself in the company of a tall dresser, an old wooden desk, and a double-door closet.

Pushing with everything I have, I scoot the bed from one part of the room to the other, reaching the dresser. Rifling through drawers, I find nothing but men's flannel shirts and faded thermal pajamas.

Moving toward the desk, I tug each drawer open, searching for anything. A knife. A gun. Anything.

But it's nothing but papers.

Old bills, yellowed greeting cards, all of them addressed to a man by the name of Jack Howard.

Checking the final drawer at the bottom, I fish beneath a stack of papers, my heart jolting when my hand comes across something hard.

Pulling it close to inspect it, I sigh. Upon first glance, it appears to be some kind of walkie-talkie. Flipping it over, I hold the label closer, making out the words NORTH STAR SATELLITE COMMUNICATIONS.

"Oh, my God," I whisper.

It's a satellite phone.

Pressing the power button, I expect nothing. For all I know, this thing's been sitting in here for months with a dead battery. Only the screen lights green, the display filling with a tiny logo and the words SEARCHING FOR NEAREST SIGNAL, PLEASE WAIT.

A million moments pass before the message disappears and is promptly replaced with READY.

My fingers shake as I try to decide if I should call Greer or Andrew first.

I imagine both of them have been working closely with the Glacier Park police, and who knows, maybe there's an officer hanging out at the house twenty-four seven in case anything happens.

If I call them and tell them Ronan took me and that I have no idea where I am, Ronan will catch wind of it. He's a clever man. He's connected. He's probably listening to scanners every second of every day when he's not here, keeping his nose to the ground. He'll know before they have a chance to assemble a search party or put out an APB. He'll be forced to run, which means he'll either take me with him or he'll take my location to his grave.

I take a seat on the edge of the bed, and my left arm throbs. I press the phone against my forehead, trying to go over my options. I'm sure my mother's with Andrew. I don't have Allison's phone number memorized— or anyone else's for that matter.

Except Harris.

We haven't spoken in months, our last conversation not going too well. He was angry with me for staying with Andrew, accusing me of wasting his time all those months. I saw his point, but I couldn't swallow my pride.

We ended the call and subsequently terminated the odd little pseudofriendship thing we had going on. It's been radio silence ever since.

If there's one person I can count on to be away from the media frenzy, away from the shit show in Glacier Park, it's Harris.

I punch his number into the phone, the thick buttons lighting with each press.

My heart beats in my ears, whooshing between each ring. Biting my lip between my teeth until I taste blood, I'm 99 percent certain he's not going to answer. For all I know, it's four in the morning in New York, and he's sound asleep.

"Hello?" His voice crackles over the line. He sounds far away—fitting, I suppose.

"Harris." I clamp my hand over my mouth, afraid to smile, afraid to get my hopes up too high. "Oh, my God. Harris."

"Meredith?" His voice is clearer now, louder. "Where are you? The whole fucking country's—"

"I don't know." My voice shakes. "Ronan took me. Ronan McCormack. He was a detective in Glacier Park. He took me, and I have no idea where I am. I woke up in this cabin. He tied me up. The windows are boarded. I—"

I realize how simultaneously hopeless and insane my situation sounds the second I breathe life into those words.

"Stay on. I'm going to call the police," he says.

"No. Don't. He'll know. He'll move me. Or he'll run. And he'll never tell anyone where I am." My words ramble on, frantic and frenzied. "I'm sure he's watching everything going on in Glacier Park. That's why I didn't call Greer. He'd know. And I don't want to put her in danger."

"Okay, let's calm down here," he says. I imagine him sitting up in his bed, sliding his glasses over his perfect nose and flicking on a nearby light. "We're going to get you out of this; we just need to figure out how the hell to get to you. Is there anything you can tell me about this cabin?"

Exhaling, I glance around the room. "It's small. Dated. I think it's an old hunting cabin? I can't see the outside. All the windows are covered. My wrist is tied to the bed, so I can't leave the room. I found this satellite phone in the bottom of a desk drawer."

"There's a desk?"

"Yes."

"What else is in there?"

"Oh, my God." I sit up straighter. "Mail. There was a bunch of mail addressed to a Jack Howard. Maybe he owns the place?"

"Get me an address."

Sliding off the bed, I return to the dresser, rifling through stacks of old paperwork. "There are dozens of addresses. It's like this guy never sat still. There are probably at least ten of them."

"Read them to me." Paper rustles in the background.

"What now?" I ask after I've read them off.

"I'm going to find you," he says.

"We have to keep this quiet. Don't tell the police. Don't tell Greer. If Ronan so much as suspects, this isn't going to work—"

"Mer, don't worry." His voice soothes, even if only for a few seconds, and it's like our falling-out never happened. "I'll be on the next plane. I'm going to find this Jack Howard and go from there. Just . . ."

He doesn't finish his thought. Maybe he's realizing for the first time that he doesn't know everything about everything.

"I don't know if I'll be able to call you again," I say, glancing around the room and realizing what I've done to it. I'm going to have to put this back together and pray to God Ronan doesn't realize a single thing is out of place.

"Don't worry about it. Stay safe. Do what he tells you to do. I'll find you, I promise."

I don't want to end the call. I want to bask in his voice, the promise of freedom.

"Get some rest, Mer," he says. "I'll see you soon."

Harris ends the call before I get a chance to respond, and I delete the call log from the phone before returning it to the bottom drawer, beneath the stack of papers. Moving the bed back, I flick off the lamp, crawl beneath the covers, and slide the cuff of my free hand back over the spindle.

I'm exhausted, but I couldn't sleep if I tried.

I'm getting out of here.

CHAPTER 44

GREER

Day Eleven

I've never seen a gun up close, and I never imagined the first time would involve the cold metal of the barrel pointed between my eyes.

I brace for the inevitable, imagining the boom in my ears, the smoky stench of gunpowder, the bright flash, and the subsequent darkness that follows—not that I would likely be conscious for any of that.

Only Ronan lowers his piece, his ear pricked toward the door.

Then I hear it, too.

Someone's knocking at the front door—stiff, attention-demanding strikes.

Thump, thump, thump, thump.

"Don't say a fucking word," he says, his voice low and controlled. "You make one sound, and I promise your sister will die cold, alone, and hungry."

I nod, heart leaping in my throat. Whoever this is, he wasn't expecting them.

Tucking his gun behind his back, he exits the room in silence, pulling the door closed. A minute later, the click and unlatching of the front door is followed by voices. A man, maybe two?

Silence comes next.

Then gunshots.

The house rattles—the walls, the windows, the doors on their hinges.

I count six, maybe seven altogether. But all it takes is one to kill a man.

Someone's dead. I know it.

I envision a local or a park ranger who happened upon a truck at an abandoned property and maybe wanted to check on it, only to be met by a psychopath wielding a semiautomatic weapon.

I also imagine a scenario in which the police somehow tracked him down, pinned Meredith's disappearance on him, and were quick on the draw the second they saw his weapon.

Only there's one problem with both of those scenarios. If Ronan lives? I die.

If Ronan dies? No one knew I was with him. I hadn't told a soul. No one would know to look for me here, behind a door hidden by a tapestry.

Looks as though I'm going to die either way.

CHAPTER 45

MEREDITH

Two Days Ago

"Meredith." He wakes me with a kiss, my name a whisper in this dark room. "I'm going to be gone for a couple of days."

Ronan takes a seat beside me, dragging his hand over his face.

"Your sister," he says, rolling his eyes, "has decided we should be looking for you in Vermont of all places. Don't ask why. It's a long story. I'm just going along with it because . . . well, it'd look odd if I didn't."

He trails his fingertips down the inside of my arm, smiling.

"We're so close," he says. "So damn close."

The hope that's been burning inside me the last few days is nearly extinguished. I thought Harris would be here by now. I thought he'd find me. Every part of me believed I'd be a free woman, and yet here I am, still tied to this bed, smiling at everything Ronan says, professing my love for him, my excitement for a lifetime spent off the grid with him.

Ronan hasn't drugged me the last couple of nights, and he hasn't noticed the broken spindle on the headboard. Had he not locked the door from the outside, I might have been able to escape by now.

I managed to dig out the satellite phone last night after I was sure he'd left, and I tried to call Harris, only it went straight to voice mail.

Wherever he is, I just hope he's okay.

"These are for you." Ronan points to a nightstand covered in bottles of water, towels, and granola bars. Three buckets rest by his feet. "This should get you through the next couple of days. It's not ideal, I know, but we have to make it work."

Dragging his fingers through my snarled hair, he gathers it into his fist, tugging gently as his mouth lifts at the corners. He looks at me the way he did before, the same look that used to send a swarm of butterflies circling my middle.

He was so normal then.

Now I know it was all an act.

"I'm going to miss you, Meredith," he says, bending forward to kiss my mouth. The familiar taste of his spearmint chewing gum lingers on my lips, and I want to be sick. "But I'll be back for you soon."

Ronan leaves, removing the knob from the inside and latching the door from the outside.

Two days.

Harris has two days to find me.

CHAPTER 46

GREER

Day Eleven

Exhaustion blankets my body, but adrenaline keeps me on edge. Footsteps shuffle outside the door, and after that a man's whispered voice. My heart gallops, heat creeping up my neck as I straddle the line between two very different futures.

Ronan's warning plays in my mind . . . if I make a sound, my sister will die.

And I believe him.

I believe him because crazy and determined make for a desperate man.

The shuffle of feet grows louder, heavier. Whoever it is must be on the other side of the wall.

My voice rests at the bottom of my throat, words choking as I fight the urge to scream for help.

"Did you check in here?" a man's voice asks.

A door opens.

It isn't mine.

The squelch of a police radio fills the empty house.

"In here!" I yell, my body shifting in the metal chair as I attempt to make as much noise as I can. My heart races and I'm breathless, but I manage to yell once more. "Hello? Can you hear me?"

My pleas are met with silence.

CHAPTER 47

MEREDITH

One Day Ago

I can't stop thinking about Greer today.

The thought of Ronan spending two days with my sister has been eating me alive, my mind obsessing over every possible thing that could go wrong, every possible thing he could do to her.

He's not stable.

And he's not one to let anyone stand in the way of what he wants.

All that time I spent with him in the past, he seemed so harmless, so benign. Never in a million years would I have thought he was capable of something like this, and if he's capable of kidnapping me, he's capable of anything, especially getting rid of the one person who knows what he did.

I can't stop shaking as a cocktail of powerlessness and anxiety takes over.

The windows rattle, which I've learned almost always coincides with the opening and closing of the front door.

He's back.

Lying in the dark bedroom, my arms tingling and asleep, I stare at the water-stained ceiling, my body sinking into the mattress. The pungent stench of bodily fluids fills the thick, stale air.

I shouldn't have placed all my hope in Harris. He's just an Ivy League–educated coffee shop owner from New York, not a superhero.

Ronan moves around the house, his footsteps shuffling from room to room, quickly, as if he's looking for something. I listen until they grow louder and then stop altogether.

A second later, the latch on the outside of the door slides, and the door swings open.

I don't look at him.

I can't.

"Meredith." The man's voice doesn't belong to Ronan.

Lifting my aching neck, I squint toward the dark figure in the doorway. When he steps closer, his face comes into focus. The glasses. The dark hair. The smug smirk permanently etched on his face.

"Told you I'd find you," he says, calm as ever. Reaching into his pocket, he grabs a tactical knife, sawing the plastic restraints until they snap.

My hands are asleep, but I manage to shake them until the feeling returns.

"Come on. Let's get you out of here." Harris glances toward the door.

"Where is he?" I ask.

He shrugs, examining the cramped room I've come to know too well. "Not sure. Not planning on sticking around long enough to find out either."

Wrapping one arm around my shoulder and hooking his hand around my elbow, he leads me outside, toward the glowing headlights of a running Toyota.

I don't know what day it is.

I don't know what time it is.

And I don't ask.

"Harris." I stop when I see a man sitting in the front seat of the car.

"That's my driver," he says with a wink. Only Harris Collier can make rescuing a kidnapped woman seem like an ordinary event. "You know I don't have a license. How'd you think I was going to get around?"

He helps me in the back seat, fastens the seat belt, and hops in front.

"Is there a park ranger station nearby?" he asks the man up front before turning back to me. "There's literally no cell service out here. We're going to have to find someone and tell them you're safe, and that Ronan took you."

"He's with Greer," I say, hands gripping the back of his chair. "He went to Vermont with her."

"Vermont?" His face wrinkles, then his eyes widen. "Oh, shit."

"What?"

"I haven't talked to her in days . . . not since I've been out here," he says. "My phone wasn't working half the time. I called her this morning, but my phone cut out." Exhaling, he glances at the clock. "My family has a cabin in Vermont. That's the only thing I can think of. Maybe she thought I was there?"

"Ronan went with her," I say. "To look for you. She must've thought I was with you?"

"Like I'd kidnap somebody." He rolls his eyes. "Your sister."

The driver veers down a hilly gravel road that cuts between two mountains before the tires hit smooth pavement. Cracking the window, I let the cold air hit my face. I make a silent vow never to take fresh air for granted ever again. Harris reaches back to pat my knee, his own way of telling me everything's going to be okay despite the fact that we have no way of knowing what's to come.

We ride in silence, and while I'm no longer locked away, I don't yet feel free.

I won't until I find my sister.

A road sign ahead welcomes us to Zion Gardens State Park, and over the hill rests a little brown cabin with a single ranger truck parked out front.

I rub the red marks on my wrists until the aching subsides, and it seems like it takes forever for the driver to slow down.

"Here, pull in." Harris points toward the station, and the driver slows. The second we're stopped, he leads me inside, where a young ranger glances up from his computer with tired, glazed eyes. His name tag identifies him as Ranger Kyle Howe, and he can't be much older than twenty-one judging by his baby face and the soft, peachy facial hair he's trying to turn into some kind of beard. "I need you to call the police. This is Meredith Price. She's been missing out of Glacier Park since last week."

The young man blinks at me, as if he's seeing a ghost, and I'm certain I look like a whisper of my former self. My hair is matted, my skin pale, my body gaunt.

"What the fuck are you waiting for?" Harris's voice cuts through the small space, and he reaches across the desk, shoving the phone toward the kid.

Tucking the receiver against his shoulder, the kid punches in a series of numbers and keeps his gaze trained on me.

"Fletcher, we got her. That missing woman. She's here," he says. "Yeah. Send medical, too."

As soon as he hangs up, he heads to a closet behind the front room, returning with a red woolen blanket, a bottle of water, and a meal replacement bar. Harris wraps me in the scratchy fabric and uncaps the drink, bringing it to my lips. I'm hungry, but I'm too tired to eat, and the meal bar feels like a rock in my hand, old as hell.

Within minutes, a white state car pulls up outside, and two troopers in brown uniforms rush inside, stopping in their tracks when they see me. The older of the two glances at Harris for a moment, but I place a hand up.

"He found me," I say. "Ronan McCormack, he's the one who did this. And you need to find him. He has my sister."

Outside an ambulance parks beside their vehicle, a pair of EMS workers hopping out and heading to the back to grab their bags.

"Do you have any idea where he is right now?" one of the officers asks, his hand resting on his radio.

I glance at Harris. "He went to Vermont. He's supposed to be back tomorrow."

Harris takes my hand. It's a sweet gesture, and one I hope to never experience again. It's weird holding his hand, basking in his sympathies. All I want is for things to go back to the way they were before. I miss the snarky Harris. The sweet one is alien and serves only to remind me of the gravity of this disgusting situation.

"We'll put a tail on him," the other officer says, his thin lips flattening. "We're going to get him, Meredith."

CHAPTER 48

GREER

Day Eleven

A blazing flashlight blinds me the second the door swings open. Squeezing my eyes, I turn my face to the side.

"Jesus." A man rushes to my side. "Found her, Robbins."

"No." I shake my head, my vision still adjusting as a gray-haired man in jeans and a thick down jacket comes into sight. "I'm not Meredith."

"Greer Ambrose?" he asks.

I sit up straighter, confused. Nobody knew I was here. "Yes?"

"I'm Agent Berwick." He snips the flex-cuffs before helping me stand. My bones ache, my muscles stiff. "Your sister's been found."

Your sister's been found.

My heart drops. "Oh, God."

"She's fine. A little dehydrated, a little traumatized. But she's fine." He loops his arm around my shoulders. "She told us you were with him, tipped us off that he was on his way back from Vermont. We've been following you since Salt Lake City this morning."

My hand cups my mouth as he leads me through the small, musty house and out the front door. An unmarked Suburban is parked behind two county patrol cars, but I don't see anyone else.

"Where's my sister?" I ask when we step outside.

"Unity Grace Hospital, few miles into town," he answers, peering over his shoulder as he rushes me to the back of his car.

"Where's Ronan?" I ask. "Ronan McCormack. He did this. He's responsible for this."

"We're aware, ma'am," he says, grabbing the door. "Watch your head."

"Where is he?"

"Took off on foot after he answered the door and realized who we were and why we were there. We've got two guys on him. He won't get far in this snow. And if he does, the cougars will get him before sunrise."

He chuckles. I can't tell if he's kidding.

The idea of wild animals tearing him limb from limb might bring me great satisfaction if I weren't so fucking terrified of that monster being on the loose.

Drawing in an icy breath, I let it go, trusting that they're going to nail him one way or another. They're on his heels. They won't let him get away.

Berwick hands me a flannel blanket once I'm situated in the back seat, and I wrap it around my shoulders.

"You thirsty?" he asks.

I nod.

Ducking into the front seat, he retrieves a thermos. Unscrewing the lid, he pours it halfway full of steaming coffee before handing it over.

It's cheap. Store brand, probably. But the strong scent comforts me. And I think of Harris.

"Harris Collier . . . ," I begin to say.

"What about him?" he asks.

My gaze narrows. "Was he with my sister?"

When I realized Ronan was behind all this, I was more fixated on getting free and finding Meredith than figuring out why Harris lied about his whereabouts.

Berwick hooks his hands on his hips, his lips pressed. "Sure was. He's the one who found her."

My jaw hangs slack for a second as I wrap my head around this. I start to ask a question when his radio sounds. He tells me to stay there and slams the car door before running toward the backyard of the little cabin.

A fogged windshield obstructs my view, but I'm able to make out the sound of men yelling, though I can't decipher what they're saying.

A gunshot.

Then three in a row.

Pop. Pop. Pop.

My heart stops cold. I don't move.

Ronan is a cop. He has access to guns. He's trained to shoot to kill.

I hit the locks like a coward, my exhausted mind crafting up some scenario where Ronan comes running toward the car, a gun pointed in my face, and a bunch of dead FBI agent bodies lying bloodied in the snow. I know a lock couldn't save me from him, but at this point, I've nothing but a blanket to hide under.

"Ten-thirty-three, shots fired. Ten thirty-three, shots fired. Suspect down, still not in custody." A man's voice plays over the agent's car radio, sending shock waves through my frozen body. "Send backup. And medical."

I realize I've been holding my breath the moment Berwick appears from around the back of the house. He jogs toward me, and I unlock the door, opening it for him.

"Stay in here," he says. "We got him. He fired at us from the woods. One of the county guys fired back. Hit him twice."

"He's still alive?" I ask.

Berwick cocks his head, his chin jutting forward. "For now. He's bleeding pretty good. Conscious and suffering, I'll tell you that much."

With that, he shuts the door and speaks into his radio before trudging back to the scene.

I hope the bastard suffers.

I hope his death is slow and painful and agonizing.

And I hope he never gets the privilege of living to regret what he's done.

◆　◆　◆

Agent Berwick insists I get an examination, but I refuse, forcing him to take me to Meredith instead.

Two officers stand guard outside her hospital room, nodding at Berwick as we pass through.

"Mer." I freeze the moment I see her. She's hardly recognizable, so faded. So fragile.

"G." Flinging the covers off her legs, she tries to come to me, but a nurse stops her before she hurts herself.

Making my way to the side of her bed, I wrap my arms around her tight. I'm not a hugger, but I could hold her forever.

"I'm so sorry," she whispers.

"You have nothing to apologize for." I pull myself away, keeping my hands on her shoulders. "You did nothing wrong."

"I didn't tell you about Ronan, about the affair. I didn't tell you I'd been talking to Harris about all the things I didn't want to tell you," she says. "I didn't tell you anything because I wanted you to think everything was fine, that you didn't have to worry about me anymore."

"None of that matters now," I say, brushing my fingers through her tangled blonde waves. On the drive over, I thought about Harris and how he rescued her. And here I was ready to strangle him for sending

264

my emotions into a spiraling free fall and me on a wild-goose chase. I've never been so relieved to have been wrong about someone. "I have to admit, I'm shocked about the Harris thing. I thought you two hated each other."

Her mouth draws into a careful smirk. "We did. And then I called him once when I wanted some nonbiased life advice, and somehow that turned into him becoming my sounding board, and . . ."

My sister rambles on, filling me in on the last eleven days, on Harris, her reasons for contacting him instead of anyone else, and how he found her by locating Jack Howard, a local business owner with hundreds of rental cabins in Utah.

"I was in the twenty-eighth cabin," she says. "He hired a driver, printed off a bunch of maps, and drove to each and every address until he found me. They're all over the state. Took days."

"Wow," I say as my fondness for Harris starts to reignite. Picturing him as some kind of hipster superhero puts a dopey smile on my face. "Who'd have thought Harris could be so valiant?"

"I know, right?" Meredith's head tilts, and she laughs through her nose. It's good to see her like this, especially when I was expecting her to be a shell of herself after everything she's been through. I should've known she was resilient. I raised her to be that way, after all. "He's been really sweet, G. But I kind of miss the other version of him."

"Where is he, anyway?"

"He went to grab a coffee, I think," she says. "He'd been trying to call you since yesterday, when he finally found a cell signal."

"Ronan threw my phone away." I exhale.

"Did they find him yet?" Meredith reaches for a plastic cup of water on a nearby table.

Pausing, I swallow a deep breath. "They haven't told you?"

Bringing the straw to her lips, she stops, shaking her head. "Told me what?"

"They shot him outside the house he was keeping me in," I say carefully. She's been through so much, and I've yet to determine how she feels about him at this point, if she's resentful, confused, or illogically compassionate. "I guess you told the police he was flying back from Vermont, and they sent a couple of plainclothes agents to tail him from the airport."

Meredith is silent, her chin tucking against her chest.

"You okay?" I place my hand over hers.

"Yeah," she says. "Just wrapping my head around all of that."

"He was a sick man."

My sister nods. "I know."

"Greer." Harris's voice calls my name from the doorway, where he stands with two cups of coffee. Striding across the room, he hands me one. "They said you were on your way."

There's a fullness in my chest, swelling as I lock eyes with him.

"Thank you." I wrap my hands around the warm Styrofoam, stuck somewhere between wanting to run into his arms or bask in how good it feels to see him again.

"Figured you'd be tired." Harris studies me. "You doing all right? You've been through . . . shit, I don't even know what you've been through." He takes a step closer, reaching toward my face with gentle hesitation before cupping my cheek. "I was so worried about you, Greer. The thought of something happening to you . . ."

Harris's words fade, and his warm palm leaves my cool cheek. He doesn't want to finish his thought.

"I'm fine," I say. I'm not sure if I'm fine or what the lasting repercussions of the last couple of days are going to be, but for now, I'm with my sister and we're both safe, and that means everything's going to be okay. "Thank you for . . . for what you did." I nod toward my sister. "You saved her life."

He shrugs, taking a sip. I love his modesty. I love that he doesn't expect accolades or attention.

"Let's not make it into a thing, all right? I did what anyone else would do." Harris steps closer, releasing a hard breath through his nose as his lips press together.

"I don't know about that," I say, the corner of my mouth pulling up. It's as if I'm looking at him in a whole new light. He saved my sister. He saved her because he knew how much she meant to me. He saved her because he's a good person with a good heart and a good soul.

I *hate* that I doubted him.

And that I doubted myself.

"I meant what I said last week." His voice is low, soft as a feather.

Resting my palm over his hand, I smile. "I know."

"You know, do you?" He chuckles, and my gaze lands on the dimple on his left cheek, the one I used to kiss when we first started dating because I thought it was so cute. He called me a "weirdo." I laughed and told him to get used to it. He told me he'd love my idiosyncrasies if I promised to love his.

"You never stopped," I say, stating it as if it were an inarguable fact.

Harris pauses before rubbing the back of his neck. "Never. Not once."

"What the hell are we doing?" I ask.

He shakes his head, exhaling. "I never should've let you go, Greer. It's just, you went so quietly, without a fight. I thought you were over me. Over us. And you seemed fine on your own, like you didn't need me."

"Harris." I bite my bottom lip, blinking away the tears threatening to fill my eyes. "You're it for me. I couldn't get over you if I tried. And trust me, I tried."

His mouth pulls wide. "Want to go somewhere and talk? Alone?"

Turning toward my sister, I watch her eyelids grow heavy. I'd hate for her to wake up to an empty hospital room.

"I can't leave her," I say. "Not yet."

"Right. Of course. Getting a little ahead of myself." Eyeing a spare chair in the corner, he takes a seat. "Then I'll just be here. Waiting. And when you're ready, I'll take you away, anywhere you want to go."

"I just want to go home," I say. "To our apartment. With you."

His face lights. "Then that's where we'll go."

CHAPTER 49

MEREDITH

"She's right in here, sir." One of the officers outside my door steps out of the way as my husband pushes past.

His eyes widen when he sees me, and he takes careful steps toward my bed, falling to his knees. His amaretto-colored gaze never leaves mine, and I see it—I see that he's sorry. He's sorry he wasn't able to protect me.

"What did he do to you?" Andrew's voice shakes, which sends a fullness to my heart. Looking at this man, I wholeheartedly believe he was beside himself in my absence, even if he didn't show it—and knowing him, he kept his cards close. Rising, he sits next to me. "Never mind. It doesn't matter. You're safe now. You're with me."

He bends forward, pressing his lips against my forehead, and I cower at first, thinking of Ronan until I inhale my husband's familiar musky aftershave.

Andrew cups my cheek. "I'm sorry I didn't worry more about you."

Shaking my head, I say, "Worrying about me never would've stopped him. He had this planned for years."

"I heard they shot him," Andrew says, huffing. "Serves him right."

I say nothing. Despite recent events, a part of me still struggles to believe that the Ronan who was once so sweet and unassuming and affable was capable of all this. He was always so normal. That was what I always liked most about him.

I know now that he was mentally ill, deeply disturbed, and he was only ever pretending to be the person I thought he was.

"How's the baby?" Andrew rests his palm across my belly, and for a flicker of a second, I imagine him holding a swaddled baby—our baby—and my chest swells. If I can make it to that day, to that moment, everything's going to be okay.

"I had an ultrasound," I say, eyes resting on his. "Everything looks good. I'm just over six weeks. Heard the heartbeat and everything."

"Thank God," he whispers, taking my hand in his. "How are you holding up, though? Other than being traumatized and wafer thin?"

My gaze follows the line of the IV drip they've had hooked to me since the second I got here. I'm guessing we're on bag number four in less than twenty-four hours. Despite the fact that nothing feels real, I've never felt more alive.

I just want to get out of here.

I want to forget this happened.

I want my life back . . . the life I signed up for.

I want to be a good person. I want to live a life void of secrets and shame and guilt.

I want to make it up to my husband, give him the wife he deserved. The one he married, the one he ravished in a Parisian honeymoon suite, vowing to love her until her dying day.

Harris and Greer watch from across the room. My sister has refused to leave my side since she got here, even forcing the doctors to examine her here, in front of me, so she didn't have to step out.

If I thought she was overprotective before, I'm guessing I haven't seen anything yet.

"The doctors say I can leave today," I tell Andrew.

He smiles, squeezing my hand.

"Where's my mom?" I ask.

"She and Wade are on their way," he says. "They got stopped by a news crew outside. Your mom insisted on answering questions."

I snort through my nose, rolling my eyes. "Must be a new phase of hers . . . wanting the spotlight."

"You should've seen her on TV last week." Andrew winks.

"I can only imagine."

The doctor who examined me last night steps in, and the room falls quiet. "Meredith, how are we feeling?"

"Homesick," I say without pause.

He chuckles through his nose before reaching for the stethoscope around his neck. "Then let's get you the hell out of here."

"Yes, let's," my husband says, moving out of the way before planting himself in the chair beside my bed. "I'm anxious to get my wife back home, where she belongs."

The doctor checks me over once more, exchanging words with one of the nurses before she hands him a clipboard and a form to sign.

"I'm so sorry," I whisper to Andrew, "for everything."

"Me, too." He presses his nose against mine, breathing me in. He's never been an emotional man, rarely letting his guard down, but when he pulls away and looks into my eyes, I catch a sliver of the man I fell in love with, the one who looked at me like I was the only thing he was ever going to need for the rest of his life.

"I want what we had before," I say, "before we started keeping secrets and hurting each other."

"We'll get there." Andrew sighs, studying my face. "Besides, I could never let you go. I'm a selfish man when it comes to you."

My husband takes my hands in his, lifting them to his mouth and depositing a single kiss against my skin. When he lets me go, I realize my sister is standing across from him now. Greer takes a seat on the edge of my bed, studying me, her mouth half-open like she has something to get off her chest.

"I've never been so scared," she finally says. Her eyes turn glassy, a rare sight on a woman whose heart has always been wrapped in impenetrable stone.

"Me, too," I say, releasing Andrew's hands and taking hers.

"I didn't know if I'd ever see you again." Greer glances at our intertwined fingers before returning her gaze to me. "How could I not know all these things about you, Mer?"

Exhaling, I flatten my lips. "I didn't want you to worry. And I was ashamed. I justified everything, all the time. And I know now that I was wrong. I'll never keep anything from you again, Greer. I promise."

We linger in silence, the two of us, and I imagine she's lecturing me in her mind right now, but I can assure her there's nothing she could say that I haven't already said to myself.

I've made mistakes. I've been selfish. I've been lost. I've hurt the ones I loved the most, and in the end, it almost cost me everything.

"I never would've stopped looking for you," Greer says.

"I know." I offer a closemouthed smile. "That Harris, huh? Guess he's not so bad."

Her lips twist at one side at the mere mention of his name.

"Let's get you home, okay?" Greer rises, dabbing her eyes with the backs of her hands and tearing herself out of her emotional stupor as if it were a scratchy polyester suit.

"G?" I ask.

"Yes?" She turns to face me, head tilted and limp blonde hair blanketing her shoulders.

"You're my best friend. And I love you," I say. "Thank you for never giving up on me."

Her eyes crinkle, and she places her palm over the top of my hand. She says nothing, but I know. The unspoken bond between us supersedes the sweetest sentiment either of us could possibly exchange in this moment.

Sitting up, I toss the hospital blanket off my legs and pull a generous breath of hospital air into my lungs.

I'm going home.

I'm finally going home.

ACKNOWLEDGMENTS

This book would not have been possible if it weren't for the amazing people responsible for the behind-the-scenes craziness. Jessica Tribble, thank you so for reaching out to me after reading *The Memory Watcher*. Your enthusiasm and passion and energy for the book world are refreshing and delightfully contagious! Jennifer Jaynes, you've been my own personal cheerleader from the moment I reached out to you. Your kindness and encouragement have been an absolute godsend. Jill Marsal, thank you for everything you do; your tireless brokering, wealth of industry knowledge, straight-shooter attitude, and impeccable communication are proof that I won the lottery of literary agents. Charlotte Herscher, your notes were amazing! You're like an intense personal trainer . . . but for books. After the first round of revisions, I was sore but in a good way, and I knew I was only going to get stronger going forward.

To my parents: Thank you for the endless love and encouragement. Mom, thank you for feeding my book addiction via Scholastic book orders growing up, and Dad, thanks for making us hang out at the library on the weekends. Because of that, I stumbled upon Stephen King at age twelve and graduated from Sweet Valley High to the dark and twisted.

To K, M, and C: You're simply the best. Better than all the rest. But seriously, you truly are. I couldn't survive this career if it weren't for you three. Your talent and friendship mean the world.

Finally, to my husband: You may have eaten frozen pizza one too many dinners or seen the light on in my office late at night more than you would have liked, but you've never once complained. You always supported me, believed in me, and did everything you could to make this dream a reality. Thank you, thank you, thank you. I love you. (And yes, you can get those golf clubs.)

ABOUT THE AUTHOR

Photo © 2017 Jill Austin Photography

Born and raised in the Midwest, Minka Kent is a graduate of Iowa State University and the author of *The Memory Watcher*, *The Perfect Roommate*, and *The Thinnest Air*. Her debut psychological suspense, *The Memory Watcher*, reached the Amazon Kindle Top 100 in March and September 2017, as well as the Amazon Most Sold chart in November 2017. Translation rights to *The Memory Watcher* have been sold in multiple countries.